THE ANGELS' SHARE

LOSERS CLUB BOOK THREE

YVONNE VINCENT

Copyright © 2022 Yvonne Vincent
All rights reserved.

By Yvonne Vincent:

The Big Blue Jobbie
The Big Blue Jobbie #2
The Wee Hairy Anthology

Frock In Hell

Losers Club (Losers Club Book 1)
The Laird's Ladle (Losers Club Book 2)
The Angels' Share (Losers Club Book 3)
Sleighed! (Losers Club Book 4)
The Juniper Key (Losers Club Book 5)
Beacon Brodie (Losers Club Book 6)

TO SHEILA & ALLEN

For a thousand kindnesses over the years.

A WEE WORD BEFORE WE BEGIN

Thank you to Barry, who told me about the angels' share, saying, 'I bet you cringe when people give you ideas for your books.' Not when they give me a cracking title, Barry.

Also, thank you to all the lovely people (Fiona, Dianne, Dawn and Louise in particular) who helped along the way. It truly takes a village.

The idea for this story began with a tour of Ben Nevis Distillery in 2021, so my final thanks go to the very knowledgeable man who showed us around and patiently answered all the daft questions. Any whisky distilling cockups in this book are purely mine.

I've peppered this book with a few words and phrases from the local Scots dialect, Doric. Most are explained in the story, but a couple are not. Kittle ma oxters means tickle my armpits and keech is poo. A sentence I never imagined myself writing!

This book is written with huge warmth for the Northeast of Scotland which, wherever I am in the world, will always be home.

PROLOGUE

Ian Henderson liked Lochlannach distillery at night. The steady thrum of the giant mash tuns, churning barley and water, was louder, somehow more forceful than during the day; as if now that the people had gone, they could get on with the job at hand.

Ian agreed with them. Life was easier without other people. These days, it seemed, you couldn't be yourself. Ever since the new owners of the distillery had introduced *values*, he'd been considering retirement. According to the twelve-year-old who was now his boss, his attitude towards his colleagues was disrespectful. After that last incident, where he'd told the lassie she should be at home looking after her children instead of bleating on at him about HR policies, they'd sent him on a training course. Being Respectful at Work. Total and utter shite. Three hours of listening to some liberal leftie blethering on about micro-behaviours and unconscious bias. What a waste of time. Judging by some of the slides, the wee bastard couldn't even spell racism if a *"person of colour"* shoved a red-hot poker up his spotty arse. And that's what he'd told them on the feedback form, too.

These days, everyone acted like being offended was a

human right, and you couldn't even compliment a woman without her getting all…what was it called again? Aye, hashtag me too. You couldn't even tell a woman she had a nice set of paps without her going all hashtag me too on you.

Ian took a moment to feel a little quiet pride that he knew about hashtag me too, even if he had no idea what a hashtag was. Something to do with the Facetwitter he supposed. And that was the problem, wasn't it? They were all out there, the outraged folk with their hashtags, bouncing off each other on the social media, winding each other up until nobody could have an opinion anymore. Or at least, that was what he'd read in the papers. Proper papers like the Vik Gazette and the Daily Mail. Now, that last one was a real newspaper. The Daily Mail saw the world as it was and gave it to their readers straight; a finely balanced blend of women in bikinis and having a go at Andrea Forglen.

Ian felt his blood pressure rise at the mere thought of the dried-up, ugly bitch that was Scotland's First Minister and turned his mind to the Daily Mail's other important news of the day; The Biggest Breasts in Britain Are Found in the North. He leaned on the guard rail of mash tun number three and recalled the accompanying picture of Marie Morne, the underwear model, in a bra. Aww, that woman should be called Marie Moan, because that was what she made him do. Aye, happy moan. Nae the grumbling kind. In the article, she'd been facing the camera, the bra just covering a perfect pair of paps. There was also a photo of yon tubby wee news presenter with her cleavage bursting out the top of what must surely have been a sequined circus tent, but he could block that out. He turned his mind back to Marie and felt a stirring below. You may be past seventy ma boy, but you've still got it, he thought, reaching down to unzip his trousers.

His fumbling growing more frantic, Ian opened the hatch to mash tun three and imagined a gaping mouth. They'd never notice a few extra enzymes in there, he decided, picturing a large-bosomed blonde kneeling on the floorboards at his feet. Come on, lassie, brace yourself. Oh yes, any minute now.

So lost in his fantasy was he, that he didn't notice the figure slip through the mash house door, the sound of approaching footsteps masked by the hiss of water entering the steel vat. He didn't feel the presence of someone behind him or sense the pair of hands reaching towards him. Faster and faster he tugged, eyes closed and his breath coming in short pants.

As Ian hit that singular moment of pure bliss, his feet left the ground, and he opened his eyes to find himself heading for the gaping maw of the machine. His mind scrambled to grasp the impending danger and his mouth, already open to groan a throaty sigh of release, instead issued a howl of pain as his forehead was jarred against the metal opening. He began to struggle as hands lifted and pushed him through the gap. Letting go of his rapidly shrinking nether regions, he grabbed at the edges in a desperate attempt to push his body away from the hatch but his fingers, slick with his own fluids, slipped on the smooth metal. Then it was too late. Ian's body bounced off the blades, unrelentingly churning the scalding hot liquid, and he felt himself sinking into the mash, the door of the hatch above him closing to cut off the light and his hoarse screams.

He knew he had minutes…seconds, even…to live and through the confusion and terror, came one clear thought. At least he'd made his point to that bitch Forglen. People were so busy shouting at each other online, they didn't appreciate the elegance of threats delivered by the postman, the good, old-fashioned way. In those final moments, as his life flashed before him, Ian paused and rewound back to himself sitting at his kitchen table, carefully cutting out whole sentences from the Daily Mail and gluing them to a sheet of plain paper. Ah, that was the best bit, right there. He wished he could have seen her face when she opened the letter; "I know what you did and you're going to pay". He wondered if she was shitting herself right now. He'd ask her when he met her in Hell.

CHAPTER 1

Penny lay on the bed next to Jim, pink cheeked and exhausted, but satisfied.

'You did a grand job,' she said. 'I was a bit worried at the end there, but when you did that wee jiggle with your whatchamadoobry, that finished things off quite nicely.'

Jim grinned at her.

'Aye, well, it's not my first time. Although nobody's ever farted in my face before. *That* was a first.'

'You were the one who insisted we try that position,' said Penny, her cheeks now a deep crimson. 'Hold my big pole and back up, you said. Anyway, are you ready for another go yet?'

Jim sighed and looked at his watch.

'Can you give me five minutes? I'm not as young and up for it as I used to be.'

'I can hear you,' came a voice from the other side of the bedroom door. 'You better not be…oh my God, old people doing it. That's too disgusting to think about.'

'You shouldn't be lugging in to other people's conversations then,' Penny shouted back.

'Aye, me and your mum are doing lots of sex. Old

people's sex, with wrinkly bits and hairs where they don't belong,' shouted Jim. 'We've only stopped for an indigestion tablet and a cup of cocoa. And on the subject of lubrication, we could do with some. Any chance you could get the Vicks from the kitchen cupboard?'

'Ew, no, ew! Ugh, I'm moving back in with Granny and Grandad.'

Penny listened to her daughter's feet thumping downstairs. She heard the living room door open then slam shut, followed by Edith's muffled voice saying, 'Alexa, play Harry Styles.'

Alexa's reply was clear. 'Playing Barry White.'

Barry's dulcet tones, informing everyone within a ten-mile radius that he couldn't get enough of your love baby, were punctuated by Edith's screams of 'Alexa! Stop!'

'It's almost a shame we were only building a bed,' mused Jim. 'I probably shouldn't have said that about the old people's sex, though. Sorry.'

'Och, it's okay,' said Penny, rolling over and getting to her feet. 'She's immune to it, really. You can't live with my mother and not develop a tolerance for the inappropriate. Come on, let's put her out of her misery. She can help us build her and Hector's beds. I can't tell you how glad we'll be to see the back of Mum and Dad's old blow-up mattresses. A month of them has almost broken us.'

Penny had been so desperate to move out of her parents' bungalow that she and the twins had settled into the cottage at Port Vik harbour the moment the keys were handed over. She silently blessed the family, friends and neighbours who had given her temporary custody of their odd assortment of deck chairs, old tables and, of course, the dreaded blow-up mattresses. All lit by a hideous standard lamp that her mother had insisted on forcing upon her as a house-warming gift.

'Still,' said Jim as they trudged downstairs, 'it was good of Kenny to lend you his work van to go to the mainland for the beds.'

Penny rolled her eyes.

'He only gave it to me on condition I take Eileen with me so he could get some peace. She's been learning Russian and managed to upset Mrs Petrenko at the baker's by asking for half a dozen cameltoes and a cream bum. Kenny had to offer Mr Petrenko a free oil change so they'd let Eileen back in the shop.'

'Why is she learning Russian of all things?'

'Remember I told you about her dark web contact from a couple of months ago?'

'Aye, Ivan Kimov.'

'Well,' said Penny, in a tone that implied something interesting was afoot, 'he's coming. His friends are too.'

Jim stopped with his hand on the living room door handle and looked at her, his eyes dancing with amusement.

'When I said Ivan Kimov, I didn't expect it to go that far.'

Penny suppressed a grin and gave him her best stern look.

'I thought we'd agreed to stop with the Ivan Kimov jokes.'

'Aye we did, but it's very hard.'

Jim's snort of laughter was cut short by Penny punching his arm. She shouldered him aside and barged into the living room.

'Alexa!' she shouted. 'Stop making that godawful racket.'

Recognising Penny's "mum-at-defcon-three" voice, Alexa promptly shut up.

'Why does she keep doing that?' Edith wailed into the silence. 'One minute she's fine and the next, ignoring everything I say and doing whatever she likes. She's so unreasonable.'

'Welcome to my world, sweetie,' said Penny with a wry smile.

'I'm bored,' said Edith. 'Chloe isn't talking to me because she thinks I broke her hairbrush, and Hector's off snogging Danny in the woods, only I didn't tell you that because I'm not a grass, and Jessica's pied me off to go to the mainland with her mum.'

'Erm, Jim and I have built my bed, so how about you come and help us build yours? The quicker it's built, the sooner you'll have a comfy bed,' Penny suggested.

Edith regarded her with horror.

'Oh my God, I can't even believe you asked me that. You just assume I have, like, nothing to do.'

She threw her hands in the air, as if to implore God to rescue her from stupid people, and stalked out. Penny and Jim winced as first the living room door then the front door slammed so hard that a fine cloud of dust descended from the ceiling and settled on Alexa. A moment later, they heard the creak of the front door opening again and Edith's head appeared around the living room door.

'Unless you'd like to maybe give me a driving lesson?' she asked in the sweetest of tones.

'I told you, we're building your–'

'You never want to do anything I want to do,' roared Edith, slamming out again.

Penny closed her eyes and hissed out a breath between clenched teeth.

'Let's begin with Hector's bed,' she told Jim. 'I have a funny feeling we might not have time to build Edith's today. Alexa, play Teenage Dirtbag.'

A few doors down, Eileen was in her element. She'd been practising her Russian all day in order to impress Ivan and his friends, and it seemed to be working. Okay, most of the conversation on her side of the Zoom call consisted of her insisting on a double room and two beers. And maybe everyone had looked slightly confused when she offered to give them a tomato with their hotel booking. But they'd got the overall message that she would sort out their accommodation on the island.

She waved cheerily into the camera.

'See you tonight, Ivan. Dad's vagina.'

'Do svidanya, Eileen.'

'That as well.'

Eileen closed the laptop and turned to her husband, who was grating cheese onto four slices of burnt toast.

'I don't see why we couldn't have the hacker collective to stay here,' she complained. 'We could squeeze four in.'

Kenny sighed and paused for a moment in his efforts to cover up the worst of the burnt bits.

'We've already been through this,' he told her. 'They're criminals and we're not having criminals around the boys. I don't want Ricky and Gervais getting any ideas. It's bad enough that they guessed your Amazon password and bought a pair of Japanese nipple clamps.'

'Och, they were only banned from Show and Tell for a term. But it's not like Ivan and his friends are baddy criminals. They're goody criminals.'

'Goody criminals who hacked the baggage system at Heathrow, sent everyone's luggage to Frankfurt and replaced Heathrow's website with a picture of a big sausage?' Kenny asked in exasperation.

'They were just trying to point out a security flaw. Anyway, everyone got their bags back…eventually. Alright, I won't ask again. I'll ring Martin and Rachel at the hotel and book a couple of rooms.'

'Aye,' said Kenny, wiping his hands on his mechanic's overalls, 'but for God's sake don't try to impress them with your Russian. I can't keep fixing cars for free every time you offend somebody. At this rate, you'll put me out of business.'

Life was trundling on as normal at Mrs Hubbard's Cupboard. Well, normal by island standards in that a six deep queue had formed as Mrs Hubbard, queen of the counter at the general store and ice cream emporium, took a moment to gossip with each customer. Her Douglas had been relegated to unloading boxes in the storeroom, his perpetual scowl being less than conducive to good customer relations. Mrs Hubbard knew all about customer relations. Mrs Hubbard had done a course. Several courses, in fact, and she was full of new-fangled ideas about branding and blue-sky thinking.

Douglas was glad to be tucked out of the way, where nobody would make him feel like he was on an episode of the bloody Apprentice. Last week she'd given him…what was it she called it? Aye, a project, that was it. A bloody project to make fliers for the ice cream side of the shop, which had needed a boost ever since Lady Sugar oot there had accidentally poisoned half the island. She'd demanded the leaflets be "consistent with the organic ethos of the business" and represent the ice cream without actual pictures of the stuff.

'Aye, and I'll just pull a unicorn out of my backside while we're at it,' he'd grumbled.

Douglas may not have done a fancy course, but he knew what outsourcing was. Mind you, he wasn't sure that giving Hector and Edith driving lessons was the best bargain he'd ever struck. He'd set up some cones down the old airfield, then set them up again, slightly the worse for wear after Edith drove over them. Three times. The lassie had clearly inherited her grandmother's driving style.

Having heaved a box of cat food onto a shelf, Douglas paused at the storeroom door to catch his breath and listen to his wife doing customer relations. He smiled to himself as he heard her asking Minky Wallace if she was doing a cake for the Vik Show. The woman did like a good blether.

Out front, Mrs Hubbard was in her element. It was important to know your customer. Find out a little information about them, the course had suggested, and you can gain customer loyalty by discreetly dropping a few personal nuggets into the conversation. And on the subject of personal nuggets, she thought, here's the ideal candidate.

'Oh, I heard about your piles, Eddie,' she said, plucking a box of All-Bran from the hand of a miserable-looking gentleman and scanning the barcode. 'A high fibre diet makes all the difference.'

'It's not for me!' Eddie protested, his face mottled pink. 'It's for the wife. She's making a bran fruit loaf for the Show.'

'That's very thoughtful of her, dearie.' Mrs Hubbard gave him a kindly pat on the arm. 'Though I'm not sure she should be baking for other people. I saw her in the chemist the other week buying scabies cream.'

'Shingles!' squeaked Eddie. 'It was shingles cream. She's had bad shingles, but she's better now.'

'Goodness me. I'm so sorry. I'm forever getting those two mixed up. Tell Margaret I'm glad to hear she's doing fine. Now, that'll be three pounds please.'

Mrs Hubbard counted the coins and smiled at Eddie, who looked even more miserable than he had a few moments ago.

'Cheer up,' she boomed. 'Her thrush must have cleared up as well by now. You have a great day, ye hear. Next!'

Eddie sloped off, avoiding the eyes of his fellow shoppers, and the queue moved forward.

'Ooh Elsie,' said Mrs Hubbard, her face lighting up at the sight of her best friend, who was next in line. She leaned across the counter, arms folded beneath her ample bosom, and nodded towards the retreating Eddie. 'Have you heard about Margaret Linklater? Terrible dose of the scabies, poor woman. Anyway, I haven't seen you for days. You're looking a bit peely wally. Is there something the matter? Are you ill?'

Elsie, a small, thin woman who generally radiated an air of quiet disapproval, did indeed look pale. And worried.

She shook her head and leaned in closer, whispering, 'There's something I need to talk to you about.'

'Is it business related?' Mrs Hubbard murmured. 'Because if you want any leaflets done for the library or the drug dealing, it turns out my Douglas is a marketing genius.'

'Keep your voice down. Anyway, it's not drug dealing,' Elsie hissed. 'It's a plant-based arthritis medicine and book delivery service. And, no, that side of things is fine provided

Kenny can keep the library van running for me. It's something else, but I can't talk here. Come round to mine after Losers Club tomorrow tonight.'

Gordon and Fiona had taken the day off from the farm to celebrate their wedding anniversary. Fiona had ditched her usual dungarees in favour of a floral-patterned dress and Gordon thought she'd never looked so bonny. With her red hair freed from its practical ponytail and the wellies replaced with a pair of pretty sandals, she was like one of those lassies from the perfume adverts.

Gordon imagined her running through the barley field, backlit by a halo of sunlight, and decided that if Fiona was a perfume, she'd be called Ginger Spice. He'd tell her later, over dinner at La Maison. She always said he didn't have a romantic thought in his head. Well, look out missus, because you're getting Gordoned tonight. He scratched his own ginger thatch as he contemplated how Fiona would react to getting Gordoned. It sounded a bit wrong, didn't it? Maybe better keep that one to himself. He wondered if other men used their forenames as a verb.

Fiona glanced over at her husband and noticed that he was smirking.

'What're you thinking about?' she asked.

'Roger Moore,' he replied.

Fiona gave a mental shrug and looked around her. The distillery was housed in an old, stone building, painted a pristine white. From its neatly trimmed lawns to its surprisingly Scandi interior, everything about it was meticulously tidy. She'd expected cobwebbed barrels and bagpipes but instead found herself in a comfortable leather armchair, gazing at a wall made from recycled whisky bottles.

From behind a beech-clad desk, the receptionist gave the waiting group a tight smile.

'Sorry, there are just two more to come then the tour will begin.'

No sooner had the words left her mouth, than the door flew open, admitting what appeared to be a six-foot fuchsia whirlwind followed by a short, harassed-looking man who was sweating profusely.

'Late, late, yes, sorry,' said the woman. 'Len, nip to the loo and tidy yourself up. You look like Danny de Vito in a tumble drier. I told you it was too warm for a tank top.'

As her husband shuffled obediently towards the toilets, the woman turned to the receptionist.

'Mary and Len Hopper. We're here for the tour. I can't believe we've lived on Vik for fifty years and haven't done the tour before. I said to Len, I said, let's do something fun. Get you out of the garden shed for a bit.' Mary paused for breath and giggled. 'That makes it sound like I keep him in the garden shed, doesn't it? I don't. Although he would make a lovely garden gnome. Can you commission gnomes? I could get him a gnome of himself for his birthday. But would a gnome version of oneself be a good present? At least it would be company for me when he's out in the damn shed all day. What do you think?'

She looked expectantly at the receptionist, who appeared to have momentarily lost the power of speech.

Receiving no reply, Mary stabbed a finger at the visitors book and asked, 'Shall I sign us in?'

Staring mutely at the verbose vision in pink before her, the receptionist slid the book and pen across the desk before picking up the phone.

'The group's ready now, and we have a lively one,' she murmured into the handset. 'Good luck.'

By the time a far tidier Len arrived back from the toilet, Mary had joined forces with Gordon and Fiona and was quizzing an older gentleman on the subject of garden gnomes. Len sidled up to Fiona and indicated Mary with a jerk of his head.

'Sorry we were late. Apparently, it's all *my* fault that *her* car ran out of petrol. There was logic to her argument but for the life of me, I can't remember what it was. Anyway, I hope we didn't delay the tour too much. What on earth is she talking to that man about?'

'He's our tour guide. Grant Hay. Mrs Hay's grandson,' said Fiona.

'Peppermint slice Mrs Hay?' asked Len.

'Yep. Only he's just been telling us that someone has pinched the recipe, so she won't be doing peppermint slices for the Vik Show this year.'

Len's shoulders slumped. 'Oh, this is the worst thing to happen on the island since the Great Fruit Scone scandal of 1984. She's been making them for decades. She must be able to remember the recipe.'

'She's about ninety-three and once turned up at the post office in her nightie,' Fiona reminded him. 'Jeeze, does Mary never stop talking?'

She leaned around Mary, who was now holding forth on the ridiculously small size of petrol tanks in modern cars, and said, 'Sorry to interrupt, Grant. I think we're all ready to start now.'

Grant looked somewhat relieved and, excusing himself, stepped back so he could address the whole group.

Besides Fiona, Gordon, Mary and Len, there were four Chinese tourists and the mysterious middle-aged couple who had bought the old hunting lodge near the Loch as a holiday home. Mrs Holiday-Homer was short and dressed in a purple poplin jumpsuit which emphasised what could kindly be described as an apple shaped middle. With her hair gathered into an enormous bun on the crown of her head, the woman reminded Fiona of something, only she couldn't quite put her finger on it. Mr Holiday-Homer, on the other hand, was tall and lean, with a large, pointed nose and a slight stoop. Despite the heat, he wore black trousers, black fleece and a black fedora, which only served to emphasise the unusual pallor of his skin and gave him a slightly sinister air.

Nobody on the island knew much about the Holiday-Homers, even though they really, really wanted to. The Holiday-Homers arrived in their big white Range Rover once in a while, never visited the shops or the pub and didn't mingle with the locals. Occasionally they appeared with a group of well-heeled guests, and the current theory among the islanders was that they were the ringleaders of a travelling satanic cult. After all, Stevie Mains told Geordie Barnes who told Pat Fisher who told Mrs Hubbard that he'd seen hooded figures in red robes when he was out poaching in the woods. Thus, Fiona, Gordon, Mary and Len stood apart from the Holiday-Homers and let the Chinese tourists take their chances.

Grant cleared his throat and began with what was clearly a well-rehearsed speech.

'Welcome to Lochlannach Distillery. Our tour today will take approximately one hour and there will be an opportunity at the end to sample the wonderful array of whiskies we produce. First, a few wee rules to make your visit a safe and enjoyable experience.'

As Grant droned on about not sticking your hands in anything dangerous, Len turned to find Mary, sparkly pink reading glasses firmly in place, absorbed in her phone.

'You should listen to this bit,' he whispered out of the side of his mouth. 'If anyone is going to get their fingers trapped, it's you.'

'Och, pish and twaddle,' Mary hissed. 'Eileen's asking if we can have the Russian hacker collective to stay now that Penny's moved out. The hotel's fully booked and Kenny won't have them in case Ricky and Gervais run away to join Anonymous. I've told her that we turned Edith's bedroom into my pole dancing room, so we'll put two in Penny's old room, one in Hector's old room and I'll ask Sandra Next Door if she'll have the last one.'

'What's an Anonymous?' asked Len.

'It's something to do with fixing computers,' said Mary confidently.

'That's good. Do you think the Anonymous do printers? I haven't been able to get ours to work in months.'

'When the hacker collective gets here, we'll ask them for their number.'

'Righty-ho,' said Len, 'and while they're at it, they could fix the oven clock too. It's been stuck on midnight since we had that power cut. By the way, what's a hacker collective?'

Mary thought for a moment then, with an air of authority, said, 'They do crowdfunding.'

'What's crowdfunding?'

'Oh, for goodness' sake Len, get with the modern terminology,' said Mary, who had absolutely no idea what crowdfunding was, or for that matter, hackers and Anonymouses. However, she fervently hoped that the Anonymouses didn't have a long waiting time for fixing oven clocks.

They followed their guide through the floor malting stage and watched the barley grist being turned into sugary wort in the giant mash tuns.

'Once we've extracted the sugary wort, it goes into one of these vessels here,' Grant explained, indicating a large steel vat, 'where we add yeast to begin the fermentation process. This can take a few days and what you end up with is a sweet beer. Here, I'll show you.'

Grant opened the hatch and dipped a flask into the foaming liquid.

'I'll pour some of the liquid into this glass and you can see for yourselves.'

He tipped the contents of the flask into a glass and lifted it to his lips.

'Erm, excuse me,' said Mary.

Having already been side-tracked by her once, Grant was determined that the big pink lady wasn't going to derail his carefully prepared show.

He gave her a professional smile and said, 'I'll be happy to answer questions at the end of this section of the tour.'

'It's just that–'

'Uh-uh. In a minute,' Grant said firmly, wagging a finger at her. He lifted the glass once more to his lips and took a long sip.

'You see, it's perfectly safe to drink. Would anyone else like to try some?'

The Chinese tourists were staring at him in horror and the holiday home woman looked like she was about to pass out. Meanwhile, Mary was eagerly leaning forward, positioning her reading glasses to get a better look at the glass.

'This tour is far more exciting than I'd expected!' she exclaimed. 'Do you normally get eyeballs in it?'

CHAPTER 2

'Why am I not surprised?' sighed Sergeant Wilson, holding up a hand to forestall Mary, who had opened her mouth to offer at least five different reasons for the police officer's lack of amazement. 'No need to answer. It was rhetorical. Whenever there's a crime, I always find one of you lot poking your noses in.'

Mary's face fell.

'It's hardly our fault!' she protested. 'There we were, minding our own business and asking important questions… well, *I* was asking important questions. Gordon was just scratching his backside. Isn't that right, Gordon?'

Gordon nodded glumly.

'Aye, it was quite itchy. I think I might have put on my scratchy pants by accident this morning.'

'It's the labels that do it,' said Mary, 'and if you cut them off, it's even worse. Have you tried a good fabric conditioner? Although you have to be careful with that. My Len has *very* sensitive skin. I used Lavender Dream on the fancy boxers Penny bought him for his birthday last year and, well, let's just say that we had ourselves a couple of extra party balloons.'

Sergeant Wilson loudly cleared her throat. 'When you're ready, people.'

They were standing at the entrance to the distillery car park, watching as Sergeant Wilson's new constable, PC 'Easy' Piecey, fixed police tape across the gateway and took up position to ward off the press hordes, which so far consisted only of Mystic Mike, the ageing hippy who wrote the astrology column in the Vik Gazette and who happened to be walking his dog past the distillery just as Sergeant Wilson screeched into the car park, blue lights and siren signalling that something was afoot. Mystic Mike had decided to hang around to see what all the fuss was about.

'It was in the stars that something big was going to happen on the island today,' he told PC Piecey.

'Technically it probably didn't happen today,' said the officer. 'It happened last night. We only found it today. So, how come your stars didn't predict that? It should have been all over the Gazette before we even knew about it.'

'Ah, the stars are full of mystery,' Mystic Mike said, airily waving a hand towards the sky. 'Tell me, boy, are you a Libra?'

'Oi, Easy,' shouted Sergeant Wilson, 'Would you prefer to a) guard the entrance or b) be sacked for giving unauthorised interviews to the local rag? Come on, son, it's multiple choice. Fifty-fifty. I'll even let you phone a fucking friend. Pick one and I shall make your dreams come true.'

PC Piecey's cheeks reddened, and his Adam's apple bobbed as he firmly closed his mouth and stood to attention, his gaze fixed somewhere in the middle distance.

Mystic Mike grinned and gave him a wink.

'Definitely a Libra. A Sagittarius would have torn her a new arsehole.'

Sergeant Wilson gave an impatient shake of her head and turned her attention back to the tour group.

'Right. Chinese people, hiv ye ony English? No?'

She pointed at Fiona.

'You there, Fred Weasley, give us a hand here. How do you work the Google Translate thingy on the phone?'

Mary stepped forward, tentatively raising a hand.

'If it's any help, I speak Mandarin.'

Sergeant Wilson thought about this for a moment then shook her head.

'No offence, Mary, but we'll be here 'til Christmas while you go off on tangents about the best way to use a wok or the human rights atrocities being perpetrated in China. Now, I doubt these people are much interested in woks or atrocities, because they've come on their holidays to get away from always having to be the one who does the cooking and the torturing, so if you don't mind, I'll stick with the Google Translate. Here we go, first question. Have you brutally murdered anyone recently?'

Eventually, having satisfied herself that the Chinese tourists were not, in her own words, "here to destabilise the Vik economy and spoil a good malt" she bade them a cheery "Off ye fuck. Och shut up, Weasley. It's not like they can understand what I'm saying" and turned her attention to the Holiday-Homers, who had become increasingly nervous during the Sergeant's exchange with the tourists.

'Right, Tinky-Winky and the Child Catcher, let's start with your names and contact details.'

Fiona gave a small gasp. A Teletubby. That was what the woman reminded her of. God, it had been really annoying her.

'Do you think we could do this somewhere more private please? Perhaps indoors, where it's cooler?' asked the woman.

She was fiddling nervously with a handkerchief. Strands of dark hair had come loose from the bun atop her head and now stuck to her face and neck in the heat of the afternoon sun.

Seeing the sceptical look Sergeant Wilson shot his wife, Mr

Holiday-Homer bravely took over the impossible task of trying to reason with her.

'Anyway, isn't it better to do these things separately? You wouldn't want us all influencing each other, I'm sure. Not that we have much to say, of course.'

Sergeant Wilson's inner bullshit detector gave a small bleep. These two were squirming. Why were they squirming?

'Why are you two squirming? Did you murder someone?'

'No, of course not,' said the woman. 'We just don't want… well, there's really no need for us to be involved.'

'Involved? Why would you not want to be involved? Is our crime not good enough for you? Would you prefer to be transferred to one of your cushy English prisons when I arrest you for failing to cooperate with the investigation? Because you're on the mean streets of Vik now, lady, and…what? What is it, Mary? Yes, you can go for a pee. Easy, will you take Mary in for a pee please and make sure she doesn't wander through the crime scene. Len, I hereby deputise you in the name of the King, God and the Brownie Guide Law. You take over guard duty and don't let anyone in. Now, where was I?'

Len's favourite burgundy tanktop took the strain as he puffed out his chest and assured the policewoman that, 'Deputy Hopper won't let you down, ma'am.'

He tipped an imaginary Stetson and moseyed on down to the front gate where, legs apart and thumbs hooked in belt, he glared at Mystic Mike and asked, 'Do you feel lucky, punk?'

Before Sergeant Wilson could return to her rant, Mr Holiday-Homer handed her a card.

'Officer, I do apologise if we seem reluctant. Please, call the number on this card and if you still have questions for us, we will endeavour to answer them.'

The Sergeant peered at the London number on the card. Bloody posh people and their fancy London lawyers, she thought. Still, sometimes it was fun to bait posh people and sometimes it was better to haud yer wheesht. The bullshit detector had gone strangely silent, so perhaps it was time for her to do the same. There was something off about the Holiday-Homers; something she couldn't quite put her finger on. And the number on the card looked familiar. She'd seen this before, but where? She clicked her fingers a few times, as if the friction would somehow spark the memory. It didn't, so she moved away from the group and called the number.

Left alone with the Holiday-Homers, Gordon and Fiona shuffled awkwardly, unsure what to say to the strange couple.

Eventually Gordon cleared his throat and asked, 'Eh, I don't suppose you have any more of them magic cards, do you? I've never found anything that could shut her up once she gets annoyed.'

The woman gave him a weak smile.

'Sorry. I know this must seem strange. If you could maybe, you know, just say nothing to anyone about it? We only wanted a nice, normal day out, you see.'

The man cleared his throat, and she stopped talking.

'Yes, well, hmm,' the man said, clearly trying to think of a way to steer the conversation onto common ground. 'So, erm, what made you decide on the distillery tour today?'

'It's our wedding anniversary,' said Fiona, proudly putting an arm around Gordon's shoulders and giving him a squeeze. 'We have the wee farm out at Braebank, and it's not often we get the chance to take the wellies off. You're not far from us. You have the old lodge near the loch, right?'

'Ah, right, yes,' the man mumbled, then he seemed to rally as a new topic of conversation sprang to mind. 'Lovely weather we're having. Most unscottish, ha ha. Bit of a change from the summer storms last year, eh?'

'You were here last summer?' asked Fiona. 'I thought you'd only recently taken over the lodge.'

Both the man and the woman looked distinctly uncomfortable. They glanced at each other, clearly coming to a silent agreement that it might be best to stop talking.

Once more, the man cleared his throat and said, 'Well, I expect your Sergeant will have made her call by now, so we'll just, you know.'

He tailed off and made a walking motion with two fingers, aiming them in the direction of Sergeant Wilson, who appeared to be having a heated discussion with the person on the other end of the line.

As the man strode towards the police officer, the woman reluctantly trailed behind, glancing over her shoulder at Gordon and Fiona and mouthing a hasty, 'Sorry.'

'Well, that was weird,' said Gordon.

'What was weird?' came a voice from behind him, making him jump.

'Mary!' he exclaimed. 'It was nothing. Just them two over there, the big weirdos with the magic cards. And now she's letting them go! She hasn't even shouted at them or anything! Is she smiling? She never smiles. Fiona, she's smiling. Do something.'

'Leave it with me,' said Mary. 'I'm an old hand at these diplomatic situations. I'll have things smoothed over in no time.'

She failed to spot Gordon and Fiona rolling their eyes heavenward.

Sergeant Wilson's smile had been replaced with her habitual scowl by the time she returned to the group, still clutching the card. Being a big fan of the status quo, Gordon relaxed. He knew where he was with a grumpy Sergeant Wilson. He never wanted to experience her full wrath, but he could cope fine with the odd bout of swearing and mild aggression. Nevertheless, he was curious about the Holiday-Homers, so he risked a telling off and cocked his head to get a better look at the card.

'Stop being a nosy fucker,' growled Sergeant Wilson, hastily tucking the card into the pocket of her stab vest.

Jeeze, thought Gordon, it's roasting hot and the woman's wearing a stab vest. She never takes the thing off. What did she think would happen today that she'd need a stab vest? Vik was hardly a hotbed of knife crime. Except all the murdered folk of course. And then there was that Australian eejit who nearly bashed Jim's brains out and put Penny in the hospital. Och, maybe a stab vest wasn't such a bad idea. But did she have to wear it all the time? She even came to one of Mary's parties with it on. Was she expecting to be brutally murdered with a cake fork? They were running a pool down the village pub, taking bets on whether she slept in it. Stevie Mains had asked her out, hoping to resolve the argument once and for all. She'd turned him down, of course. Said she was looking for someone who cooked Jamaican food and would take her dancing, not a cheesy wee bell-end whose mum still did his washing for him. What sort of man was he? Forty-two and his mum still did his washing! Although, on the subject of washing–

'Gordon! Earth to Gordon!'

Gordon started at the sound of his name. 'What? Sorry, I was thinking.'

'What were you thinking?' asked Fiona.

'Just that I've almost run out of clean boxers.'

'I'll wash some for you when we get home.'

'Thanks. I don't know what I'd do without you.'

'Right, now that we've fully established the current and future state of Gordon's underwear, we can get on with the questions,' said Sergeant Wilson.

'I have a question,' said Mary. 'Why were you smiling at the Holiday-Homers?'

'I was not smiling. I was…stretching my lips.'

'You were definitely smiling. We saw you.' Mary turned to the others. 'We saw her smiling, didn't we?'

Gordon clocked the expression on Sergeant Wilson's face, which he suspected may herald the full wrath he'd rather not experience, and hastily looked away, murmuring a noncommittal, 'Hmm.'

Sergeant Wilson decided to put an end to this line of

enquiry because at some point, she did have to get on with an actual investigation.

'You can stop being a nosy fucker as well, Mary. And where's Len? Len! Stop distracting my officer and get your arse over here.'

Len didn't hear the Sergeant calling for him. He was very busy being an important deputy, briefing PC Piecey on all the interesting things that had happened in his absence; Mrs Mackie came past with a new tartan shopping bag, Frankie from the farm tooted his tractor horn on the way by and Paula McAndrew from the paper shop had stopped to let him know that his Cruising Monthly hadn't come in yet. The policeman was quite disappointed to have missed Paula because he could have saved himself the trip to check if this week's copy of Flower Arranging Today had arrived. The conversation had just moved on to whether it was still worth ordering Cardigan World since they'd put the price up, when Len spotted something out of the corner of his eye and shot a foot out to intercept it.

'Oh, good save, Len,' said Sergeant Wilson, arriving at his side.

She peered down at the photographer from the Vik Gazette who was sprawled on the tarmac, his feet scrabbling to push himself away from the policewoman with the dangerous glint in her eye. After all, she did have a reputation for taking no prisoners. Or was it taking prisoners? He wasn't sure.

Sergeant Wilson made a low sound in her throat, something akin to a growl.

'I was coming over here to tear a strip off Len, but I think I might tear something off you instead. Now, where shall we begin? I usually prefer the genital area but I'm a reasonable woman. I'll listen to other suggestions.'

The photographer gave a squeak, rolled over and got to his knees. With fumbling fingers, he picked up his camera and shuffled backwards through the car park entrance.

'You can't get me. I'm in den! I'm in den!' he wailed from the other side of the police tape, for all the world like a giant, badly dressed child in the safe zone in a game of Tag.

Sergeant Wilson turned away from him and contented herself with barking at Easy to stop blethering and do his job. Or at least that was how Len would later summarise it to Mary. He had mentally blocked out the worst of the swearing. Nevertheless, he felt a sense of pride that he'd done his bit, and he positively glowed when Sergeant Wilson told the group he was a "have-a-go-hero or some such fucking nonsense." He'd never thought of himself as a hero before. He resolved to do more heroic things in future. All he had to do was think of some.

'Right,' said Sergeant Wilson in her firmest voice, 'Everyone stay still, don't go anywhere and speak only when you're spoken to. I need names and contact details. I'll start with the Weasley twins over here. Fucking whatchamacallthem. Fred and George.'

'Fiona and Gordon,' said Fiona.

'Nope. They were definitely Fred and George. I saw the films.'

'We're Fiona and Gordon, and *you're* being gingerist.'

'I'm what?' barked Sergeant Wilson.

Fiona shook her head and looked uncomfortable.

Sergeant Wilson gave a sharp laugh and said, 'Listen here, Weasley, I have checked the Police Scotland diversity form and I can assure you that there is no ginger box. Now, names and contact details.'

'But you already know our names and contact details,' interjected Mary.

Sergeant Wilson pursed her lips and glared at the woman.

'Mary Hopper, Valhalla, a mile up the road from the village,' mumbled Mary, cowed for quite possibly the first time in her life.

Len was impressed by Sergeant Wilson's ability to silence his much adored but somewhat strident wife. Len made a mental note to invite his new friend Sergeant Wilson over for tea on a regular basis. Len had completely forgotten that he had a bright yellow shed full of cannabis in his back garden and that he and Elsie had a burgeoning business supplying the local pensioners with "plant-based arthritis medicine" from the back of her library van.

By the time Sergeant Wilson had extracted personal details from the group and established to her satisfaction that they knew very little and were unlikely to be murderers, the sun had moved west and a rumble in her belly told her that the afternoon was drifting towards teatime. She finally put her notebook away and told everyone to bugger off, before making her way back into the distillery to speak with the manager.

As they wandered towards their vehicles, quietly contemplating the unexpected turn of events and looking forward to getting home to a nice cup of tea, Mary suddenly stopped in her tracks and tutted.

'Oh, I can't believe I forgot to tell you!' she exclaimed.

Used to her dramas, the others ignored her and carried on walking.

'No, stop,' she called after them. 'This is actually something important. I know who died and why Sergeant Wilson thinks it's murder.'

The other's wheeled around and walked back to her.

'Okay, I'll bite,' said Fiona. 'Spill the beans.'

Making the most of her moment in the spotlight, Mary launched into her tale.

'Well, you know how I needed a pee? And Sergeant Wilson sent Easy Piecey to make sure I didn't escape?'

The others nodded and she continued.

'The loos just have these partition walls. They're not solid stone like the other rooms because they're modern additions, you see. Someone at some point has carved a big room up into smaller rooms and popped in a few pipes.'

'Mary, stop wittering on and get to the point,' Len warned.

He was desperate to get home to make a list of all the heroic things he could do.

'The point is that I could hear people talking through the wall. I assume they were some of the distillery workers. Anyway, I heard them saying that it was Ian who died. Ian Henderson. They've all had a peek in the mash tun and he's in there with his wee lad hanging out of his trousers. They reckon he was…how can I put this politely?...tossing the caber when he went in.'

'Oh, Jesus,' said Gordon. 'You mean he was, you know, into the whisky? Oh, Jesus. I'll never be able to look at a blended malt again without wondering "blended with what?"'

'Couldn't he have just fallen in? If you were doing, erm, *that*, you could get a wee bit excited and lose your footing,' Fiona suggested.

'You saw the hatch. It's not that big,' said Mary. 'It would be quite hard to accidentally fall in. No, from what I heard, everyone thinks he had to have been helped through it.'

'I suppose he could have been peeing into the mash tun,' said Fiona, glancing sideways at Gordon and flashing him a wicked grin.

'Oh, no,' said Gordon glumly. 'I'm not sure which is worse.'

'I didn't think of that,' admitted Mary. 'They mentioned something about a forensic team coming over later, so I'm sure we'll find out. Obviously, the results will be secret, so half the island will have them in full within fifteen minutes.'

'Did anyone know Ian very well?' asked Len. 'Does he have any family?'

'I haven't spoken to him since 1979,' said Mary. 'He was an odious man then, and I don't imagine he improved with age. Grabbed my backside when I was queueing in the chemist with Penny in my arms. He was probably used to women who didn't make a fuss, and I expect he thought there wasn't much I could do about it, with the bairn there. I broke his nose with her rattle. Anyway, I heard he got a wife from a catalogue.'

Len frowned and shook his head.

'A mail order bride? How do you get one of those to Vik? We're in the back of beyond.'

'I don't know,' said Mary. 'She probably came in a box, and he had to build her. She'll be dancing a jig right now though, assuming he screwed her legs on properly. She gets rid of the filthy old beggar and presumably inherits everything.'

'Which makes her our chief suspect,' Fiona pointed out. Then, seeing the confused looks on the faces of her companions, she added, 'Well, we're not going to let Sergeant Wilson do this on her own, are we?'

CHAPTER 3

Penny and Eileen were setting out the chairs while Jim ran around the church hall, kicking a football.

'He shoots. He scores! And the crowd goes wild!'

Jim stared expectantly at Penny and Eileen. Hands on hips, they stared back.

'Aye, well, it was a tricky goal,' he said.

Penny eyeballed him, her expression betraying her scepticism.

'I can see that. Fairly sure the Scotland manager will be straight on the phone offering you a place on the team and taking up your suggestion that for next World Cup, they replace the goalposts with your old painting jumper and a coat.'

'Girls just don't understand the beautiful game,' said Jim, gathering up his makeshift goalpost and pulling it over his head.

His face emerged through the neck, grinning and Penny couldn't help but be reminded of a naughty scarecrow. There he was, mucky sweatshirt and hair standing on end…well, most of his hair. The bit they'd shaved in the hospital still hadn't caught up with the rest and he was refusing to get the whole lot cut until the short patch grew longer.

She could see the scar where they'd operated. Everything had been going so well until he had that aneurism and had to be rushed to the operating room. The blow to the head had caused far more damage than the doctors realised, and he was lucky to be alive. Had he not already been in hospital, well, Penny could hardly bear the thought.

Having realised that they had become more than friends, they'd agreed to sit down and have the Big Talk when he got home. As it was, they'd spent much of Jim's time in hospital Facetiming each other, with the occasional visit from Penny at the weekends. Her heart had almost burst with excitement when Aberdeen Royal Infirmary said he was stable enough to move back to the hospital on the island. Finally, they'd have the chance to explore these feelings. These feelings which were consuming her and making her every atom crave him. These feelings that she thought she would never have again after her divorce from Alex. These feelings that made her giddy and giggly and light and hopeful and…Then he had the aneurism, and her world crashed.

Of course, Jim had no memory of this or of the past couple of years. Sometimes she wasn't even sure he remembered that he had forgotten, if that made sense. He could recall things from a long time ago and, upon being told, was happily surprised to discover that he had moved back to the island to help his dad with the vet's practice. Yet as well as the recent past, day to day he struggled to make new memories. Oddly, he appeared to be blithely unaware of the problem most of the time. He simply accepted his current reality and didn't seem at all perturbed by the fact that he'd had to be introduced to Elsie three times in the same day. It was all very strange. The doctor said his memory would probably recover in time, but for now they should go with the flow. As far as Penny could tell, the only other side effect of having his head bashed in was that Jim had taken an inexplicable dislike to the colour blue, hence he was using the time off work to redecorate his house.

Penny hadn't told him about their budding relationship because, after all, to him she was a new person. It wouldn't be fair to expect him to love her, to take on this virtual stranger with her two teenagers, this woman who had once snogged him at a school disco then unexpectedly dropped back into his world when they were all grown up, this woman who claimed to be his pal and was apparently the one whom he was defending when, in his words, "some bastard caved my fucking head in." Yet every time they were together, it was all Penny could do to resist the urge to touch him. The need to bury herself in him was overwhelming and, oh God, she wanted to be held. She just wanted to…everything.

Aaaand breathe. Penny clenched her fists, digging the nails into her palms to stop the tears that were threatening to well up.

In general, he was the same old Jim. He looked the same (except the baldy patch), laughed the same and had the same interests as before. She simply had to have faith that if he loved her once, he would come to do so again.

Penny was brought out of her reverie by a comforting hand on her arm. Eileen, her best friend since forever, knew exactly what she was thinking right now and how very hard this was.

'What?' asked Jim.

'What do you mean what?' said Penny.

'You were looking at me funny, like you'd just secretly farted and followed through.' He held his body rigid and crossed his eyes to demonstrate.

'I did not look like that,' laughed Penny. 'Now, stop messing about and help us set things up. The rest of Losers Club will be here in ten minutes.'

They busied themselves laying out pamphlets and copies of this week's superfood star recipe.

'Did you hear that someone stole Mrs Hay's peppermint slice recipe?' Eileen asked.

Penny instinctively turned to Jim, expecting him to be

horrified. Every church sale, fundraiser and island event, he was always to be found at the front of the peppermint slice queue. Jim was a slave to the peppermint slice. Except he didn't look horrified. He didn't look anything other than mildly interested.

'You love Mrs Hay's peppermint slices,' she reminded him.

'I do?'

Penny nodded. 'You said you'd marry Mrs Hay for her peppermint slices alone.'

'She's a Mrs. Isn't she already married?'

'She was,' said Eileen, 'but Mr Hay died a few years ago.'

'Is she very attractive?' Jim asked, his face lighting up at the prospect of a single woman who could cook.

For a brief moment, an image of a confused elderly woman in pink negligee and green bed socks, banging on the post office counter to demand her pension, her false teeth forgotten in a jar at home, flitted through Penny's mind. Poor Mrs Hay had been on strong medication at the time, and it had taken her neighbours months to persuade her to show her face in public again. How to summarise for Jim?

'She's a bit scantily dressed for my taste, but she does have a regular income.'

'Aha! Sexy, rich and available. She sounds like my kind of woman. Do you have her number?'

'I think she's on Tinder,' Eileen offered, her face a picture of innocence.

'Eh? Like stuff you use to start a fire? No way am I shagging a pyromaniac. I'm looking for a…,' Jim clicked his fingers, 'What's the word?'

'Woman you can love and respect?' suggested Penny.

'Nymphomaniac. Aye, one of them nymphomaniacs would be just grand.'

By the time they'd explained the concept of swiping right to Jim's satisfaction, a small crowd had filtered into the church hall. Originally, Losers Club had been Penny,

Jim, Eileen, Fiona, Gordon, Sandra Next Door, Mrs Hubbard and Elsie. These days, Penny ran multiple sessions on different nights across the island and her business had expanded to take in Scotland's cities. However, each Wednesday night, the original Losers stayed behind to share a picnic and a good old-fashioned chinwag. Tonight was no different, or at least so it seemed until after the session, when Penny looked up from her notes to find only six originals and one new Loser passing round the tub of carrot sticks.

'Sergeant Wilson, what are you doing here?' asked Penny.

'I won't lie to you, Penny. I can't get my backside into my uniform trousers, and I've decided to do something about it.'

'But you're wearing your uniform trousers.'

'I've been secretly buying trousers that look like my uniform trousers.'

'For how long?'

'Fifteen years. There's no way I'm submitting a uniform order form with my arse size on it to that bastard McCulloch in Aberdeen. He'll have it posted on the front page of the intranet. Anyway, they've put the price of fake police trousers up, so it's cheaper to join you lot. At least until McCulloch retires.'

'How old is McCulloch?'

'Thirty-five. I'm in it for the long haul, Penny. I can tell you're pleased.'

Penny had some doubts about Sergeant Wilson's detective skills on that score. Nevertheless, she took a deep breath and smiled.

'I hope you enjoyed your first session. This,' Penny gestured to the group, 'this is just a get-together afterwards for friends. You're welcome to stay, of course, but you don't have to.'

'Long haul, Ms Moon,' said Sergeant Wilson, raising her eyebrows and wagging a finger at Penny. 'If it means fucking making friends, I suppose I'll give it a go.'

She helped herself to a paper plate and began to load it with snacks.

'It's good that you're here,' said Fiona. 'How are you getting on with the Ian Henderson murder?'

Mrs Hubbard's gasp was louder than she'd intended and all eyes in the group turned to her.

'Ian Henderson has been murdered?'

Fiona swallowed a lump of celery and humus before replying, 'Aye, sorry, I thought you would have heard at the shop. He was…oh, Mrs Hubbard, I'm too embarrassed to say it to you. He was,' she paused for a moment, her brain scrambling for a polite word to describe what Ian had been doing, 'pleasuring himself into a vat when someone shoved him in.'

'My goodness, dearie. He always was,' Mrs Hubbard paused for a moment, her brain scrambling for a polite word to describe Ian Henderson, 'a complete wanker. I suppose I should cancel his paper. Have you spoken to his wife, Martisha?'

'It's Sergeant Wilson, Mrs Hubbard. Always on duty. Always Sergeant Wilson. And yes, I spoke to his wife, but I'm not at fucking liberty yada yada yada, so you can mind your own nosy business.'

'Martisha Wilson, don't you get high and mighty with me. I remember you spending your pocket money on spot cream and Smash Hits. Your mum was one of my favourite customers and your dad was on the Bowling Club committee with my Douglas. If your dad was still with us, he'd be ashamed of you for speaking to me like that. Now, what did Ian Henderson's wife have to say for herself?'

The others held their breath, waiting for the usual Sergeant Wilson bout of swearing and bad temper. However, nothing came. If anything, Sergeant Wilson looked slightly unnerved.

Gordon leaned over to Fiona and whispered, 'Maybe Mrs Hubbard makes the magic cards.'

The silence continued, Sergeant Wilson shifting

awkwardly in her seat and twiddling the knobs on her police radio, until eventually she said, 'Eh, I'm, ah, what's the word? The one I don't use. Aye, eh, sorry. The wife said she was at home. No alibi. She's one of them Latvians or something, so it was a bit difficult to get much information out of her.'

'I'm fluent in Russian, if that helps,' Eileen offered.

Penny snorted.

'You only know the swear words and make the rest up so it sounds a bit Russian.'

'Feckov,' said Eileen, giving her friend a wicked grin. 'I have some Russian friends visiting. I'm sure they wouldn't mind doing the interrupting. Do you think we could borrow Ashov, Sandra Next Door? I know Geoff's had him doing his website, but this is more important. I think Ashov used to live in Latvia.'

Sandra Next Door rolled her eyes and corrected Eileen.

'Interpreting, not interrupting. Yes, please take Ashov. It'll give me a chance to get the house back in order. The man keeps leaving the toilet seat up and, even worse, never uses a coaster. He's an absolute nightmare.'

'Given how Ian died, I can see why you didn't offer the services of Ivan Kimov,' said Jim, his dead-pan expression belying the inner twelve-year-old which snickered at every mention of the name.

'He's very busy consulting with Anonymous about Len and Mary's oven clock. It has them all stumped,' Eileen told him.

She turned to Sergeant Wilson.

'So, that's settled then. You can have Ashov Manin.'

Beside her, Penny could feel Jim tense then almost vibrate as he tried valiantly to contain his mirth.

'Aye,' he squeaked, his voice trembling, 'Because that's far more appropriate.'

Trying to keep a straight face, Penny discreetly elbowed him in the ribs.

'For once you're not being fucking useless, Eileen,' said

Sergeant Wilson, regaining some of her usual brio. 'Phone me in the morning and we'll arrange it.'

'I don't have your number,' said Eileen.

'999, get me in any time. Right, is that all the being friendly done for today? If so, I'll get myself off.'

'What about the forensics?' asked Fiona.

'What about them? The man was bashing his wee bishop into a vat of mash, and somebody pushed him in. End of. The body went back to Aberdeen and I'm sure they're pissing themselves laughing right now.'

'You're not a very sympathetic person,' sniffed Sandra Next Door.

'And you're clearly not a fan of irony, Margaret Thatcher's evil twin. Have you all finished quizzing me on my job? Because there's a serial killer documentary with my name on it at home.'

Gordon's eyes widened.

'They made a film about you?'

'Ha fucking ha,' sneered the Sergeant as she zipped her fleece over her stab vest. 'Right, you lot, no meddling. This is police business, and I don't want you sticking your noses in. I know what you're like.'

'Just one more question,' said Penny. 'Did you find out who was in the distillery at the time Ian was murdered?'

'That is also none of your nosy business, but I'll give you this for free. The new owner's solicitor is a hardened turd-nugget in the backside of Lady Justice and won't let any of his staff cooperate with giving us distillery records. Worry ye not. I'll be shoving some laxative up there tomorrow, in the form of the Procurator Fiscal.'

With that, Sergeant Wilson strode confidently towards the door, a trail of cheap, church hall toilet paper stuck to the heel of her police boot.

Penny turned to the others and asked, 'Is it just me, or does she not want us looking into this?'

'I'm not surprised,' said Jim. 'Could be dangerous and

who are we to be running around the island, looking into murders?'

'You do remember I told you about us solving the last two murders on the island?'

'Really?'

Penny shook her head, exasperated.

'I'm not explaining again. You'll have to go with the flow on this one and trust that we know what we're doing.'

'Strictly speaking, we fly by the seat of our pants,' said Sandra Next Door. 'We usually mess with crime scenes, take the corpse to the pub and break into people's houses until the solution presents itself.'

'But it's all part of a plan. Sort of,' said Penny. 'And this time we have something that the police don't.'

She paused for dramatic effect.

'Underpants with wings?' suggested Gordon, who had stopped listening when Sandra Next Door mentioned pants.

'Will you shut up about pants for once in your life!' Fiona scolded him.

'I was only thinking of ways you could fly by the seat of your pants,' Gordon protested. 'I mean, the wings would have to fold in, of course. Or you'd have to get really big trousers.'

Jim nodded sagely. 'Aye. And they'd have to be multidirectional wings. Otherwise, how could you turn your pants inside out and wear them for a second day?'

'You're a wise man, Jim. You wouldn't want a wing tip in the goolies.'

'Both of you shut up about underpants,' said Penny. 'No, our secret weapon is–'

'Ooh, ooh, I know,' said Eileen, putting her hand in the air like a schoolchild desperate to impress the teacher. 'Is it the gun Sandra Next Door found in Old Archie's kitchen that time and never handed in?'

'You didn't give the gun to the police?' asked Penny, shocked.

Sandra Next Door was the sort of woman who had plastic covers on her sofa and folded the end of the toilet roll into a neat point. A woman with the emotional range of a cat getting a belly rub, without the nice purring bit at the start. A woman with an unshakeable belief in the birch when it came to rowdy teenagers and people who didn't take their shoes off at the door. In short, not a woman who should be in charge of a gun.

Sandra Next Door fixed her eyes on Penny's and said in a menacing tone, 'Perhaps now you'll take me seriously when I tell you I'm sick of your mother's cat shitting in my begonias.'

The implied threat slightly lost its edge when Eileen piped up with, 'It's okay. She doesn't have any bullets.'

'Och, Eileen, you had to spoil it,' said Sandra Next Door. She gave Penny a thin smile. 'Nobody ever asked for the gun, so I kept it as a souvenir. Not to remember killing that man, even though he deserved it. No, it was saving Ricky and Gervais that I wanted to remember.'

'You're a scary babushka sometimes, but I'm glad you're on our side,' Eileen told her. Then she paused and raised her hand again. 'Ooh, ooh, is it Sandra Next Door? Is she the secret weapon?'

Penny sighed. 'We don't really do dramatic reveals here, do we? It's the Russian hackers. I thought we could ask them to look into Ian and the distillery. If the new owner isn't cooperating, our hacker friends can go places the police can't.'

'Good thinking,' said Jim. 'That's far less dangerous. Who are the hackers again?'

'You can meet them if you like,' Penny offered. 'I'm calling an extraordinary meeting of Losers Club at my mum and dad's house in half an hour.'

She glanced at Mrs Hubbard, who had been uncharacteristically subdued and was currently leaning forward in her chair, peering gloomily at her mobile phone.

'Mrs Hubbard, you've been very quiet tonight. Are you okay? Mrs Hubbard? Mrs Hubbard!'

To the surprise of everyone present, Mrs Hubbard removed a pair of wireless earbuds and looked around her, slightly befuddled.

'Hmm? Oh, sorry dearie. Maybe I'm not using these earmuffs right. It's just that I've been calling Elsie but she's not picking up. She asked me to come round to her house after Losers Club. I thought she'd be here, then I thought maybe she meant she wasn't coming and to meet her afterwards. If you don't mind, I'll pop round to Elsie's and check on her.'

Penny frowned and checked her phone. No messages from Elsie to say she wouldn't be at Losers Club tonight. Maybe she was ill.

'You're right, Mrs H. We best check on her. We can all go.'

'Och, there's no need,' Mrs Hubbard protested. 'She'll only get embarrassed about folk making a fuss.'

'How about Gordon and I go with you, then?' Fiona suggested. 'That way, you'll at least have someone to give you a ride home if Elsie's not up to it.'

With that agreed, Losers Club went their separate ways, not for one moment suspecting that their evening was about to descend into turmoil.

CHAPTER 4

Mary was in her element. She'd spent the afternoon inventing sausage cupcakes and here at her kitchen table was the perfect captive audience. Captive in that they had no escape because she'd locked the back door.

'And the topping?' asked Jim in a strained voice. He had just swallowed his first bite and was determinedly ignoring its attempts to reappear.

'Brown sauce icing, dear. Do you want to try one of the pink ones?'

'Strawberry?'

'Ketchup.'

'Just be glad you weren't here last week,' said Len sombrely. 'Fajita trifle.'

'You barely touched yours,' protested Mary. 'You spent all evening in the toilet, refusing to come out.'

'That wasn't *me* refusing to come out, dear. It was the night before's haddock and marmalade curry.'

'Where's Ivan, Mum? asked Penny. 'We were hoping that Ivan, Max, and Victor could help us with something. Sandra Next Door and Eileen are coming over with Ashov in a minute.'

Mary arched one eyebrow, a trick Penny dearly envied.

'Intriguing. Ivan's here, but Max and Victor have gone to the pub. Said they wanted to meet the pretty girls. I didn't have the heart to tell them that the only people in the place on a Wednesday night will be Bertie the barman and Stevie Mains. Stevie has long hair and a cracking pair of man boobs, but I'd hardly call him pretty.'

As if on cue, Ivan appeared in the doorway, all suntan, muscles and tousled dark hair. He was wearing a black t-shirt, which had ridden up to partially expose a smooth, taut stomach, and looked far more bad boy rock star than expected.

'Penny,' he cried, walking over and enveloping her in a tight hug.

He smelled of cigarettes and spice, with an undertone of citrus shampoo. Penny felt a small, surprising rush in what she thought of as the lingerie department, and quickly closed her legs. She supposed it was probably a reaction to how very sexy the Russian was and oh my God he smelled so good, but with a pelvic floor like one of her mother's leaky airbeds, she couldn't discount it being a tiny wee.

Smiling broadly, Ivan held her away from him, his hands on her shoulders. 'I am so pleased to finally meet you, Penny. And I can see that you are so very pleased to meet me.'

Penny looked down at her own black t-shirt, which hid a slightly doughy belly lined with the permanent reminders of a giant twin pregnancy, and was horrified to see that the girls had perked up. Traitors, she thought, pulling her cardigan across her chest, although you make a good point there, Ivan. Two of them, even. Note to self – for all future meetings with Ivan, wear the big padded bra that looks like a couple of blancmanges. Why couldn't he be a normal nerd, like you see in the movies, all spots and pale skin from too much junk food and not enough daylight?

Her thoughts were interrupted by the arrival of Sandra Next Door and Eileen, who had a far more appropriate specimen in tow. Ashov was a tall, thin man with a fierce shaving rash, and eyes made large behind bottle-thick spectacles. He peered uncertainly around the room, taking in its occupants, before raising a hand and greeting everyone with a faint, 'Hi.'

'Ashov his English is not so good as me,' Ivan explained. 'He is, how you say it, very quiet man. Does not like people. But he is very good on the computer, even better than me.'

'Well, maybe you can tell him in Russian to put the toilet seat down once in a while and eat some vegetables. He looks like a short-sighted vampire with herpes,' snapped Sandra Next Door. 'Mary, have you decorated again?'

'Yes,' said Mary, beaming at her neighbour. 'When Penny and the twins moved out, we decided it was time for a refresh. Dark Olive and Moody Mustard. Bit of a departure from my usual colours. Sausage cupcake?'

'No thanks, Mary. I tried your Marmite fancies the other day and they came out the other end, well, a bit like this kitchen, I suppose.'

Undaunted, Mary offered Ashov a cupcake and ushered him onto one of the wooden chairs around the table.

'Right, placebo for coming, everyone,' said Eileen, settling herself down on the stool that Len used to reach high cupboards.

'Spasiba,' Ivan corrected her.

'That as well. Now, because Ivan and Ashov are my guests, I should be in charge of this bit. So, Penny, what are we doing?'

Penny smiled at the two Russians.

'Ivan and Ashov, we need you to dig up anything you can find on Ian Henderson and the Lochlannach distillery. Ian has been murdered and we're trying to find out who was at the distillery when he was killed, any enemies he might have, that sort of thing. Eileen and Sandra Next Door will give you details.'

'Yes,' said Eileen, taking charge again. 'We will definitely do that. And tomorrow, Ashov, could you come with us to speak to Ian's widow? She's Lavatorian.'

'Latvian? Or perhaps Lithuanian?' asked Ivan.

'That as well,' Eileen confirmed. 'Sergeant Wilson will be there, but don't worry. She's good police. Okay, grumpy police. With psychopathic tendencies. But she won't arrest you unless you've done something really bad. Probably.'

Eileen looked at Penny for confirmation and Penny nodded.

'We've broken into loads of places, and she's never arrested us, has she Jim?'

Astonished, Jim stared back at her, a sausage cupcake halfway to his lips.

'We have?'

'Honestly, you used to be the vaguely normal one around here. Does everyone understand their jobs? Any questions?'

Penny paused for a moment and looked around the table, giving Ivan, who was hurriedly translating for Ashov, a chance to catch up.

'Da,' said Ashov. 'Understand. Hack computers like guid loon. Dinna fash yersel.'

'Has Eileen been teaching you Doric?' said Penny, referring to the local dialect.

'Da. Gie's a bosie, Ivan, and skelp ma dowp.'

Ivan frowned at his friend, who seemed unfazed by the fact that Jim had almost headbutted the kitchen table in his haste to bury his head in his arms. Penny could see Jim's shoulders shaking as his efforts to contain his laughter emerged in a strangled wheeze. She was struggling to keep a straight face herself and was quite relieved when her father intervened.

'Hack computers like a good boy. Don't stress. Give me a cuddle, Ivan, and spank my bottom,' Len translated. 'Eileen, what have you been teaching the poor man?'

Eileen was beaming proudly at her protégé.

'The interesting bits,' she declared, giving Ashov a thumbs up.

'Kittle ma oxters,' said Ashov.

Len ignored him, instead turning to Penny and saying, 'I have an investigation of my own. I've decided to find out who stole Mrs Hay's peppermint slice recipe. I'm going to see her in the morning.'

Jim's head shot up, a look of intense interest on his face.

'I could come and help you,' he tentatively suggested, his eyes wide and hopeful.

Len, who had given considerable thought as to which heroic deed should come top of his list, was unsure how to explain to Jim that he wanted to do the hero stuff on his own, so he politely paid no heed to Jim's offer and continued.

'Once I've established where she kept the recipe and who might have access, I'll draw up a list of suspects and start interviewing them.'

'I could come and help you,' Jim repeated, a little more forcefully.

Len sighed.

'Alright, but you're the deputy and I'm the chief.'

'Woo hoo!' Jim exclaimed. 'I am swiping right on that saucy little minx.'

'There will be no swiping anything,' Len retorted. 'The poor woman has suffered enough already. And make sure you pack some lunch. It's going to be a long day.'

'Ooh,' said Mary, 'I have the perfect thing.'

She reached into the fridge and withdrew a wide, shallow pie dish.

'Gooseberry and liver quiche.'

Elsie's house was nestled at the end of a lane, by a clump of trees, a short walk from the church hall. It was a low, two storey semi-detached stone cottage, with a front door directly onto the lane. Elsie had placed planters beneath the windows either side of the door and by the path which led around the side of the house to a small garden at the rear. They had vainly tried knocking on both front and back doors.

Despite the lateness of the hour, daylight prevailed, and Fiona, Gordon and Mrs Hubbard did not expect to see any lights on inside the house. It therefore came as a surprise when Mrs Hubbard, peering through the letterbox, said, 'That's very strange. The kitchen light's on and I can see a pan on the stove.'

Fiona and Gordon, who were at the windows, attempting to glimpse the rooms beyond through the haze of Elsie's pristine net curtains, gently nudged Mrs Hubbard aside and took turns to look through the letterbox.

As Fiona stood to make way for Gordon, she was frowning. She had confirmed Mrs Hubbard's observations but had spotted something else; something that had made her stomach drop and a feeling of quiet dread pass through her.

'Mrs H, can you try her phone again please?'

'Dearie me, I've already tried it about fifty times,' said Mrs Hubbard. Yet she took her mobile phone from her pocket and jabbed at the screen.

'I don't think there's anyone in,' said Gordon.

'Shh!' Fiona hissed sharply. 'Just listen.'

They stood absolutely still for five, ten, fifteen seconds, and Gordon had just started to say, 'What are we–' when they heard a faint buzzing noise inside the house. Fiona lifted the letterbox, and the buzz immediately grew louder. Bending to look through the gap, she could see Elsie's phone vibrating on the small table in the hall, its screen momentarily bright before fading into darkness as the buzzing stopped.

'Voicemail,' said Mrs Hubbard, putting her phone back in her pocket. 'I never know what to say to those things. I panic and have a whole conversation with myself. And the ones where they make you choose fifty numbers before they'll put you through to a real person are even worse. I once tried to make a doctor's appointment and ended up buying caravan insurance from a lovely young man in Mumbai. I don't even own a caravan! But he was such a nice man. We still keep in touch, and I went to his cousin's wedding in Skegness last year.'

'Mrs H! Focus!' Fiona barked, the stress making her impatient. 'Elsie's phone is on the hall table. We need to get in and check she's okay.'

Fiona tried the front door handle, but it was unmoving.

'Damn. Locked. Come on, we'll try round the back.'

The trio made their way past the planters and down the path to the back garden. Fiona tried the back door handle but once again it was locked fast. She stepped back and stood in the middle of the patch of lawn, surveying the house for a point of entry.

'Gordon, you're skinnier than me. See that little open window? It's probably the bathroom. I'll boost you up then you hold onto the drainpipe, reach in and open the bigger window below it.'

It took several attempts, but eventually Fiona managed to boost Gordon high enough so that he was able to get a foothold on the drainpipe and, clinging on precariously, stretch an arm through the window.

'That's it,' Fiona encouraged him. 'Shift your foot onto the windowsill and get your shoulder through the gap.'

'It's nae that easy, woman,' said Gordon, his voice reduced to a croak by exertion.

He had managed to wedge the small window open with the back of his head and push his shoulder and face through the gap. Fiona could see his hand scrabbling for the lock on the inside of the larger window.

'Hurry up, Gordon,' said Fiona impatiently. 'It can't be that hard. Penny's broken into loads of houses.'

'If you're that keen, you bloody try it. Shit. I think my head's stuck. Fiona, I'm really stuck here. The window has shut a bit and won't open again.'

'Oh, for goodness' sake,' said Fiona, sighing dramatically

as she looked up at her husband's dungareed bottom waggling frantically. 'Try turning your head sideways and… what the ffffudge!'

Fiona started and only just managed to curb her language as Mrs Hubbard suddenly appeared through the back door.

'How the flibbertigibbet did you get in there?' she said.

Mrs Hubbard smiled and patted her stiff leather handbag, a doughty specimen which had once felled a would-be mugger in Aberdeen and put him in a coma for three weeks.

'I forgot I had a key, dearie. Elsie used to ask me to look after her budgies when she went to visit her cousins in Forfar every year. Wingo Starr and Mr Tiddlywinks.'

'Seriously?'

'The birds, not the cousins. I've had a look around the house and she's definitely not here.'

'Do you mind if I come in?' Fiona asked.

Mrs Hubbard looked doubtful. 'Elsie wouldn't like people nosying inside her house. She's a very private person. Maybe we should wait until Sergeant Wilson comes.'

'Aye, but Gordon's got his head stuck in the bathroom window. We can hardly leave him with his backside hanging out. It's going to rain and that's a new pair of dungarees he has on.'

As if to emphasise her point, one of Gordon's wellies sailed past her and hit the lawn.

'Sorry, foot slipped,' came a muffled voice from above.

'Och, I suppose it'll be okay,' said Mrs Hubbard, reluctantly standing aside to let Fiona past.

Fiona was about to make her way in the direction of the stairs when she veered off course towards the fridge.

'Just in case we need to grease him out,' she told Mrs Hubbard, extracting a large tub of butter and closing the fridge door with a soft thump.

'You could use soap,' Mrs Hubbard suggested. 'I'm not sure how Elsie would feel about you using her butter.'

'Mrs H, I'm not being funny, but your friend is missing

and there's a man upstairs with his head stuck in a window, one wellie on and the imminent threat of a wet arse. Did Sergeant Wilson say how long she'd be?'

'I haven't phoned her yet, dearie. I was hoping you would. She'll only shout at me for interrupting the serial killer documentary they made about her. You young ones are much better with things like shouting. Everything's shout, shout, shout these days. You hear them in the street, shouting to their pals, and the whole world gets to hear their business. I blame the social media. There's no privacy anymore. I was just saying to Elsie the other day–'

'Mrs Hubbard!' snapped Fiona.

The older woman's brow was creased with worry and her fingers twisted the stiff handles of her handbag.

'Sorry. I just get so chatty when I'm anxious. I'll phone Martisha. You see to Gordon.'

'Sorry for being short with you,' said Fiona, her voice softening. 'It would be a huge help if you could phone Sergeant Wilson. Probably best not tell her about Gordon, though. She'll only invent a rude name for him and leak the official police report to the Vik Gazette.'

A minute later, Mrs Hubbard heard the creak of the floorboards in the bathroom above her, followed by Fiona's muffled voice telling Gordon, 'Keep still while I butter your ears.'

Left alone with her thoughts, Mrs Hubbard felt panic grip her as she tried to imagine what could have happened to her friend. There was no way Elsie would have left without a word. She certainly wouldn't have left Mr Tiddlywinks with nobody to look after him. Elsie loved that bird. Mrs Hubbard loved Elsie. They'd been joined at the hip for half a century and…oh good lord, Elsie, what's happened to you? Mrs Hubbard stared at the phone, her breath coming in short, shaky rasps as she tried to focus on stemming the flow of tears that threatened at any second to overwhelm her. She didn't think she could cope with an ear-bashing from Martisha Wilson right now.

Mary was part way through her monologue on the health benefits of gooseberry and liver quiche when Penny's phone rang. Relieved to have an excuse to get away from what would surely morph into a lecture on incorporating the banana and prawn smoothie into one's morning routine, Penny left the table to take the call in the relative quiet of the living room; relative because she could still hear her mother happily droning on in the background about irons in the blood.

She looked at the name of the caller and smiled warmly. A few minutes later, that smile was gone as she made a call of her own.

As soon as Penny walked back into the kitchen, Eileen knew something was terribly wrong. Her friend's face was pale, her lips pursed and her short, dark hair askew from where she had run a jittery hand through it.

'What's up, Rubber Duck?' asked Eileen, using the familiar nickname in a vain attempt to make Penny look a tiny bit less like the time she'd gotten a false positive on a pregnancy test aged seventeen.

'Bad news, Winnie the Pooh,' said Penny, taking a deep breath in through her nose to calm herself.

The hubbub in the kitchen quickly faded to silence and everyone stared at Penny, waiting for her to explain. She steeled herself, wishing to her very marrow that she didn't have to say what she was about to say.

'You know how Gordon, Fiona and Mrs Hubbard went to check on Elsie? They couldn't find her, and Mrs Hubbard was in a state, so she phoned me to ask if I'd call Sergeant Wilson. While she was on the phone, she realised she'd forgotten to check the pantry. She opened the pantry door and found… God, there's no easy way to tell you this. Elsie's dead.'

. . .

'Well, bugger me with a six-foot python,' said Jim, breaking the stunned silence that followed Penny's announcement. 'Obviously I didn't know her as well as everyone else here, but still.'

'You did know her,' said Penny. 'You just don't remember.'

She took another deep, shaky breath and allowed some of the shock she was feeling to seep through; the horror of hearing her friend break the moment she opened that door.

'What will Mrs Hubbard do without her? To find the body of your best friend of fifty years. She'll never get over this. I better call Douglas and let him know.'

'Has Mrs Hubbard called Sergeant Wilson?' asked Mary, biting back her own tears in an effort to be strong for her daughter. Mary loved to make a fuss over nothing but in a real crisis, she was a rock. All thoughts of avocado crumble fled from her mind as she squatted down beside her daughter's chair and stroked Penny's hand, Len hovering uncertainly behind her.

'I phoned her. She's on her way there now with Doc Harris. They've sent an ambulance,' said Penny, hot tears finally spilling over as her voice rose to a strangled squeak, 'but there's no point. It's too late.'

Beside her, Sandra Next Door was comforting a sobbing Eileen. Sandra looked up and her eyes met Mary's, a silent understanding passing between them. It was time to do what one always did in a crisis.

'I'll put the kettle on,' said Mary.

CHAPTER 5

For possibly the first time in forty years, Mrs Hubbard's Cupboard was closed. Douglas had opened the shop briefly in the early morning, long enough for the locals to pick up their milk and newspapers, yet he was reluctant to leave Minty alone, so he had flipped the sign to "Closed", locked the door and brought his wife her third cup of tea. She'd be peeing like a broken tap by lunchtime, but at least it would keep her busy.

Douglas wasn't quite sure what to do for the best. He knew he ought to be doing something. He couldn't bear to see Minty in this state and felt compelled to look after her. Yet there were all these people in his front room, making a fuss and eating fondant fancies, even though it was only just gone nine and far too early for cake. Douglas didn't do chit chat and polite entertaining. In fact, Douglas didn't do people, which was why Minty preferred it when he was out of the way, not scowling at customers and putting them off their morning rolls.

With all the folk attending to his beloved, Douglas felt somewhat redundant and wondered whether anyone would mind if he watched Antique Bargain Hunters Fix Houses. He pointed the remote at the telly and settled back on the sofa, intent on finding out whether the Art Deco taps the blue team bought at auction yesterday really were the ideal solution to Judith and Dean's plumbing problems. Unfortunately, Douglas had overlooked one thing. Daytime TV adverts. The stairlift and the over fifties' life insurance plan were fine, as were the appeals for "just three pounds a month" to save donkeys, dogs and schools in far flung lands. However, the advert for Crockett & Cooke "direct cremations from only £14 per month – over eight thousand five-star reviews on Happy Customers dot com!" drew an ominous glare from the wife.

'I don't know where they're getting all these five-star reviews from anyway,' he grumbled, switching the television off. 'Does anybody want another cup of tea?'

Mrs Hubbard shook her head.

'No thank you, darlin'. I've drunk that much tea this morning, my tonsils are floating. I expect the three of you will be ready for another.'

She looked at Fiona, Gordon and Penny, who all politely declined.

'In that case,' Douglas declared, 'I'll go and tidy up the shop. A new order of stretch mark cream has just come in and I'm going to put it beside the condoms.'

He tapped the side of his nose.

'For those in the know, it's called a psychological nudge. Mrs Hubbard did a course.'

After he'd left, Mrs Hubbard breathed a sigh of relief and slipped on a pair of sandals.

'Thank goodness he's found something to do. Now, let's get out of here before he comes back offering more tea.'

'But I thought you would be grieving and staying in and such like,' said Penny.

'Dearie, I'm devastated. It's hard to think of a world without her. But she wouldn't want me moping around, crying and drinking cups of tea. She'd want me to find out who did this terrible thing and cut their dangly bits off. We'll

53

have a wee Losers Club meeting, just the four of us, but not here. I need to get out.'

'Where then? Cuppachino doesn't open until ten,' said Fiona.

Mrs Hubbard pulled her emergency cardigan from her handbag and brusquely shook out the wrinkles. She tutted impatiently at Fiona.

'Haven't I just said I don't want more cups of tea? That goes for coffee too. No, we're going to bang on Bertie the barman's door until he opens up the pub for us, then I'm going to have the biggest cocktail with the rudest name and all the umbrellas.'

Fifteen minutes later, Fiona, Gordon and Penny sat at a table in the empty pub, eyeing the vibrant concoction in Mrs Hubbard's enormous glass with awe.

'What's it called again?' asked Fiona.

'Sex on the Beach with a Porn Star with three Slippery Nipples,' said Mrs Hubbard. 'Bertie invented it on the spot.'

Bertie, still in his pyjamas, doffed an imaginary cap at Mrs Hubbard and put three lemonades on the bar.

'How come you get the fancy cocktail, and we get lemonades?' asked Fiona.

'I didn't know who was driving, so I just played it safe.'

Using two hands, Mrs Hubbard raised her glass.

'Let's have a toast to Elsie.'

Gordon hurriedly collected the lemonades, and they clinked their glasses together, safe in the knowledge that wherever she was, their friend was looking down at Mrs Hubbard's cocktail and shaking her head in utter disapproval.

'Okay,' said Penny, 'Dad and Jim are off investigating the mystery of the peppermint slices, Eileen and Sandra are busy looking into Ian Henderson's murder and now, sadly, we've got one of our own to lay to rest. Tell us what you want us to do, Mrs H.'

Mrs Hubbard took a hefty slurp of her cocktail, going

slightly cross-eyed as the combination of alcohol and tangy fruit hit her tastebuds.

'Sergeant Wilson arranged for Elsie to go to Aberdeen last night. The forensic team were already here because of Ian, so she called them out straight away. Goodness, I hope they don't put Elsie next to Ian in the morgue. There weren't many people on this earth she didn't like, but she never could stand that man. There was just something about him. Once, when we were much younger, he–'

'Mrs Hubbard, I don't mean to be indelicate but if you keep digressing, we'll be here all day,' said Fiona. She had taken out a notebook and pen. All she had written down so far was "Who killed Elsie?"

'Oops, there I go again,' said Mrs Hubbard, with a small hiccup. The cocktail seemed to be kicking in, although Fiona wasn't sure if the alcohol or stress were to blame for the fact that getting any relevant information out of the woman was like performing colonic irrigation on a constipated elephant. An awful lot of the brown stuff had to come out before things became clear.

'Maybe it would help if I sum up what we know so far,' Fiona suggested, turning to Penny. 'Elsie was lying in the pantry. The pantry has a hook on the outside that slips over a nail in the frame to keep the door closed. Mrs Hubbard hadn't looked in the pantry before because Elsie could hardly have shut herself in there and if by some accident she had, she could have shoved a bit of cardboard in the gap and knocked the hook back off the nail again. That's why it has to be murder. Someone stashed her body in there.'

Fiona took a sip of her lemonade and gave Mrs Hubbard a sympathetic glance before continuing.

'As Mrs Hubbard said, Elsie's off to the pathologist in Aberdeen and the house has already been gone through by the fingerprint boys. While we were waiting for Sergeant Wilson last night, Gordon and I took a closer look at her.

There was bruising around her neck, which suggests she was strangled, but obviously we're no experts.

'Mrs Hubbard told Sergeant Wilson that she saw Elsie in the shop the other day and she seemed rattled about something. She wouldn't tell Mrs H what had got her so worried, but said it was nothing to do with her cannabis deliveries.'

Fiona put a hand up to forestall Penny's protestations.

'Yes, yes, we know. Mrs H told us all about your dad and Elsie's gardening sideline. Why didn't you tell us before? Your dad's like the Pablo Escobar of the Northern isles. It's quite cool, really.'

Penny looked slightly shamefaced.

'Sandra Next Door. If she found out, she'd have the police straight round. Anyway, they only sell to the sick and pensioners. It's not like he and Elsie were hanging around the school gates dishing out jellies from the back of the library van.'

'Nonsense, dearie,' said Mrs Hubbard. 'It's only Sergeant Wilson and she'd have to arrest her own mother for being one of Len and Elsie's best customers. Terrible arthritis, poor woman, and they ration the painkillers in that care home. Elsie slips…*used to* slip her an extra baggie inside an Agatha Christie.'

'What about anything else that could have worried Elsie?' asked Penny.

Mrs Hubbard took a sip, then another, of her cocktail while she considered her reply.

'I can't think of anything. She knew a lot of people through working at the library, but she was also very private and kept herself to herself. There were no enemies, if that's what you're getting at. She was seeing Old Archie on and off for years and I'm sure there was nobody else. There never was, for either of them. She must have seen or heard something though, because she seemed almost scared when she asked me to come to her house after Losers Club. It sounded very serious, whatever it was.'

'I've been thinking,' said Gordon, ignoring Fiona's muttered aside that this better not be about underpants. 'Did she keep a diary?'

'She did, although I expect Sergeant Wilson took it. I still have her keys if anyone wants to have a look round the house.'

Mrs Hubbard leaned down to retrieve her handbag, the sudden pressure on her stomach eliciting a small burp. After a quick rummage through the assorted tissues, pens and receipts, she emerged triumphant with Elsie's keys.

'Mind you,' she told the others, 'we'll have to sneak in without being seen, or Sergeant Wilson will have our guts for garters. Don't worry about messing up the crime scene, though. I have everything we need in the shop.'

An hour later, four very strangely dressed people, one of them smelling strongly of spirits and slightly unsteady on her feet, slipped in through Elsie's back door. They were covered head to toe in an assortment of bin bags, rubber gloves and shower caps, all secured with the aid of clothes pegs and rubber bands.

As they stopped at the threshold to put shower caps over their shoes, Penny reflected that, despite their intention of being discreet, four adults driving around dressed in bin bags and bright pink shower caps may have attracted some attention.

Precisely on cue, her phone rang.

'You're fucking up to something, with "fucking up" being the operative words in that sentence,' declared Sergeant Wilson, without preamble.

'Just a spot of shopping,' Penny lied, gesturing frantically at the others to be quiet.

'Stevie Mains' mum told Ailsa Brody who told Marie Knox who told me that four arseholes dressed in bin bags and shower caps were spotted driving through Port Vik in a vehicle that sounds suspiciously like yours. If I find out you're lying to me, Penny Moon, I'll sink my police boots so far up your arse you'll be shitting kneecaps. Are we clear?'

'Transparent,' Penny snapped. 'I don't suppose you have–'

It was too late. Sergeant Wilson had rung off.

'Was that Sergeant Wilson?' asked Gordon. 'She scares the pants off me. When she asked for my number the other day, I gave her Jim's so if she ever phoned, she could shout at him instead.'

'Yeah, well, she suspects what we're up to, so for the sake of my backside, we better be quick before she decides to come and check up on us,' said Penny.

They divided the rooms between them and spent the next fifteen minutes going through drawers, lifting mattresses and checking under cushions to no avail. Eventually, they congregated in the small living room, where Mrs Hubbard was gazing thoughtfully at the fireplace.

'If I was Elsie and wanted to hide something, I'd put it in here,' she said, slowly struggling to her knees and reaching an arm up the chimney.

Other than a shower of sooty debris, this achieved nothing. However, as she knelt on the hearth, Mrs Hubbard felt one of the tiles wobble beneath her knee. She shuffled backwards until she felt the soft hearth rug beneath her aching joints and bent over to peer at the loose tile.

'Can you get a knife please, Gordon?' she instructed, holding her arms out so that Fiona and Penny could hoist her back to a standing position.

Gordon returned with the knife and pried up the loose tile. The three women gasped as he lifted it to reveal a letter and a necklace.

'I thought if she had a hidey hole, it would be somewhere close to her chair,' said Mrs Hubbard. 'That's the necklace her mother gave her when she went off to university. It was the last time she saw her mum. It's nothing fancy, but even the cheapest things can be priceless.'

Gordon passed the letter and necklace to Mrs Hubbard, who passed the letter to Fiona, saying, 'You read it, dearie. I can't.'

Fiona cleared her throat and began to read out loud.

Dear Minty,

If you're reading this, I'm either dead or you're being a nosy parker as usual. If it's the latter, put this letter back where you found it.

We've been friends for most of our lives, and you and Douglas are like family to me. I've left a will with the solicitors in Cowpit Yow Lane, but you'll be pleased to know I've bequeathed everything to you. Could you see to it that my books are donated to the library or to a good cause? Please burn my diary. I kept it so that if I ever went ga-ga, I'd have something to remind me of who I was. However, I don't like the thought of it being read by strangers.

I realise you'll be reeling right now because I know how I'd feel if something happened to you. Take comfort from the fact that I had a good life, and you were a big part of that. Don't do anything stupid like getting drunk on cocktails with rude names, or I might come back to haunt you.

I've never told you how grateful I am for our friendship. I count myself lucky to have had you by my side through the best and worst of times. Please remember the best times – they're the ones that really count.

I'll be in heaven with Archie, I hope, and always looking down on you with love, my friend.

Until we meet again,

. . .

Elsie

By the time Fiona had finished speaking, there wasn't a dry eye in the house. Tears ran freely down Mrs Hubbard's cheeks, splashing with little plops onto her bin bag. Even Gordon, a man not prone to outbursts of emotion, found his beard suddenly damp and itchy. Wordlessly, the four friends came together, arms tightly clasping each other, a small island of comfort in a stormy sea of grief.

CHAPTER 6

Jim smoothed his hair down and checked for about the fiftieth time that he hadn't accidentally put on his old painting jumper this morning. He was looking forward to meeting Mrs Hay. This memory thing was sometimes very frustrating, and he could feel it slowly eroding his confidence. Whilst he was grateful for friends like Penny, who had patiently kept him on the right track, he needed to start getting out again. He had tried going back to work but had got everything muddled up and prescribed worming tablets for Mrs Cruikshank's cockatoo instead of Mr Newbank's cockapoo. Thankfully, Dad was keeping the vet's practice ticking over until his brain untangled itself. And he felt that there was some progress on that front, with small flashes of familiarity and fewer episodes of having to be introduced to the same person five times. Nevertheless, he had somehow managed to order flowers to his own house on six consecutive days, and he still didn't know who they were for! He had simply handed them back to the delivery man with a cheery, 'Consider this a gift from me.' Each day, the delivery man grew more suspicious that something was going on until, on day six, he blurted out, 'I'm not being funny, but have you got a thing for me?' The Petal Palace in Port Vik now had Jim on a watchlist, like some sort of floral predator.

Although most of the time he forgot that he had forgotten, all these inconveniences knocked the old self-esteem, and he was becoming increasingly anxious about making mistakes. The only antidote, he had decided, was to put himself out there, meet new people, do stuff and keep buggering on. Which was why he was sitting here in Len's Volvo, clutching a gooseberry and liver quiche and pinning his hopes on Penny's assurance that "Mrs Hay will be delighted to go out with you. She's been going through a bit of a dry spell lately."

'Do I look okay?' he asked Len. 'I mean, I know I'm no Johnny Munroe, but I think I've got a certain rugged charm.'

Len briefly flicked his gaze away from the road. 'That's the third time you've asked me. I'm not being funny, but have you got a thing for me? Because I'm batting for team Mary, in case there's any doubt. Anyway, I always thought you and Penny–'

He stopped before he said something that Penny would make him regret. Jim looked at him, eyebrows raised.

'Me and Penny what?'

'Make a great team, yes, that's it, a great team with Eileen, Sandra Next Door, Fiona, Gordon, Mrs Hubbard and poor Elsie, a great, great, smashing team who are just lovely, lovely friends,' said Len, inwardly congratulating himself on an excellent recovery.

It wasn't an excellent recovery, but Jim decided to let it pass. He suspected he knew what Len had been about to say because he couldn't believe that he'd been friends with someone as beautiful, clever and funny as Penny for nearly a whole year without asking her out. Only he didn't want to bring up the subject, in case it turned out he'd made a complete tit of himself. After all, she seemed to only want to be friends, so either he didn't fancy her, or she'd turned him down.

'It's not a gay thing. I just want someone to think I look

nice,' said Jim glumly. 'Although there was this time at university when I thought I was bi-curious, but it turned out she had polycystic ovaries and didn't give a shit about the beard.'

'I think that's one of those things we're not supposed to talk about because we're men,' said Len, who had once nearly lost his dangly bits when he had suggested to Mary that she was making fuss about the menopause. She'd been carving the Sunday roast at the time and the knife missed his crotch by an inch. He'd never forget it. That was the day he wasn't allowed any roast potatoes.

'I'm not being rude about her,' Jim protested. 'She was inspiring. It took real guts not to conform and to own it like that. We were together for a year. Weird that I can remember it all so clearly but I've no memory of my last birthday.'

'It'll come. Look, we're here.'

Len pulled up in front of a small row of terraced houses across from the market green. The street was far busier than usual, with a constant stream of people and vehicles entering and exiting the green, where a large marquee was being erected in preparation for the Vik Show. A man in a yellow jacket tapped on the car window and gestured to Len to park further down the street, away from the entrance.

With a sigh, Len moved the car forward and rolled to a halt at the end of the street.

'Looks like it might rain,' he commented as he stepped onto the pavement. 'I hope it clears up for the Show. Come on, then. Let's see what Mrs Hay has to say about this recipe business.'

He marched off purposefully towards a house in the middle of the row.

Jim, his hands full of quiche, wasn't quite as quick off the mark. He carefully laid the quiche aside and gave himself a quick once over in the vanity mirror before getting out of the car and following Len.

The creak of the garden gate must have alerted Mrs Hay

to her visitors because by the time they reached the front step, the door was already opening.

'Good morning, Mrs Hay. Long time, no see.'

Len's smile was warm as he explained why they were there.

Jim's smile, on the other hand, faltered slightly as he regarded the small, grey-haired figure in the pink housecoat. Bloody Penny, he thought. If there's one thing I mustn't forget, it's that I am going to get you back for this.

They entered the narrow lobby, carefully wiping their feet on the mat and hanging their coats on the end of the banister. Mrs Hay took them through to a small living room, where every surface, from windowsill to a wooden 1970s electric fire complete with fake flames, was covered with ornaments. She settled herself into an armchair by the fire and gestured to Len and Jim to make themselves comfortable on the sofa.

No sooner had they sat down than Mrs Hay was levering herself back out of her chair, saying, 'You must think I'm very rude. Would you like a cup of tea and a peppermint slice? I still have some peppermint slices left over in the freezer and I defrosted a few this morning because Grant's coming over later with his girlfriend. Have you met my grandson? He's a nice boy but a bit easily led, if you know what I mean. That girlfriend of his is…well, she's a Wallace.'

'It's not Poopy Wallace, is it?' asked Jim. 'She was in my year at school.'

'No, it's her younger sister, Minky.'

'The one with the brown teeth?'

'You're thinking of Manky. Minky's the blonde one. She owns the café on the High Street now. Cuppachino. The rest of them moved to Aberdeen, and last I heard, the father was doing fifteen years for arson. Right, enough gossip. I'll put the kettle on.'

Mrs Hay shuffled off towards the kitchen, waving off offers of help, and Jim turned to Len.

'Poppy, Mindy and Mandy Wallace. There's a blast from

the past. Poopy and Manky were hard as nails, but Minky was okay. Do you think Minky could have stolen the recipe to use in the café?'

'She's certainly at the top of the suspect list,' Len declared, writing "1. Minky Wallace – café owner, illicit baked goods provider?" in a small notebook.

By the time Mrs Hay shakily deposited a silver teapot, complete with hand-knitted orange tea cosy, onto a low coffee table, Jim and Len had drawn up a list of Minky related questions.

'Is Cuppachino making a profit?' Len asked.

'Heavens, how would I know?' said Mrs Hay, depositing a china milk-jug in front of him. 'I suppose she must be doing okay. She bought that son of hers a car for his seventeenth birthday, even though the little beggar had already been banned for three years for stealing Randy Mair's tractor and joyriding it through the window of Linda Loves Laces. Poor Linda. Shirley Newton told me she had to close the shoe shop for a month. Shirley's my carer, so she brings me all the news.'

'And, eh, does Shirley like a peppermint slice?' asked Len.

'Can't stand them, though she'll sometimes take one home for her brother.'

'Does anyone else come in and out of the house regularly?' asked Jim, struggling to capture a lump of sugar with a pair of tiny silver tongs. He gave a satisfied grunt as he finally managed to deposit one into his cup, then thanked Len, who had caught the others as they had pinged off randomly around the room.

Mrs Hay paused for a moment, silently counting on her fingers. Eventually, she nodded to herself, seemingly content that she had a complete list.

'Jimmy Gupta and Mrs Petrenko from the bakers deliver bread on a Monday. They always come in for a cup of tea. I don't know the new postman very well. Michael something. He's a good boy, though. Pops in and leaves the post on the hall table to save me bending down. Carol-Anne Green does my hair on a Friday. Then there's my neighbours, Jeanie Campbell at number seven and Ernie on the Other Side. They're always in checking up on me. I can't imagine either of them wanting to steal my peppermint slice recipe. Ernie on the Other Side can't cook, and Jeanie won't cook.'

'Jeanie Campbell is Eileen's mum, your dad's girlfriend,' Len reminded Jim. 'I suppose Gupta and Petrenko could have hatched a cunning plan to sell peppermint slices in the shop.'

He made a note – "2. Gupta and Petrenko – international heads of The Floury Baps crime syndicate?"

They stayed awhile, exchanging island news with Mrs Hay, but elicited no further useful information. She said she kept the recipe in a drawer in her kitchen and any visitors could have accessed it. She was unable to think of anyone else who had stopped by in the days before she noticed that the recipe was missing. Thus, Len and Jim drained their cups and set off to interview their list of suspects.

It was raining heavily by the time they left Mrs Hay's house, and Jim marvelled that Len, despite his advancing years and the back of his burgundy tanktop pulled over his head to protect his balding pate, could still manage a decent sprint to the car. He caught up just as Len wrenched the driver's door open, launched himself inside then immediately sprang back out again, howling, with half a liver and gooseberry quiche attached to his backside.

'Ah, bugger, I should've put it in the back seat,' said Jim, attempting to help Len scrape the brown, green and yellow mass from the seat of his trousers. 'Here. Bend over the driver's seat and I'll give it a wipe with this cloth.'

It was unfortunate that Jeanie Campbell from number seven chose that moment to emerge from her garden gate.

She stood under a large pink umbrella for a few seconds, pondering the sight of Len, his bottom poking out of the car while the younger man, muttering darkly about "fucking corduroy, everything sticks to fucking corduroy," frantically rubbed it.

'I'd recognise that bum anywhere. Is it you Len Hopper?'

'Oh God, Jeanie Campbell,' came a muffled voice from inside the vehicle. 'Is there any chance of you keeping this to yourself?'

'None whatsoever,' declared Jeanie. 'Anyway, it eventually comes to all of us.'

'What?' asked Len.

'Needing somebody to wipe your bum. I'm just away to meet your Mary at Cuppachino. I'll let her know in case she wants to swing past the supermarket for a packet of adult nappies on the way home.'

'It's quiche!' Len squeaked.

'Aye, it's definitely keech,' said Jeanie, giving Jim a wicked wink as she sauntered past.

'Quiche!' Len yelled after her

'Do you want to go home and change?' asked Jim, eyeing the smeared mess.

'There's no point,' said Len. 'I came out without my house keys and wild horses couldn't drag me into Cuppachino right now to borrow Mary's.

He did a passable impression of his wife loudly informing everyone within earshot, 'This is exactly like the time you sneezed too hard in the lift, and we had to go seven floors with eight strangers pretending not to notice. Of course, by the time we got to the seventh floor, there was only you and I left. Do you remember? Such a shame that white trouser were all the rage that summer.'

Jim smirked.

'You, um, really? In a lift?'

'I probably shouldn't have used that example,' said Len, miserably. 'Come on, let's hope it dries and we can rub the rest of it off. Should we start with the bakers, the hairdresser or the postman?'

· · ·

Eileen, Ashov and Sandra Next Door pulled up next to Sergeant Wilson's police car outside Anna Henderson's house, a squat two-storey building at the end of a farm track about two miles from the village. As they got out of their vehicle, Sergeant Wilson strode over, puffing herself up to deliver a sound telling off for tardiness. Sandra Next Door, however, was in no mood for one of the Sergeant's temper tantrums today.

'I know we're late,' she snapped, pointing a thumb over her shoulder at Ashov. 'Boy genius here can write a computer programme but can't work a bloomin' toaster. Set it on fire, threw it in the sink and blew every fuse in the house.'

'I nae a guid loon the day,' mumbled Ashov, staring miserably at the grass verge.

'What's he saying?' asked Sergeant Wilson.

She raised her voice and slowly shouted, 'I no speak Russian. You yes speak English?'

'It was Doric,' sighed Eileen. 'He said he isn't a good boy today. He speaks Latvian, Russian, English and basic Doric.'

'Why didn't Ivan come?' asked Sergeant Wilson.

'Because he doesn't speak Latvian and he's…erm…busy.'

'Busy?'

The Sergeant fixed Eileen with her very best hard stare. Eileen duly squirmed and looked around, as if hoping the right answer would leap from behind the Henderson's shed shouting, 'Here's some keech she'll totally buy.'

It wasn't in Eileen's nature to lie or evade, so she inwardly cursed herself for a traitor as she mumbled, 'Ooh, well, hmm, you'd have to ask Penny about that and she's not here.'

'Aye, that's because she's running around the island in fucking bin bags, up to no good. You're not the sharpest pencil in the box, Eileen Bates, and you're a poor liar.'

Sandra Next Door drew herself up to her full five-foot-four and stepped in front of her friend.

'You leave her alone, Martisha. *I'm* the only one who gets

to talk to Eileen like that. We're here to do you a favour, so we either get on with it or we're going home.'

'Aye, we'll get on with it, but you two can stay in the car,' growled the Sergeant, stabbing a finger in Sandra Next Door's chest.

'Skelp ma dowp!' shouted Ashov, going with the first phrase that sprang to mind.

He had no idea what was going on, but the scary lady who kept yelling at him about toilet seats seemed to be squaring up to the police lady and he didn't want her to be arrested because, despite the toilet seat yelling, she brought him cups of tea in bed and made scones for him. Anyway, the skelp ma dowp seemed to have worked. Both women were now staring at him like he'd lost his mind, which he quite possibly had on this weird island where people seemed to be dying at an alarming rate.

Sergeant Wilson glared at Sandra Next Door and snapped, 'Keep him under control,' before turning on her heel and knocking on the front door of the granite clad monstrosity before her.

Anna Henderson was a tiny, pale woman with lank blonde hair and deep, dark circles below her eyes. Age, or perhaps marriage to Ian Henderson, had not been kind to her, and even Sergeant Wilson, used as she was to shouting everyone into submission, lowered her voice and politely asked if they could come in.

Having declined cups of tea, the group settled themselves on Anna's sofas while Ashov explained the reason for their visit. Anna's face lit up when she heard her mother tongue.

'How on earth did she and Ian communicate?' Sandra Next Door muttered to Eileen. 'It must have been a lonely life for her, stuck on this rock in the middle of the North Sea with that awful man and not being able to talk to anyone.'

'Ask her if Ian had any enemies,' Sergeant Wilson instructed Ashov.

After a lengthy exchange, Ashov said, 'No. He is loved and respected by whole island. This is what he told her.'

Sergeant Wilson caught herself just as she was about to roll her eyes.

'Was there anything unusual about his behaviour recently?'

'He is writing to First Minister, may she be toasted and buttered in Hull,' came the reply.

Then, after a moment's thought, 'Sorry, my English, roasted and battered in Hell.'

This time Sergeant Wilson did roll her eyes although, with the island not being a hotbed of Latvian speakers, she decided that if she had a forgiving nature buried somewhere deep inside her, now would be the time to dig it up.

Therefore, she confined herself to, 'For fuck's sake, Ashov. What does Anna have against the First Minister?'

Ashov consulted with Anna, the explanation seemingly long and complex.

'Ian says First Minister bad woman who is doing bad thing. He writes letters to tell her he knows about the bad thing and then policeman from London come to speak to Ian. He told policeman to go away.'

'Was Anna there when the policeman came? Does she know the policeman's name?' asked Sergeant Wilson.

'No,' said Ashov. 'Ian told her to stay in bedroom like guid loon. She sees bald man leaving with Ian's laptop but that is all she sees. Ian said he is policeman but not why he is here, and she think it is about letters to that bitch First Minister.'

'What bad thing did Ian think the First Minister did?'

'She does not know. She hear Ian say Andrea Forglen, may she be eaten by randy frogs–'

He was briefly interrupted by Anna, then corrected himself.

'Sorry. Is angry dogs. So, Andrea Forglen is on island and Ian is seeing her in a house with other man. Ian does not understand because this other man should not be there. Then

Ian is on the internet and he is very angry. This is all she knows.'

Anna plucked at Ashov's arm and said something in Latvian.

'She is asking how she does funeral.'

'I'll send her some information and perhaps you could translate it for her?' said Sergeant Wilson. 'Can you ask her if Ian had any friends?'

Ashov asked and Anna shook her head, saying, 'No friend,' before explaining further in rapid Latvian.

'No. She is thinking he is not so much liked as he tell her,' said Ashov. 'He always working late because he hate the people at work. No people there at night. They have no visitors to house. She is only allowed to supermarket. This is why her English is very bad. He is sometimes at work all night and he is sometimes at village pub.'

Anna gave Sergeant Wilson a wan smile and asked a question.

'She is asking what will happen to her now,' Ashov translated.

'I'll give her the number for the solicitors in Cowpit Yow Lane. They'll be able to help her with sorting things out,' said Sergeant Wilson, giving Anna what she believed was a kindly smile but what Sandra Next Door privately considered a rictus grin.

Nevertheless, once Ashov had explained, Anna smiled back at the police officer and, eyes brimming with tears, said, 'Thanks you.'

As they left, Eileen made a mental note to take Ashov back to see Anna as soon as possible. Her very warm heart went out to the poor woman. Perhaps she could take her shopping and introduce her to people.

Eileen felt a small pang of sadness as she thought how Anna was exactly the type of stray that Elsie would have taken under her wing. She remembered how Elsie had adopted Johnny Munroe when the Hollywood A-lister was filming on the island, and how she'd taught him to knit. She knew they'd kept in touch since, with Johnny asking Elsie to be his "plus one" at the UK premiere. Elsie had been so looking forward to that. This determined, rather stern, yet good-hearted woman, who never expected anything other than a quiet life on the island, had become quite pink-cheeked when she'd delivered the exciting news to her Losers Club friends. Eileen wondered if Mrs Hubbard had told Johnny yet.

CHAPTER 7

Following the interview with Anna Henderson, Sergeant Wilson returned to the police station in Port Vik. She was still waiting to hear back from the Procurator Fiscal in Aberdeen but hoped he had been able to make some headway with the distillery owner. She was also waiting for his mobile phone data, and it would be the knees of the bees and the danglies of the dog if she could find his laptop. Who the hell had taken it? Because she was bloody sure that if it had been the police, she'd have known about it.

Sergeant Wilson didn't like people being on her patch without her knowing about it. She didn't even like them being on her patch when she did know about it. What with Ian and Elsie, the Major Investigation Team would be here any minute, upsetting the finely balanced relationship between police and locals; the one where she shouted at folk, and they did as they were told. Bloody MIT. It would be a good thing if she could wrap this up before she had some Detective Inspector with a hard-on for promotion politicking the fuck out of the situation because it would look good on his CV. Sergeant Wilson was perfectly capable of diplomacy and giving interviews to the press. Arseholes, the lot of them.

As it stood, she was nowhere near wrapping anything up.

She was still waiting for results from Elsie's house, but forensics hadn't turned up anything useful at the distillery and the work rota only showed Ian Henderson and Kylie Jackson on the late shift. Kylie was four-foot eleven, and Sergeant Wilson had done turds fatter than her. She doubted Kylie would have had the strength to push a struggling man through the hatch of the mash tun. Which meant that someone else was on the premises.

The security guard on patrol was about as much use as a fart in a wind tunnel. He claimed to have seen nothing unusual while doing his rounds, but Sergeant Wilson suspected he'd been sitting in the wee security office blethering with the man who watched the CCTV, who had also allegedly seen nothing unusual.

Sergeant Wilson had viewed the CCTV footage from that night. Unfortunately, only the exterior of the building and the warehouse were covered and even then, there were blind spots. If you were at all familiar with the layout, you could easily avoid the exterior cameras. Of course, the only place that anyone would want to break into would be the bonded warehouse, where the maturing whisky was kept in casks stacked on wooden shelves for anywhere between twelve and seventy years. A cask of seventy-year-old Lochlannach would be worth tens of thousands, so the warehouse was well-guarded. However, the fact that there hadn't been a robbery and that the killer had avoided being caught on CCTV, initially inclined Sergeant Wilson toward this being an inside job, quite possibly directed specifically at Ian. Whoever did this had known where the cameras were. Perhaps they came across Ian by chance and took their shot, or perhaps they knew he'd be there and planned it. Hard to say. It sounded as though he didn't get along with his co-workers and, from what she had heard of the man, he was a creepy, miserable old bastard. Yet today's interview had given her different food for thought.

'This motherfuckery with the First Minister only makes

things more complicated,' she muttered as she removed her stab vest, lifted her shirt and inspected the underside of her breast. Buggering vest. She was starting to suspect she had a fungal infection. It was so itchy last night that when she saw Elsie's knitting needles sitting by the armchair, she'd been tempted to pinch one and stick it through the armhole of her vest to give the old left boob a bit of relief.

PC Piecey chose that moment to wander in. He looked up from the witness statement he was perusing, stared for a few seconds, then wheeled around and made a quick exit in the direction of the tearoom.

'Get the teas in, Easy,' Sergeant Wilson shouted after him, 'and bring the good biscuits. Jammie Dodgers or caramel wafers. Not the twatting ginger snaps. What sort of fucking psychopath buys fucking ginger fucking snaps anyway? Though, at least they come in a long cylindrical packet. It'll hurt less when I shove them up your–'

She picked up the phone, which had been ringing for the past thirty seconds, and yelled, 'What?'

She listened for a few seconds then took a seat at her desk, knowing that this call could take a while.

'So that's a chicken korma with egg fried rice, a banana naan and a spring onion bhaji,' she confirmed. 'Do you want poppadoms or prawn crackers with that? Okay, hoi sin sauce or mango chutney with the poppadoms? Righty-ho, it'll be with you in half an hour. Aye, everything's fine. My eldest is starting at the Academy and she got a new bike for her birthday.'

Easy sauntered in bearing two mugs of tea and a packet of bourbons. He plonked the "World's Best Sergeant" mug on the desk in front of Sergeant Wilson and settled himself behind his own desk, half an ear on the conversation across from him.

'Who was that?' he asked when she eventually hung up the phone.

'Old Benny from the care home putting in his Thursday

takeaway order. Mind you, he's a bit early today. They must be running late with his lunch.'

'Why don't you tell the carers to stop him phoning?'

'Och, what would be the point in that? I'm the only one outside that place he ever gets to speak to. He'll have forgotten the whole conversation inside five minutes. I always pop by his room with a bag of spring rolls in curry sauce when I go to visit my mum. He doesn't have a clue who I am, but it makes his day. Now, what's with the fucking fake chocolate biscuits?'

Penny, Fiona, Gordon and Mrs Hubbard stood in Elsie's back garden, stuffing their bin bags, shower caps and gloves into yet another bin bag.

'Is there anything we can do for you, Mrs Hubbard,' Penny asked.

'No, dearie,' said Mrs Hubbard, shaking her head sadly, 'I suppose it's all in the hands of the police now. Such a shame we didn't find anything.'

Penny patted Mrs Hubbard's arm reassuringly.

'At least we do know one thing. Whoever killed Elsie, it was likely someone she knew. There was no sign of a break in, so presumably she let them in.'

'I can't think who she would know that could do this,' said Mrs Hubbard, gazing around her. 'The neighbours are nice people. There's Grant Hay on the right and Jimmy Gupta the baker two doors down.'

Fiona perked up at this.

'Grant Hay? Peppermint Slice Mrs Hay's grandson? That's odd. He was at the distillery when Ian Henderson's body was discovered. Did Sergeant Wilson talk to the neighbours?'

'Yes, but only briefly. I don't know what they had to say for themselves, but I heard her telling Grant that Easy Piecey would be by to take his statement today.'

'I don't suppose it would be inappropriate if the grieving

friends had a wee word with the neighbours? Just to console them if they need consoling, of course,' suggested Penny.

Mrs Hubbard nodded enthusiastically, her silver curls glinting in the sunlight.

'I think that would be entirely appropriate,' she said, then leaned in towards Fiona and lowered her voice to a whisper. 'Plus, I really need the bathroom. It's the water tablets, dearie. Ever since Doc Harris put me on them, it's been like Fairy Glen Falls down there. Only with less fairies.'

'Shall we start with Grant, then?' Penny suggested, making as if to leave.

Fiona and Mrs Hubbard followed her down the path towards the side of the house, leaving Gordon alone in the garden, unsure if he should follow.

After a moment's quiet contemplation, he looked up at the clouds and put his hands together in prayer.

'If you're up there, Elsie, could you have a wee word with God and ask him to make Sergeant Wilson not shout at us, thanks and amen?'

He hurried along the path and caught up with the others just as Fiona rang Grant's bell for a second time. She was about to peer in the windows when a front door to her left opened and Jimmy Gupta's head peeked out.

'He's not in. I heard him and Minky leaving half an hour ago. They've probably gone to see his granny.'

Penny smiled warmly at the man who had once given her a free sausage roll to cheer her up after his son, who had promised to take Penny, asked Lorraine Shaw to the school disco instead.

Jimmy was well-known in the Northeast of Scotland for his butteries, the bread rolls popular throughout Aberdeenshire. When he and his parents were kicked out of Uganda by Idi Amin in the 1970s, he never imagined that he would reach the dizzying heights of winning the World Buttery Championship. The newspaper articles documenting his win took pride of place on the wall behind the counter of his baker's shop in Port Vik.

More recently, he had opened a shop in the village, leaving his business partner, Mrs Petrenko, to look after the Port Vik shop. This was where Hector worked part-time. Penny had expected Hector to throw in the towel by week two, disgusted by the early starts. However, to everyone's surprise, he'd taken to baking like a duck to water. Nobody, least of all himself, knew he had this in him. Recognising talent, Jimmy had taken Hector under his wing and there was talk of an apprenticeship when he left school. Penny had hoped that Hector would go to university, but it seemed the fates had other ideas and, she reasoned, happiness was more important.

'Hello, Jimmy,' she said. 'We were just over at Elsie's and thought we'd see if you or Grant had any news after last night.'

It sounded lame even to Penny's ears.

Clearly Jimmy thought the same because, with a soft chuckle, he said, 'Aye, you want to know what we told the police.'

He suddenly stopped smiling and looked directly at Mrs Hubbard, his brows furrowed.

'I'm so sorry for your loss. She was a good, good person. It's simply shocking that this happened.'

'Thank you,' said Mrs Hubbard. 'If we can find out who did this, I will feel like I at least brought her some peace.'

'I don't think I can help you much. I heard a car stop outside around teatime and looked out in case it was Mrs Petrenko. All I can tell you is that it was a big, white car. That's as much as I know.'

'Did you see the driver?' asked Penny.

'No. The windows were dark and I don't even know if the driver went to Elsie's. Sorry. Now, stay where you are, Penny. I have something for you.'

Jimmy scuttled off, leaving his front door open and Mrs

Hubbard hurried after him, issuing urgent pleas about using the bathroom. The smell of freshly baked pastry wafted down the hall and filled Penny's nostrils, making her stomach growl. Her mind was overwhelmed by a sudden desire for anything with carbs, and she had just turned to the others to suggest they get some lunch, when she heard the sound of a vehicle turning into the lane.

A red Volvo pulled up next to her, Jim's face scowling from behind the window. Oh lordy, she'd forgotten he was seeing Mrs Hay earlier.

Jim wound down the car window and pointed at her.

'You, Penny Moon, are a piece of work.'

'So, are you taking Mrs Hay to the marquee dance on Saturday?' Penny asked innocently.

'Apparently her hips aren't what they used to be,' said Jim. 'I have a special act of revenge in store for you.'

He paused.

'If I could only remember what it is. Anyway, what are you doing here?'

'We're asking Elsie's neighbours if they saw or heard anything last night. What are you doing here?'

'Trying to find out if Jimmy Gupta stole Mrs Hays recipe. Then we're going for lunch because your dad sat on ours.'

Len gave Penny a little wave.

'Hello, Pennyfarthing. I sat on your mother's quiche, and I'm waiting for my bottom to dry off. We went in past Carol-Anne Green's hairdresser shop to ask her about Mrs Hay's recipe, and she let me wash my trousers. She blow-dried my bum, but it's still a bit damp. Oh, hello there, Fiona and Gordon. Sorry, I didn't see you. I was just telling Penny, I sat in some quiche. No matter what Jeanie Campbell says, it was quiche.'

Penny sensed movement behind her and stepped back to see Mrs Hubbard arrive back. She was closely followed by Jimmy Gupta, an envelope clutched tightly in a hand permanently scarred by the burns from a thousand ovens.

'It's Hector's first certificate,' he told her, grinning proudly. 'Food Hygiene and Safety.'

Penny knew she ought to be proud of her son but, if she was quite honest, she'd been secretly hoping for a bag of sausage rolls. Nevertheless, she took the certificate and thanked Jimmy.

'Have you met my dad and Jim Space?' she asked.

Jimmy bent down and beamed at Len.

'I hear you shit your pants, Len. Jeanie Campbell told everyone at Cuppachino and Mary says she is divorcing you for the third time this week. But I haven't had the pleasure of meeting the boy who wipes your bottom.'

He winked at Jim, who was visibly torn between mirth and mortification. Jim's cheeks flushed as he got out of the car and shook Jimmy's hand.

'Aye,' he said, grinning wryly, 'that's the island grapevine for you. Download speeds of more than two hundred megapensioners per second. And on that note, did you hear that Mrs Hay's peppermint slice recipe has been stolen?'

Jimmy looked shocked.

'No, that's one thing I hadn't heard.'

'We've told her we'll look into it and you're...Len, what is Jimmy again?'

'One of the people who regularly goes to her house,' said Len, leaning over to make himself heard through the open passenger window. 'Not that we're accusing you of anything, Jimmy. Just wondering if you have any ideas about who might have taken it.'

'None. We don't do tray bakes, so it won't be anybody at the bakers. It could be a rival in the baking competition for the Vik Show,' Jimmy suggested.

'Good thinking. That hadn't occurred to us,' said Jim, before turning to Len and checking, 'Had it?'

'No,' Len told him. 'Well, that's the postie, the hairdresser and the bakers ruled out. We may as well talk to Grant while we're here.'

'He's out,' said Jimmy, Mrs Hubbard, Penny, Fiona and Gordon simultaneously.

'Grant and Minky are probably at Mrs Hay's,' Jimmy explained.

'Och, bugger me with a ballpoint pen,' said Jim, his frustration evident. 'We're getting nowhere with this.'

'Why?' asked Penny.

'We're running out of suspects to interview.'

'No, I meant why a ballpoint pen?'

'Well, it's quite thin and smooth, so it wouldn't hurt too much.'

'You could ask the organisers,' said Gordon.

'At the ballpoint pen factory? I don't think it's a service they offer, do you?'

'No, the Vik Show committee. They organise all the judging and prizes.'

Jim frowned, confused.

'What? Is there a new prize for how many you can get up there? I'm not doing that in public.'

'Are you saying you'd do it in private?' asked Gordon, momentarily side-tracked.

He caught himself before the conversation could go any further downhill and explained, 'The Vik Show committee will know who is entering the baking competition. You must have to fill in forms or something. You could find out who Mrs Hay's rivals are.'

'Ah, right. Good idea, pal. I'll do it after lunch. Is anyone going for lunch? All this talk of baking and the smell coming from your house, Jimmy, my stomach's starting to think my throat's been cut.'

'I'm not going to Cuppachino in case Mary's still there,' said Len. 'Can we go to the café by the loch?'

'I'll ring Eileen and Sandra Next Door and tell them to meet us there,' Fiona offered. 'I don't know about you guys, but I'm dying to find out if they got any useful information from Ian Henderson's wife. Shit, dying, sorry Mrs Hubbard. I meant desperate.'

'Don't mind me, dearie,' Mrs Hubbard yawned. 'Ooh, I've no idea why I'm so tired.'

'I suspect the reason had six tiny umbrellas and came in a big glass,' said Penny wryly. 'I'll drop you at home and you can sleep it off.'

By the time Penny poured Mrs Hubbard through her front door and drove to the loch café, Eileen and Sandra Next Door had joined the others and were tucking into cheese and ham toasties.

'Is Mrs Hubbard okay?' asked Fiona between mouthfuls of baked potato.

'She'll be fine,' Penny assured her. 'Alcohol on top of a big shock. A few hours sleep will do her the world of good. Now, where are we with all our investigations? Dad and Jim, let's start with you.'

'Right,' said Jim, leaning forward as if to impart important, secret information. 'This morning we visited Mrs Hay, who told us a bunch of stuff, which led us to go other places.'

'None of which you can remember,' stated Len.

'Not a scooby,' Jim confirmed.

Len took up the reins.

'It looks like someone has taken Mrs Hay's recipe from her kitchen. We've cleared all the regular visitors to her house except Jeanie Campbell, Ernie on the Other Side, Grant Hay and Minky Wallace. Did you know that Grant and Minky are seeing each other?'

'Rather him than me,' said Gordon. 'She was the island arm wrestling champion three years in a row and chucked a rude American tourist out of Cuppachino last month. And by chucked, I mean she picked him up and threw him into the street. I'm not sure who's scarier, her or Sergeant Wilson.'

'I don't know,' said Jim. 'I quite like a strong woman.'

'Aye, but Sergeant Wilson?'

'Aye.'

'You would?'

'Maybe.'

Penny shifted awkwardly in her seat and cleared her throat.

'Enough nonsense. I presume your next steps are to speak to Jeanie, Ernie on the Other Side, Grant and Minky? Then find out more about her rivals in the baking competition?'

'I might be able to help with that,' said Sandra Next Door. 'I'm on the Show committee. I'm in charge of the flower arranging competition and have joint responsibility for giant vegetables, but I can get you the list of baking entrants. Peppermint slices will come under Biscuits and Small Bakes, which is Mrs Mackie's domain. In return, we're short of judges for the giant vegetables and I suppose you two will have to do.'

'We don't know anything about giant vegetables,' Len protested.

'Well, Jim has asked to be buggered by a half-cut cauliflower, a bag of broccoli and a moist courgette in the past week alone,' Gordon pointed out.

'You don't have a choice. Not if you want the information before the Show on Saturday,' said Sandra Next Door. 'Although, you could go through official channels. Write to the chairperson, ask them to add it to the agenda for the next meeting, wait while it's delayed so the committee can take advice on data protection etcetera, etcetera.'

'How long would that take?' asked Len.

'Months,' declared Sandra Next Door.

'How do you know?' asked Len.

'Because I'm the chairperson.'

Len's shoulders drooped and he breathed a disappointed sigh.

'Oh. Okay. We'll judge the big vegetables.'

With that agreed, Sandra Next Door filled the group in on what they'd found out from Anna Henderson.

'To sum up, Ian Henderson was staying out late at night, possibly work or pub, he's seen the First Minister up to something she shouldn't be doing along with someone else who shouldn't be there, he writes letters to her, then some baldy police mannie comes along and seizes the laptop.'

'I don't think it was a policeman,' said Eileen.

'Why not?' asked Penny.

'If you think about it logically, Sergeant Wilson would have known if a strange police mannie was on the island. She seemed as surprised as the rest of us.'

'Who could it have been, then? And if you say aliens, I'll tell your mum that you let Stevie Mains feel your boob in the bus shelter after school that time.'

There was a clack of teeth as Eileen, who had opened her mouth to reply, quickly clamped her jaw shut. Penny turned to Sandra Next Door.

'You didn't happen to spot a router in Ian Henderson's house, did you?'

'Router? What's that? Some sort of vegetable? Aye, I took a minute out to conduct a thorough search of the grieving widow's fridge,' Sandra scoffed.

'Eileen, it's safe to talk,' said Penny to her friend.

'There was a router on the sideboard in the living room, next to the house phone,' said Eileen. 'Are you thinking what I'm thinking?'

'Does it have anything to do with the fact that even though the laptop is gone we might still be able to find out what websites Ian visited if we get the hackers to go into his router?' asked Penny.

'No,' mumbled Eileen, gazing at the floor.

'Does it have to do with aliens or little men inside the router?'

'Maybe. But let's say we go with your idea for now and keep mine in the bag for later.'

'Good suggestion, Winnie the Pooh.'

'I'm full of them, Rubber Duck,' Eileen beamed, giving Penny a high five.

Penny's face became serious again.

'The murders may or may not be linked and there's a lot to do if we're going to find any answers. We need to divide and conquer. Sandra Next Door and Eileen, you take all the computery side of things with the hackers. Dad and Jim, carry on with the recipe. Fiona and Gordon – find out everything you can about Ian. Does anyone know who can supply us with the distillery rota?'

There were blank looks all round until Len tentatively put a hand up.

'I don't know anyone, but I bet Mrs Hubbard will. She's the biggest goss…I mean, the most informed person on the island.'

'I'll team up with Mrs Hubbard on the distillery rota,' said Penny.

'What about Elsie's murder?' asked Fiona. 'Is there anything to follow up about that?'

'Not at the moment. All we have is Jimmy Gupta's sighting of a big, white car. We don't even know if that's connected.'

'Mrs Hubbard is going to be so happy that we're doing nothing for Elsie,' said Sandra Next Door, sarcasm dripping from her sharp tongue.

Penny sighed and rubbed her forehead.

'There was no evidence of a break-in at Elsie's, which makes me wonder if she knew her killer and let him or her in. Sergeant Wilson will no doubt be waiting for the DNA and whatever else the forensics team might have turned up on Elsie, and hopefully we can persuade her to tell us the results. But until then, I'm not sure what we can do. I suppose you could ask the hackers to get the names of anyone on the island who owns a white car.'

'I'll add it to the list,' snapped Sandra Next Door, clearly still not satisfied that they weren't pursuing big leads to catch Elsie's killer but, Penny noted, not offering any suggestions of her own.

Penny decided it wasn't worth arguing.

'Okay,' she said, 'We'll all meet back here at the loch café for breakfast tomorrow. I'll invite Sergeant Wilson because we need her information and she'll need ours.'

'Sergeant Wilson?' asked Jim. 'She's the angry, sweary one, right? Are you not worried that she'll shout at us for doing this stuff?'

Penny snorted. 'What's she going to do? Once she's calmed down, she'll see that we can go places she can't. She can treat it all as intelligence and get herself a big, fat commendation from the Chief Constable for solving two murders. And if she doesn't stop shouting at us, we'll just set Sandra Next Door on her.'

'Oh, you're good at this,' said Jim.

He turned to Gordon and winked.

'Have I ever told you I like a strong woman? I really fancy Penny right now.'

Under the table, Eileen squeezed Penny's hand in sisterly solidarity.

'By the end of this, he better be snogging the face off you or there'll be a third murder,' she whispered.

CHAPTER 8

Penny's brain felt like there were three pipe bands in there, trying to play Scotland the Brave as a round. This was by far her most complex case yet - akin to trying solve a jigsaw puzzle picture-side down. And boy, she missed having Jim with her.

It felt so strange not to be sitting in the passenger seat of his car, berating him for driving too fast or bickering about whether molecules counted in a game of I Spy because you couldn't actually see them. His ability to retain information seemed to have improved, though. Despite the enormity of their task, he seemed to have followed the conversation. Even a couple of weeks ago, he'd have struggled to remember the beginning by the time they reached the end. Nevertheless, he was better off trundling around with Dad for the moment. The hunt for Mrs Hay's recipe was the least of their worries, but she really couldn't bear the thought of Jim being injured again, and whoever was behind these murders was clearly a very dangerous man…woman…people. Were the two murders even linked? Oh, bloody hell. She didn't know. They just had to plod on and hope that some of this started to make sense.

By the time she arrived at Mrs Hubbard's, the village

church bell was ringing four o'clock. Penny hoped that Mrs H had slept off the cocktail by now. Douglas was probably raging about them letting her sneak off to the pub, but what could they do? Nothing came between Mrs H and what she called her "sweetie juice." Not even a sprained ankle. Poor, strait-laced Elsie had had to suffer the ignominy of going to the bar and asking Bertie for a Slow Comfortable Screw. Penny smiled at the memory. She suspected that Mrs Hubbard had done it on purpose, but she also suspected that Elsie hadn't really minded. Especially when Bertie winked and said how he was glad to see her dating again. Elsie had giggled like a teenager and swapped her usual soda and lime for a risqué vodka and pineapple juice.

The shop was open, Penny noted. Douglas must have got bored watching reruns of Strictly Come Dancing while he waited for Mrs Hubbard to surface. She would check with him whether the good Mrs, as he often referred to his wife, was up and about, rather than knock on the house door and risk an encounter with Mrs H in her Marks and Spencer's finest winceyette.

'I don't know what you think you were doing,' said Douglas as soon as he spotted Penny lurking behind what appeared to be a small fortress built using tampon boxes. 'Minty came home exhausted and smelling of sweetie juice. How many did she have?'

'Just the one,' said Penny, neglecting to mention that "the one" consisted of about nine shots. 'Who built Tampax Tower?'

'That was me,' said Douglas proudly. 'Minty said we needed an impactful display targeting the female demographic. I didn't have a clue what she was on about, but I supposed it was something to do with women, so I spent the afternoon building this.'

'I like that you've started with the super plus at the bottom then worked your way through regular and used lights for the crenellations. And the bars on the windows, are they…?'

'Strings. Aye. I had to open a box of the applicator-free ones, but I didn't waste the absorbent bits.'

'I can see that!' Penny exclaimed. 'Tiny cannons. This is genius!'

'Aye, well,' said Douglas, pink-cheeked and slightly flustered by the praise. 'I wasted half an hour and a 99p set of pens colouring them in black. You can't dip them in black dye, you see.'

He paused for a moment and Penny could see him wondering how to steer the conversation back to him giving her a telling off. Eventually, he relented.

'Och, on ye go. She's in the back.'

As Penny made her way through the storeroom to the house behind the shop, she heard Douglas' voice follow her.

'I don't know what you two hellions are up to, and I probably don't want to know, but you keep her safe, ye hear? We've been practicing the rumba for weeks and we're going to win first bloody prize at the Show even if she's in crutches.'

Mrs Hubbard was in her favourite armchair by the fire, fully dressed and fully absorbed in re-reading Elsie's letter. She jumped, startled by Penny knocking gently on the open door.

'Goodness me, dearie. I thought you were Douglas here to deliver another lecture on the evils of the Woo-Woo. Have you seen what he's built out there? I hope it's not the start of another hobby. He took up Lego a few years back but had to give it up when I turned my ankle on Obi-Wan Kenobi's Starfighter. It was either the Lego or our dreams of winning Strictly – one of them had to go. Listen to me, blethering on. Where are we up to with the murders?'

Penny explained that they'd worked out a plan over lunch. Mrs Hubbard was naturally disappointed that there were few leads to follow with regards to Elsie, but shared

Penny's hope that working on Ian's case might throw up some leads on Elsie's.

'Now, who do I know at the distillery that I could blackmail into talking to us?' said the older woman. 'Graham Hardy has been having an affair with Ruth Morrison, but his wife has cancer so it might be a bit insensitive to threaten to tell on him. Oh, how about this one? Lisa Brady spent thousands on a new sofa and told her husband she got it for five hundred in the sale.'

'I don't know,' said Penny. 'It feels like breaking the women's code.'

'You're right. Then we'll have to go with Billy Dent. He accidentally emailed a naked picture of himself to the Bowling Club committee last year. It was all hushed up at the time, and Douglas swore me to secrecy, but things can be unhushed, if you get my meaning.'

Penny was surprised that Mrs Hubbard had managed to keep it to herself for this long.

'What does Billy Dent do at the distillery?' she asked.

'He's a manager. He's also chairman of the golf club and runs the parish newsletter. Sees himself as a pillar of the community and has been talking about running for local councillor. I'd never actually tell anyone about the picture. I think the threat would be enough.'

'Mrs H, you're a wicked woman.'

'Only when I need to be,' said Mrs Hubbard, shrugging on her raincoat and wrapping a pink headscarf over her rollers. 'Let's go and see what the esteemed Mr Dent, prospective OBE, has to tell the redoubtable Mrs Hubbard, fully fledged KBO.'

'KBO?' asked Penny.

'Keep Buggering On, dearie.'

. . .

Billy Dent, a round-cheeked man with a slight paunch straining the buttons of his twill checked shirt, seemed surprised to find Mrs Hubbard on his doorstep.

'Erm…hello.'

The rise in tone at the end of the statement almost turned it into a question, inviting Mrs Hubbard to explain her unexpected visit.

'Hello, Billy. Have you met Penny Moon?'

Billy tentatively put a hand out to shake Penny's, all the while gazing confusedly at Mrs Hubbard. She didn't waste time on further pleasantries.

'I was wondering if we could have a quick word with you. It'll just take a wee minute. Can we come in?'

'Is everything okay?' said Billy, stepping back from the door to make way for an advancing Mrs Hubbard. 'It's not Douglas, is it? Has something happened with the Bowling Club?'

'Let's just say it's Bowling Club related. Through here?'

Mrs Hubbard, trailed by Penny, gestured towards the first door on the left, and Billy scurried after them, hurriedly sweeping a pile of papers off the sofa and depositing them on the coffee table. He paused for a moment, then turned the papers face-down and gestured to Penny and Mrs Hubbard to sit.

'Parish newsletter,' he muttered, before assuming the cheerful bluster which Penny decided must be his aspiring politician voice. 'What can I do you for?'

'Well, you could give us the distillery work rota for the night Ian Henderson was killed,' said Mrs Hubbard, coming straight to the point.

'I could what? Sorry, I'm…I'm not allowed to do that. I can't give work information to anyone who isn't employed by the distillery.'

'Yes, we heard,' said Penny. 'We hoped you'd make an exception. Did you hear about Elsie from the library? She was killed last night and we're wondering whether the murders are linked. If we can find out who killed Ian, we might also find who killed Elsie.'

'I'm sorry. It's more than my job's worth. The new owner has been very explicit about this.'

'Yes, I can see that.'

'What do you mean?' asked Billy, his cheeks flushing.

'I mean the email at the top of the pile of papers there on the coffee table. The one where Ted Hyatt has ordered the deletion of the swipe card records,' said Penny. 'Unless you were planning on including that in the Parish newsletter, of course.'

'It's nothing,' said Billy, reaching out to grab the papers then, thinking better of it, withdrawing his hand and crossing his arms. 'Ted Hyatt's the new owner. He's American and he's just doing a clean sweep in line with company policy. The Americans do things differently. Anyway, it's none of your business. I'm sorry, I don't know what you think you're going to achieve here, but I…well…maybe the shock of Elsie…yes, I'm sorry about Elsie. I'll phone Douglas and ask him to come and get you. Sorry, but I really think you need to go home.'

'You're awful sorry for a man who sent a naked picture of himself to the Bowling Club committee,' said Mrs Hubbard, a quiet menace in her voice that Penny had never heard before.

Jeeze, she's been taking lessons off Sandra Next Door, Penny thought. She sat back and watched a range of emotions play across the face of the pompous man. The journey from shock to outrage was reflected in the colour of his fleshy cheeks, from an initial pallor to a mottled purple as his blood pressure rose. He ran a hand through his hair, dislodging a comb-over so that it flopped back from his crown, revealing the beginnings of a tonsure.

'You wouldn't,' he spat, the comb-over flapping wildly atop his bobbing head.

'Yes, I would,' said Mrs Hubbard mildly.

'Douglas. Bloody Douglas. Who else has he told?'

'Only me. And only because I was looking for our club membership details and opened the email by accident. I hope there are no more accidents. Like my finger accidentally slipping on the keyboard and forwarding it to the Parish Council. Goodness, that would make an awful headline in the next parish newsletter.'

Billy breathed out and slumped back on the sofa, defeated.

'Alright. I'll give you the rota. But I'm not giving you anything else.'

'Make it the rotas for the whole month and we have a deal,' said Mrs Hubbard.

Without saying another word, Billy got up and left the room. A few minutes later, Penny and Mrs Hubbard heard the gentle whirr of a printer from somewhere in the house.

'That was awesome, Mrs H,' breathed Penny.

'I'm not just a pretty face,' said Mrs Hubbard, patting her rollers self-consciously.

As they left the house, clutching a sheaf of papers, Billy seemed to regain some of his brio, shouting after them, 'And your finger better accidentally hit the delete button on that email or I'll…I'll call the police.'

'Feel free,' Penny shouted back. 'I'm sure Sergeant Wilson will be the soul of discretion.'

However, she wasn't sure if Billy heard above the resounding slam of his front door.

The light drizzle sent Mrs Hubbard speed-walking towards the car. Penny wasn't surprised that, despite her age, the woman could go at a fair pace when she wanted to. All those salsa classes with Douglas presumably kept her limber. By the time Penny reached the car, Mrs Hubbard was in the front passenger seat, seatbelt plugged in and ready to go.

'Let's have a look at the rota,' said Penny as she got behind the wheel.

'Not here,' hissed Mrs Hubbard. 'I can see him watching us from behind his net curtains.'

Sure enough, the silhouette of Billy filled the centre of the living room bay window.

'You'd think he'd have the sense to turn the lamp behind him off before he spies on folk,' Penny commented. 'Do you want to go back to yours? Or mine? Though it's not very comfy yet.'

'The pub,' declared Mrs Hubbard. 'As Billy said, dearie, I'm clearly still in shock.'

The pub was quiet when they arrived. It was still early evening and, as Bertie noted, the usual Thursday crowd would be saving their pub pennies for Show night, when watering holes across the island would be heaving, ahead of the big marquee dance.

Being allowed to go to the marquee dance, teetering across a muddy field in stilettos to spend a week's wages on warm beer, was a teenage rite of passage on Vik, one which the current crop had missed due to two years of cancellations during the pandemic. This Saturday was, therefore, predicted to be the marquee dance to end all marquee dances. By Sunday, it would be standing room only in the cells and a parade of parents would be marching on Vik's tiny police station to collect their worse for wear miscreant offspring.

Hector and Edith had pleaded relentlessly to be allowed to attend. The dance, not the police cells, obviously. Penny hadn't wavered in her steadfast refusal, telling them that seventeen wasn't eighteen and she had no desire to do the parental walk of shame the next morning to collect them when they got pinched for underage drinking.

'It's not like we've never had alcohol before,' wailed Edith, her little orange face a mask of frustration.

Penny couldn't wait until Edith grew out of the fake tan stage. What with the short, blonde hair and the constant stream of complaints, it was like being hounded by a miniature Donald Trump.

'Mother, you're being ridiculous,' said Hector, the pompous wee twat building himself up to deliver a lecture on her failings. She'd stopped him in his tracks when he got to the one where she'd bought long-life instead of fresh coconut milk for his chai latte and completely ruined his morning.

'I expect this sort of thing from Granny because she's old. You, on the other hand, should understand the disruption to one's day,' expostulated the fruit of her loins, beloved cherub and light of her bleedin' life.

'I'll tell you what,' she'd said in an icy tone that belied the burning in the pit of her stomach, 'from now on, you're in charge of sourcing and paying for whatever form of milk you like on this godforsaken island with its one supermarket which thinks that mince and tatties is a delicacy and that halloumi is how you greet yourself in the mirror first thing in the morning.'

Aaand breathe. Truth be told, Penny would be glad to stretch this investigation out until Sunday night so she could stay out and avoid more "you never let us do anything *everyone* is going you're such a bad parent" followed by wails of "oh my God, it's on now *everyone* is there we're not there we hate you forever our lives are over" finished off nicely with "*everyone* went we were the only ones who didn't this is so embarrassing we will never forgive you."

'Shall we have a look at this rota?' she asked, setting down a pink gin spritz in front of Mrs Hubbard.

'I had a quick peek while you were at the bar. Ian was scheduled on a late shift to clean some of the equipment. Kylie Jackson was doing some work on the computers, presumably while it was quiet, and there were two security guards on duty. That night's rota doesn't tell us much, but if you look back through the month...'

Mrs Hubbard handed the pages to Penny, who flicked through them then shook her head, unsure as to what she was supposed to be seeing.

'When you were bringing me up to speed earlier, you said

that Ian Henderson's wife told Sergeant Wilson he was working a lot of late shifts,' said Mrs Hubbard.

Penny looked at the rota once more then gasped.

'Oh, you clever, clever thing. He's not scheduled for any late shifts. So, if he wasn't at work, where was he?'

CHAPTER 9

Len and Jim felt energised by their lunch. They followed Sandra Next Door home to collect the baking competition list and, with the paper still warm from the printer, Len hurried back to the car, his mission to interview all the recipe suspects uppermost in his mind. He handed the piece of paper to Jim and started the engine.

'Maybe you should go home and change your trousers,' Jim suggested, jerking his head towards Valhalla.

'Not a chance,' said Len, slowly backing out of the drive. '*She'll* be in there, thinking up trousers and poo jokes. You can hardly see the stain now anyway.'

'Alright. Let's see who we've got on Sandra's list?'

Jim scanned the names, his eyes alighting on one of particular interest.

'Aha! Only one of our suspects is a regular visitor to Mrs Hay's house *and* has entered the baking competition.'

'Don't keep me in suspenders,' said Len. 'Is it Jeanie? I'd love it if it was Jeanie Campbell. Obviously, it would be a shame for Eileen. A stain on the family name that will go down in island history, never to be forgotten. But it would be very satisfying for me.'

'Why?' asked Jim.

'She's very annoying. Touchy, bossy. She's been like this since we were at university. Always thought she knew best. The only good thing that woman ever did was pour a drink over Ian Henderson's head when he grabbed Mrs Hubbard at the third year dance.'

'Ian Henderson was at university with you?'

'Yes. He was an odious little man even then.'

'Well, sorry to disappoint you,' said Jim. 'It's Minky we're after. We should speak to her first. Where do you think she'll be?'

Len glanced at the clock.

'Most likely Cuppachino. They close soon and she'll be cashing up. We better hurry'

He signalled left in the direction of Port Vik, gunned the engine and took off at speed.

Two miles and twenty minutes later, they pulled up outside Cuppachino, Len muttering curses about Frankie and his damn tractor.

'I mean, what sort of idiot chooses rush hour to take his tractor out?' he asked, gazing around the High Street which, like the rest of Port Vik, was hardly a seething mass of jostling vehicles. The only traffic jam in sight was a Corsa desperately trying to overtake Moira Craig, who was gaily trundling up the middle of the road on her mobility scooter.

She gave them a little toot of her horn and a wave.

'I heard about your accident, Len,' she called as she went past. 'Don't worry. I once shit myself in the butchers. I was only three at the time, mind you, but still…'

'It was quiche!' Len shouted after her.

'Aye, it was keech right enough,' she cackled, steering further towards the centre line to thwart the Corsa.

A figure at the door of Cuppachino was just turning the sign to "Closed" when Len and Jim tried the handle. A woman with blonde, curly hair and deep frown lines scowled at them through the glass, mouthing, 'Go away. We're shut.'

'Minky, it's Jim Space. We just want a quick word.'

Minky fiddled with the lock and opened the door.

'You may as well come in. I'm just cleaning up,' she grumbled. 'I haven't been able to get anyone to do the cleaning since yon Ukrainian mannie was killed.'

Jim realised he probably hadn't seen Minky since they left school. She still had that hard face which made her look older than her years. Her forearms were thick yet sinewy, tattoos snaking from her wrists and disappearing into the sleeves of a plain black t-shirt. She looked like someone who stood for no nonsense, yet her voice was surprisingly soft.

'They always moan that there are no jobs around here,' she continued, 'yet I've advertised three times for a cleaner and had no applications.'

'Penny's been looking for a part time job for Edith. I could let her know,' Jim offered.

Len looked at him, surprised.

'How…I mean, you remembered.'

Jim frowned. He really had remembered. Things, well, more of a sense of things, had been slowly starting to come back over the past few days and he'd noticed that he was able to keep track of conversations and who people were more easily. But this was something Penny had told him months ago when they'd been eating an ice cream in the park, in the snow. He hadn't even felt himself remembering it. It had simply sprung up out of nowhere and he had this sense that because it was important to Penny, it was important to him. He tried to capture the feeling and remember more. Oh God, he thought, his stomach lurching. She'd looked so bonny sitting on the swings, her face framed by the fur of her hood and her little nose red from the cold. She was laughing and saying how the twins were desperate to earn some money so they could buy a car, and that they'd fallen out with her when she'd suggested that a bumper car should be top of their list.

He was brought out of his reverie by Len asking if he needed to sit down.

'Thanks,' said Jim, sinking gratefully into a chair at a table for four. He felt quite discombobulated.

'I'll get you a cup of tea,' said Minky, not quite sure what was going on but realising by the look on Jim's face that something hot with three sugars was called for.

Jim looked at Len, tears in his eyes.

'I remember. Only one thing and mostly it's a feeling. But she was so cold and so bonny in her red coat. I felt...I don't know...like this was the best ice cream in the world. Like I'd never properly tasted ice cream until that moment. I wanted to hold it all, frozen, like a postcard in my mind so I'd never forget. And then I did forget. I'm sorry. I'm probably making no sense.'

Len sat down beside him and laid a kindly hand on his arm.

'You're feeling overwhelmed, son. It's only natural. The doctor said the brain might start building new pathways. He also said not to push yourself. Things will come back in their own time. Do you want me to call your dad or take you home?'

'No, I'm fine,' said Jim, sniffing deeply and wiping away the tears. 'It's just...Penny...did I...no, never mind, I'm fine.'

Minky brought through three cups of tea on a tray, along with a large slice of chocolate cake.

'Here you go,' she said to Jim. 'I baked it for the cake competition at the Show, but you probably need it more. Eat up. A shot of sugar will help you.'

'I'm sorry,' said Jim through a mouthful of sponge. 'I didn't mean to make a fuss. And your cake...'

'Och, I'll make another one tonight. I make fresh bakes for the shop every day anyway.'

'The icing is lovely.'

'My own special recipe,' said Minky proudly. 'Now, what was it you wanted to talk to me about?'

'I'm not sure we need to ask you very much at all,' said Len, eyeing the rapidly disappearing chocolate cake. 'We're looking into Mrs Hay's recipe and wondered–'

'If I pinched it?' Minky waved away Len's protests. 'With a family like mine, I'm used to assumptions being made.'

'It wasn't your family we were thinking of,' Len admitted. 'It was more the fact that you're a regular visitor to Mrs Hay's house, you own a business that sells cakes and you're entering the baking competition for the Show.'

'I suppose I should say it's refreshing to not be judged on the sins of my father for once, but I'm still a wee bit insulted. Look, think what you like. Obviously, I didn't steal it for the baking competition.'

Minky gestured to Jim, who was proudly sporting a chocolate moustache.

'Yer man there looks like he runs a rimming service at the IBS clinic. The only other motive I'd have for taking it would be to sell it in the shop, and I think folk would notice, don't you? I'd have to modify the recipe and sell it as something else.'

She handed a menu to Len, adding, 'And as you can see, I don't sell anything like it.'

Len studied the menu for a moment then took a desultory slurp of his tea.

'You're right. We're running out of suspects, though. We still have to speak to Jeanie, Ernie on the Other Side and Grant. Then there's all the other baking competition entrants. I'm starting to worry we might let Mrs Hay down.'

Minky sighed, put her hand out and said, 'Give it here.'

Then, in response to Len's baffled expression, she clarified, 'The list of entrants. I'll take a look and see if any of them stand out. Mind you, they'd be idiots to enter a batch of Mrs Hay's peppermint slice. Barry Merry's been a baking judge for about the past five hundred years and given Mrs Hay the first prize in traybakes for four hundred and ninety-nine of them. There was that one year, 1997 I think it was, where Doc

Harris' wife won with a very nice caramel slice, but they had a judge's enquiry and found out she bought it on the mainland. That's why a lot of the old folk don't trust Doc Harris. Like I said, sins of the father, or in this case the husband. Small island, long memory.'

She pored over the list, muttering observations such as, 'Collapsed pavlova 2003,' and 'Soggy brandy snaps 2017,' until eventually she put the list down and gazed intently at Len.

'You know your wife's on here? I expect you'll be giving her a thorough investigation when you get home.'

Minky gave Len a saucy wink and nudged him in the ribs with her elbow, somewhat harder than he'd expected.

'Do any of them look like suspects,' he asked, rubbing the sore spot.

'Nobody jumps out at me. They're all ordinary folk, not criminal masterminds, although everyone would have said the same thing about Doc Harris' wife prior to 1997. None of them have any connection to Mrs Hay, that I know of. Which puts you back with Ernie on the Other Side, Jeanie and my Grant.

'Speak to Grant if you like. Though I can't see how he'd benefit from taking his granny's recipe that he could have asked to borrow or copy at any time. Ernie on the Other Side survives on Wheels on Meals.'

Jim, who was feeling slightly high on sugar, leaned forward and interjected, 'I thought the council stopped Meals on Wheels about fifteen years ago.'

'Wheels on Meals,' said Minky. 'Linda Wheels from the shoe shop took over and organised it.'

'I never understood why she called her shop Linda Loves Laces,' commented Len.

'Me neither,' said Minky. 'Wheels' Heels would be much better.'

'So, your recommendation would be to speak to Jeanie

Campbell?' asked Jim, in an attempt to bring the conversation back on course.

'You can try, but you know what she's like. She gets bad tempered. Maybe you could soften her up with a new broom or a fine cauldron. I hear the supermarket has stuff in for Halloween already.'

They thanked Minky and retreated, Jim giving her a grateful thumbs-up as she firmly shot the bolts in door behind them.

Once outside, Len took a deep breath, as if to steel himself for the prospect of Jeanie Campbell, and said, 'You're braver than you believe, stronger than you seem and smarter than you think.'

'Churchill?' asked Jim.

'Winnie the Pooh,' said Len. 'Now, let's see what Jeanie Campbell has to say for herself.'

CHAPTER 10

Fiona sauntered into the village pub, and without a word, Bertie poured her a vodka and coke.

'Bit quiet in here tonight,' she observed, waving at Captain Kev, who was propping up the other end of the bar. 'Give this one to Kev please, Bertie. I'll stick to plain coke.'

'It's picked up a bit from earlier,' said Bertie, expertly sliding the glass down the bar so that it stopped directly in front of the captain. 'I had Mrs Hubbard and Penny in about half four. They were sitting over there at the fire like two evil geniuses who'd stolen the nuclear codes and had just found a Big Red Button shop on Etsy. Except it wasn't Etsy. It was a bit of paper and they looked quite excited about it. Now, what do you suppose that was all about?'

Fiona beckoned him closer.

'We're investigating Ian and Elsie's murders,' she told him, keeping her voice low. 'I thought I'd ask around in here. See if anyone knows who he was friendly with.'

'Oh, I can tell you that,' said Bertie. 'It was Stevie Mains, Geoff Fisher and their lot. He was often in here with them, playing pool and darts and the like.'

Fiona wasn't sure what else there was to do in the pub that was like pool and darts.

'And the like?' she asked.

'Keep this to yourself,' whispered Bertie, resting his elbows on the polished wood of the bar. 'They were taking bets on whether Sergeant Wilson sleeps with her stab vest on.'

'I know,' whispered Fiona. 'Half the island knows. The question is whether they were up to anything else they shouldn't have been.'

'Well, *I* wouldn't know that,' said Bertie, straightening up and giving the bar a quick wipe with a towel. 'Give it half an hour and you can ask Stevie Mains yourself. Another drink?'

Three cokes later, Stevie Mains finally barrelled through the pub door, laughing at something his companion had just said. Fiona did a slight double take. She'd never seen Stevie with a woman before. His reputation for sleaziness usually preceded him, not helped, of course, by the long, greasy hair and the beer baby he seemed to be nurturing under a seemingly limitless supply of t-shirts with slogans such as "I Don't Have a Dirty Mind, I Have a Sexy Imagination" and "Sex Instructor, First Lesson Free."

The woman even looks normal, thought Fiona with a stab of pity. She heard Gordon's voice in the back of her mind, telling her, 'Maybe she's one of them serial killers. Aye, nae the Coco Pops kind. The ones that murder folk in their sleep and take home trophies. Though it would be ironic if a serial killer took home boxes of Coco Pops. But if you were doing that, like, you'd have to target people that buy the multipacks of tiny wee boxes of cereal because you wouldn't have the cupboard space for the big boxes.'

Fiona told her inner Gordon to shut up and watched as Stevie pulled out a chair for the woman, as if he was an actual gentleman, then got her settled at the table by the fire from which Penny had called her earlier.

When Penny rang, Fiona had been standing on the doorstep of Alec Carmichael's house, trying to persuade the man to dish the dirt on Ian. She knew Ian had been in the Freemasons because Sandra Next Door had spotted a ring on the sideboard when they visited Anna. She also knew Alec Carmichael was a big boy in the organisation. Obviously, it was a secret but this was Vik, so everyone knew.

'Och, come on,' she pleaded in the face of the man's refusal to divulge any information. 'As Chief Warlock, you must have known him pretty well. Did he have enemies? Did he say whether he was worried about something?'

Alec Carmichael was a man whose mind was in keeping with his stature, or lack thereof. A man who had two pleasures in life; being outraged about everything and lording it over those he considered his inferiors. From the moment he opened his mouth, Fiona knew she had definitely been marked out as an inferior and a source of outrage. Two for two, she thought as the man sputtered a thin mist of what she could only assume was pure bile.

'You come round here in wellies and dungarees, not even making the effort to dress like a normal woman. And I suppose you have your lesbian partner in the car!'

'No, he's at home in the twenty-first century, making the tea, while I'm here in 1953 speaking to a pompous wee homophobe who's more worried about a woman in trousers than the fact that his sorcerer's apprentice has been murdered.'

Her phone rang, momentarily distracting her, and Alec Carmichael took the opportunity to slam the door in her face. Fiona, in turn, took the opportunity to yell, 'I'm telling Sergeant Wilson on you,' before answering the call with a polite, 'Hello, Braebank Organics, how can I help you?'

'Is that you, Fiona? Sorry, I didn't recognise the posh telephone voice.'

'Penny, you've called me on my work mobile. I'm always posh on the work mobile. Mrs H is forever on at me about customers' first impressions. She must have a flamin' PhD in business by now, she's done that many courses.'

'You're on speaker and Mrs Hubbard's here.'

Fiona could hear the amusement in Penny's voice.

'Oh, crap. Sorry, Mrs H.'

'Just joking,' said Penny. 'You're not on speaker. We've managed to get hold of a rota for the distillery and Ian Henderson wasn't scheduled for late shifts in the month before he was killed, except for the night it happened, so we were thinking about where he could be. The other place Anna said he went to a lot was the pub. And who do we know that goes to the pub a lot and is out late at night?'

Fiona turned the question over in her mind, picturing all the regulars at the pub and eventually stopping at one.

'Stevie Mains! He's a poacher. Drives Laird Hamish round the bend because he's always setting traps and breaking fences on the estate.'

'Exactly,' said Penny.

'Aaand,' said Fiona, drawing the word out for emphasis, 'isn't he the one who started the rumour that he saw hooded figures at the Holiday-Homers lodge?' I'm just thinking that if Ian Henderson saw the First Minister in a house with someone who shouldn't be there, could it tie in with Stevie Mains saying he saw weird stuff at the Holiday-Homers' place?'

'It's not a strong connection, but it's worth a shot,' said Penny. 'Mind you, the lodge used to belong to Laird Hamish. It's right on the edge of his estate; prime poaching territory for Stevie. How about you go to the pub and find out what Stevie knows, and me and Mrs Hubbard will call on the Holiday-Homers?'

Which was how Fiona now found herself standing in the pub, trying to figure out how she was going to get any information from Stevie when all his attention was directed towards the slim brunette in the cropped jeans and vest top.

Sometimes, Fiona told herself as she mulled things over, it's quite handy to have Gordon's voice in your head. Aside from organic farming and spouting nonsense, he was obsessed with military history. Normally, she ignored him droning on about code breakers and D-Day, but a recent monologue on tactics must have broken through the barrier somehow, because she could hear him saying, 'What they did was, instead of coming at it head on with the infantry, they sent an agent in to turn the Italian minister. They knew he couldn't possibly be going along with Mussolini, and all they had to do was figure out what he wanted, then get him out of the way so they could put their own man in. So, what they did was...' She'd tuned out again at this point. The brunette couldn't possibly be enamoured of Stevie Mains. If she was going to get Stevie on his own and find out what he'd been up to, she had to befriend the brunette. Find out what the brunette wanted and get rid of her.

Fiona listened as Stevie ordered drinks for himself and the woman he told Bertie was called Lisa. A pint of lager and a dry white wine spritzer.

Interesting, Fiona mused. Doesn't want to get drunk. Yet happy to see Stevie get off his man tits, she observed ten minutes later, as she watched Stevie polish off his pint in double quick time and return to the bar, Lisa waving away his offer of a second drink.

Fiona gave it another ten minutes, enough time for Stevie to sink half his drink, then ordered a pint, a dry white wine spritzer and a fifth coke for herself.

'What's with the no vodka tonight?' said Bertie the barman, astonished.

'I think I need to stay sober,' said Fiona. 'But put it in one of the glasses you use for the vodka cokes and only fill it halfway.'

'I see. Tricking Stevie Mains into thinking you're just as pissed as he'll be in the next hour, you sneaky bugger,' said Bertie with a wink.

'Watch and learn, Bertie,' said Fiona, winking back.

She sauntered over to Stevie's table, tray of drinks in hand, and asked, 'Mind if I sit here for a bit? Glad Bertie's put the fire on. You wouldn't think it was summer. I really should have brought a coat, but when the days are warm, you forget the nights are so cold.'

She shivered, as if to emphasise her suffering.

Stevie Mains didn't look happy about the intrusion, but his glower soon turned to a smile when Fiona handed him the pint.

'A wee something to apologise for me interrupting,' she said, sliding the spritzer across the table and settling herself into a chair.

The fire at her back was, if anything, too warm, and she hoped that neither Stevie nor Lisa noticed the beads of sweat she could feel forming on her upper lip.

'I'm Fiona,' she said, extending a hand towards the other woman.

'Lisa Jennings,' the woman said, shaking the proffered hand. 'Are you from the island?'

'Yes. We have a smallholding and sell organic fruit and veg. Is that an Edinburgh accent I hear?'

The woman smiled. 'You have a good ear. I'm just here for a few days, seeing what's what.'

Fiona smiled back then sipped her drink, allowing a silence to stretch. She'd heard that when you were silent, people rushed to fill the void. Unfortunately, Lisa must have heard the same thing because she seemed content to gaze around the bar and eventually, it was Fiona who broke.

'So, and tell me to mind my own nosy business, but we're a nosy lot here on Vik, how do you two know each other?'

'We only met today,' said Lisa, suddenly seeming fascinated by the rows of glasses above the bar.

Refusal to give detail and avoiding eye contact, thought Fiona. My psychology may be limited to helping Douglas Hubbard work out which Strictly contestants are shagging their dance partners, but I would say she's hiding something.

'Aye and it's amazing how you can know a woman for a short time and really click,' said Stevie, pulling his t-shirt down to prevent the beer baby making an unscheduled appearance. 'Lisa was looking for someone with local knowledge to give her a tour of the island.'

'You found the right man, then,' Fiona told the woman. 'Stevie here is born and bred Vik. Knows the island like the back of his hand. What have you seen so far?'

'Oh, so many things. I can't begin to remember them all,' Lisa said in a breathy voice and reached across the table to put a hand on Stevie's arm. 'He's been my knight in shining armour.'

'I don't know about that,' said Stevie. 'I only stood around while you took photos of the distillery and went to the shop for you while you chatted to the World Buttery Champion. I never thought of Jimmy Gupta as a tourist attraction.'

'And which newspaper are you from?' asked Fiona, her eyes fixed on Lisa.

The woman's eyes met Fiona's and she slowly blinked. Fiona could almost hear the cogs whirring as she debated whether or not to come clean. Across from her, Stevie Mains' face bore a stunned expression exactly like Gordon's when Fiona had gently broken the news that Carol Vorderman had left Countdown in 2008 and the woman he'd been watching for the past nine years hadn't "taken the plastic surgery thing a wee bit too far, like." Contrary to Gordon's eventual response, which was to mull things over then declare, "I wondered why they kept calling the lassie Rachel," Stevie Mains stood up and left the table, heading in the direction of the men's toilets.

'It was cruel to string Stevie along,' said Fiona.

'Aye, and it was hardly nice of you to burst his bubble,' Lisa retorted. 'He was having a good time, and I'd have left him happy with a peck on the cheek and a promise to call.'

'He'd have come into the pub tomorrow with some tale of a night of passion and everyone would have been laughing about him, knowing full well that nothing happened. You were making a fool of him. Why are you here?'

'The murders. I got a tip off from a friend on the Vik

Gazette that a couple of locals had been killed, so I came up to see what was going on for myself.'

'Have you got much so far?'

'Stevie told me about going poaching with the first victim and seeing something in the woods. I was hoping to get more details after he'd had a few pints.'

Fiona considered her options. Stevie was probably feeling quite annoyed with her right now for ruining his night, and she needed him to tell her about Ian. Two murders on a small island were bound to come out anyway and soon there would be reporters all over the place. Why not kill all the birds with one stone?

'How about you apologise to Stevie and offer him some good money for his story?' she proposed. 'If there's one thing Stevie likes almost as much as women, it's free money. He's always skint. A group of friends and I are looking into the murders, so if you let me sit in on your interview with Stevie, I might be able to offer you an exclusive once the police have arrested the killer…or killers.'

'So, you think the murders might be linked?' asked Lisa eagerly.

'I'm not telling you anything until the cases are solved. Now, do we have a deal?'

They shook hands on it and Fiona went to find Stevie in the men's toilets.

'Come on, man,' she said, battering on the door of the single stall. 'I've made a deal with Lisa, and we have some good news.'

A muffled squeak came from behind the door, followed by a sniff.

'Are you crying? What are you crying about? You've just spent a day with a bonny lassie who's still interested in you.'

'She's not interested. Nobody's interested in me. I'm just a fat dude who still lives with his mum.' That last came out as a wail.

'I'll not lie. Being in your forties and still living with your mum doesn't make you ideal boyfriend material. But it's all stuff you can change if you want to. Maybe…definitely get rid of the t-shirts as well. Anyway, I thought you were seeing Irene Miller. What happened there?'

Stevie sniffed loudly. 'We were going to rent the flat above the chip shop then my mum told her she was punching above her weight with me and holding me back.'

Fiona put her hands in her dungaree pockets, looked up at the stained ceiling tiles and sighed.

'If you can't see what's going on there, you big eejit, then there's no hope for you. Phone Irene, tell her you're sorry and that neither of you will take any notice of your mum again. Now, how would you like to make quite a lot of cash for no effort?'

Stevie eventually emerged from the stall, his eyes red rimmed.

'Do you think anyone will notice I've been crying?' he asked.

'Nah,' Fiona assured him. 'You always look that shit after a few pints anyway.'

'Thanks. You're a pal,' he said, brightening.

By the time they got back to the table, Lisa had refreshed their drinks and two perfectly poured pints sat on the table in front of Stevie's chair.

'I'm really sorry,' said Lisa, having the grace to look genuinely shamefaced. 'You're a nice guy and I should have been honest with you.'

'Aye, I am a nice guy,' Stevie said stiffly. 'What's this I hear about money?'

Lisa offered him a sum for his story. Stevie reminded her what a nice guy he was. She upped the offer. Stevie said he was a really, really nice guy. Lisa looked pleadingly at Fiona, who said, 'Even for nice guys like yourself, there's a limit. Take the damn money. It'll more than pay for half a year's rent on that flat above the chip shop.'

Stevie took the deal.

'Right, get your tape recorder oot, Lois Lane, and prepare to be blown away,' he said.

Lisa laid her phone on the table and tapped the screen.

'Tell me how you knew Ian Henderson.'

'I see what you're doing there. Easing me in gently. Och, I met Ian about twenty years ago in this very pub. He offered to score the darts then started giving me some tips. I got quite good, and we started up a darts team, playing the other pubs on the island.'

'What sort of man was he?'

Stevie thought for a moment before replying, 'I'll be diplomatic about this, what with him being dead. He was a bit of an arsehole. Somewhere to the right of Hitler, ye ken. In fact, him and Hitler are probably up there now, playing a game of darts together.'

'I doubt Hitler's up there,' commented Lisa.

'Aye, you're probably right. He had some weird views. Always lusting after young lassies and getting his dander up about foreigners. He once staged a one man protest against Jimmy Gupta's sausage rolls in the town square.'

'Hitler protested about sausage rolls?'

'Don't be daft. What would Hitler be doing standing in Port Vik wi' a placard saying "Jimmy Gupta's sausage rolls are made of cats"? Anyway, Ian had a right thing about that Ukrainian laddie who was killed at the museum. He made a dossier about him on his computer. Aye, a *dossier* he called it. I'm thinking to myself leave the poor lad alone. He was probably a doctor or something in Ukraine and then he was cleaning the museum toilets. No, says Ian, poor nothing. He wasn't even Ukrainian. How do you know, I asks. He just taps his nose and refuses to say another word. That was two weekends ago, the last time I saw him.'

'What do you think made him suspicious of the Ukrainian?'

Stevie paused and Fiona could see him debating how to answer the question. Eventually he pursed his lips, leaned forward and whispered, 'If I tell you, it can't get into the papers that it was me. It's nae strictly…eh…legal.'

Lisa nodded and whispered back, 'If necessary, I'll say I got this bit from an anonymous source.'

Satisfied, Stevie leaned back in his chair and took another sip of his pint. It had lasted remarkably well, given that he was the current holder of the pub record for fastest pint downed.

'Me and Ian used to go poaching at night, mostly out on Laird Hamish's estate. I know it's bad, but we weren't the only ones. We were just setting traps, but there were idiots out there with guns. At first, we didn't go often but a few months ago he started wanting to go out nearly every night. I wasn't too keen because the nights were getting lighter. We'd have to wait until later to go, and we'd end up out into the wee hours.

'One night, we went a bit further than usual, right to the edge of the estate by the old lodge. It was pitch dark, and we were setting the last of the traps when we saw a light through the trees. We must have been further out than we thought because it was the porch light of the lodge and, there on the steps, were a woman and a man. They were having an argument about something. Then this other couple come out and the woman must have told them to get back inside because they go back in and the woman and man walk towards the trees, nearer us. We were shitting ourselves, like. Thought they were going to come into the woods and spot us. I was too scared to move.'

'Why were you so scared?' asked Lisa.

'Well, for a start we were poaching. Then there was the woman. And this is the bit that will shock you. It was that wifie Forglen.'

'Andrea Forglen?'

'Aye, the First Minister. We could hear her telling the man that now he'd had a demonstration, she expected to receive a final offer within a week. She said, "Do the smart thing," and laughed. The man got on his phone and said something in foreign, then they went back to the house.'

Lisa put a hand on Stevie's arm to stop him.

'Foreign? What sort of foreign?'

'How should I know. I only speak two languages, sweetheart. Scottish and the language of love.'

Fiona silently gave Lisa top marks for managing to keep a straight face. It was very hard to stay annoyed with Lisa for humiliating Stevie when the man himself so adept at it.

Lisa withdrew her hand and asked, 'Who was the man?'

'No idea, but the whole thing shook Ian. He was really quiet on the way back. The next night, I started to tell the lads in the pub what had happened. Ian was standing behind them signalling to me to shut up, so I turned it into a story about seeing devil worshippers. He wouldn't tell me why he wanted it kept quiet. Said it was better if I didn't know. After that, Ian wanted to go out poaching all the time, and always near the lodge. I'm telling you, something weird is going on at that lodge.'

Fiona decided that she'd heard enough. She could see that Lisa was poised to ask more questions, but she knew she had the bones of it.

'Excuse me,' she said, pushing back her chair and standing up. 'I need to make a phone call. Right now.'

CHAPTER 11

The sudden blast of "You are my one and only" made Penny oversteer, narrowly missing the middle-aged man in yellow lycra. She checked the rearview mirror and saw that he was now cycling hands-free behind her, fists in the air and middle fingers extended. She waved to say sorry then gestured towards her mobile phone, which continued to blast Chesney from the cup holder.

'Would you mind getting that for me?' she asked.

Mrs Hubbard picked up the device and held it as though it was an unexploded bomb.

'It doesn't have any buttons,' she said. 'I don't do the ones with no buttons.'

'See the wire there? Plug it in.'

A few seconds later, Sandra Next Door's voice came over the car speakers.

'The boys have done some of the research we asked for. I took Ashov back to Anna Henderson's and he's getting whatever he needs from the router. There isn't much to report on Ian yet. No debts or taxes outstanding. The distillery owner is an American company with a CEO called Ted Hyatt. Not much known about him. Graduated with a first-class degree in business and economics, never married, parents both deceased.

'Now onto the interesting bit. The white cars. Lots of them on the island, but the boys didn't just hack the DVLA, they went one step further and looked at car leasing companies in Aberdeen. The distillery has a few, but what caught our eye was that one is being leased to a company called Dìon. Eileen texted a picture to Jimmy Gupta and he confirmed that the make and model are the same as the car he saw the night Elsie was killed.

'The reason Dìon caught our eye is that the company address is the old lodge. We checked Companies House then followed a trail of shell companies back to James and Marion Treadwell. And here's where it gets really interesting. Marion Treadwell is the daughter of none other than the First Minister, Andrea Forglen. Remember what Anna Henderson said about Ian seeing the First Minister at a house with a man? What if that was the lodge? We think it's worth taking a look at the Holiday-Homers.'

'Funny you should say that,' said Penny. 'Fiona had the same idea. You know the rumours about the Holiday-Homers being devil worshippers? They were started by Stevie Mains. Ian Henderson wasn't working late at the distillery except the night he died, so we wondered if he was going out poaching with Stevie Mains and saw something at the lodge. Fiona's at the pub now, hoping to find out, and Mrs Hubbard and I are on our way to visit the Holiday-Homers. Hang on, give me a second to think this through.'

Penny's mind whirred furiously, trying to make all the connections. *We have a white car*, she thought, possibly seen at Elsie's the night she was killed. This links to a company which links to both the lodge and the First Minister. Then we have Ian probably seeing the First Minister at the lodge doing something she shouldn't. That's the connection between the murders. Both of them must have found out about something they weren't supposed know and the answer is somewhere at that lodge.

'Do you know what Dìon is? What they do?' she asked.

Eileen's voice came over the speaker, sounding worried.

'It's a defence research company. Looking at their website, they seem legitimate, but the trail of finances behind it looks shady. The boys are still digging for more information, but I'll text you the link. Be careful, Rubber Duck. And you, Mrs Hubbard.'

No sooner had Eileen hung up, than Penny's phone rang again. This time it was Fiona, and she sounded even more worried than Eileen.

'We were right. Stevie Mains and Ian saw the First Minister with another man outside the lodge. The other man spoke a foreign language. It sounds like the Holiday-Homers came out of the lodge to speak to them, and the First Minister told them to go back inside, so they were definitely there when the First Minister was there. Stevie doesn't know what was going on, but it sounds like Ian figured it out. Whatever it was, he wouldn't tell Stevie.

'Also, something else just struck me. It seems quite suspicious that the Holiday-Homers were at the distillery when Ian's body was found. Were they there to admire their handiwork? They seemed far too nice to be murderers, but I suppose they could have hired someone to do it. The one thing I do know is that everything is pointing to the Holiday-Homers being dodgier than a twelve pence piece.'

Penny agreed and brought Fiona up to speed on everything that Eileen, Sandra Next Door and the hackers had discovered.

'The car's the connection,' said Fiona. 'Ian and Elsie must have been killed over something they knew about whatever was going on at the lodge and this Dìon company.''

Mrs Hubbard, who had been content merely to listen until now, decided that it was time to throw a little common sense into the mix.

'But what would Elsie have known, dearie?' she asked. 'How could she have come to know anything? There's no connection at all between Ian and Elsie themselves, so where on earth would she find out information about the First Minister serious enough to get her killed? The car isn't a strong lead either. I'm sorry, but we don't even know if the car was someone going to see Elsie and, as Sandra Next Door said, there are a lot of white cars on the island.'

Penny sighed deeply as the wind left her sails.

'You're right. We need something more solid to link this to Elsie, but everything we have so far keeps pointing us to the Holiday-Homers. Let's carry on with them because the connection to Ian is definitely there.'

'I do know one thing that might help,' said Mrs Hubbard with a sly smile. 'Although I'm very surprised there was someone foreign on the island without me knowing. I suppose if he was just a day tourist, I might not know. But if they're staying for any length of time, you usually hear something. Paula McAndrew from the paper shop in Port Vik normally phones to warn me, just in case we need to order in any newspapers in foreign and such like. She's a lovely woman, that Paula. Last Christmas she–'

'You're blethering rubbish again, Mrs H!' Fiona warned.

'I was getting to the point,' said Mrs Hubbard, sounding slightly miffed. 'I went to university with Ian Henderson and guess what subject he took?'

There was a long pause as Penny and Fiona waited for the answer to what they assumed was a rhetorical question. Eventually, it became too much for Fiona.

'Are you actually asking us to guess?'

'No, it was a dramatic pause, dearie. Ian Henderson studied…wait for it…keep waiting…and some more waiting… now a drum roll please…Russian language and literature. Which means that if Ian understood what was going on, your mystery man was probably speaking Russian.'

'Och,' breathed Fiona, her disappointment evident. 'If

there's been a Russian on Vik and *you* haven't heard about it, Mrs Hubbard, it's going to be hard to trace him. I'll have to go back to the pub and ask Captain Kev for the ferry manifests.'

'I doubt we'll get anything from those,' said Penny.

'Why not?'

'Because we've just arrived at the lodge and there's a flippin' helipad on the front lawn. Try getting the manifests anyway and while you're at it, could you let Sandra Next Door and Eileen know about the Russian and the Stevie Mains story please?'

Fiona hung up just as Penny brought the car to a halt on the gravel drive. Before Mrs Hubbard unfastened her seatbelt, Penny ran through the plan they had agreed upon earlier.

'Everything we've heard makes this riskier. Are you still okay to go through with it, because we can leave now if you're not?'

Mrs Hubbard confirmed she was ready and willing, so Penny continued.

'Remember, you're the nice old lady, so you take the lead. Do you have the shortbread? Right, you say you heard they met our friends at the distillery, and we thought it would be neighbourly to come and say hello when we were passing.'

'It still sounds like a rubbish excuse,' said Mrs Hubbard. 'We just happened to be driving around with a box of shortbread and thought we'd drop in on some strangers? They're not going to believe a word of it.'

'Okay, then back to plan B; tell them we're recruiting for Losers Club. I've got some leaflets in the boot.'

'Say we're recruiting for a weight-loss club and give them a box of shortbread?'

'Of course not,' said Penny, trying not to let her exasperation bleed through. 'We'll leave the shortbread in the car.'

A hopeful gleam entered Mrs Hubbard's eyes.

'Oh, good. Can I have it?'

'No, you bloomin' well can't. It cost me four quid from your shop! Once we're through the door, I'll ask to use their toilet and you keep them talking. While you're doing that, I'll poke around the house for anything suspicious.'

They were interrupted by a knock and the sudden appearance of a face in the window next to Mrs Hubbard.

'Hello. Can I help you? Are you lost?' said a short woman in an orange jumpsuit.

Mrs Hubbard yelped. Not so long ago, she'd had a brush with the law and Elsie had made her watch every episode of Orange is the New Black in preparation for what everyone assumed would be a stint in jail. Even though she was eventually cleared of poisoning half the island and a fair chunk of Police Scotland, the sight of an orange jumpsuit still brought back memories of what was surely the worst time of her life. Well, perhaps second worst, but she really didn't want to think about that.

'Wind the window down,' said Penny, failing to notice the beads of sweat forming on Mrs Hubbard's temple.

The older woman mutely shook her head then stared fixedly through the front windscreen, as if frozen in place. This time Penny did notice that something was wrong. She pressed a button to her right and Mrs Hubbard's window slowly slid down, letting in a waft of J'adore.

'Sorry to bother you,' she said in her best nice lady voice. 'My friend's not very well and I was wondering if we could trouble you for a glass of water.'

'Of course.' The woman opened Mrs Hubbard's door and bent to take her arm. 'Let's get you inside, dear.'

Mrs Hubbard flinched and let out a small squeak as soon as the woman touched her.

Penny rushed around to Mrs Hubbard's side of the car, apologising to the woman, and spoke soothingly to her friend.

'This nice lady is going to give you some water. Can you swing your legs out of the car? That's it. Now, feet on the ground, take my arm and puuuuullll. Well done! Hold onto my arm and we'll get you inside.'

Penny didn't have a clue what was happening and supposed that Mrs Hubbard must have come up with a Plan C.

'Great acting,' she whispered.

'Not acting. It's the orange jumpsuit,' Mrs Hubbard muttered hoarsely.

'Lordy, I'd forgotten about the jail thing.'

'Thank you so much,' said Penny once she had got Mrs Hubbard seated on what was possibly the largest sofa she had ever seen.

With the woman busy in the kitchen pouring water and making tea, Penny took the opportunity to look around what was a truly stunning room. Whilst the exterior of the lodge was a traditional arrangement of turrets and large bay windows, the interior was a triumph of old meets new. Someone with a keen eye for design had introduced clean, modern lines without losing any of the period features.

'There's no shortage of money here,' she whispered, lifting a vase and peering at the engraving. 'Lalique.'

Penny replaced the vase. Very, very carefully.

'Stop touching things,' hissed Mrs Hubbard, who seemed somewhat perkier than she had a few minutes ago. 'Lovely to look at, delightful to hold, but if you break it, consider it sold.'

'You're such a shopkeeper,' grinned Penny.

They were interrupted by the woman, who placed a tray on the enormous glass and wood edifice that Penny assumed must be a coffee table. She handed Mrs Hubbard a glass of water then peeked inside what Penny had thought was a fancy toilet roll but turned out to be an Orla Kiely teapot.

'I think the tea's ready. I'm Gemini,' said the woman, proffering a hand.

'Libra,' said Penny, thinking how much Eileen would love the concept of introducing yourself by star sign.

'Scorpio,' said Mrs Hubbard gamely.

'Oh, gosh. I mean my name's actually Gemini,' said the woman, sitting down on a pouf at the end of the table.

'Ah, right. In that case, Penny and Mrs Hubbard,' said Penny. 'You have a lovely home. Do you live here alone?'

'Thanks. No, my husband's at the supermarket. You can't get any of the usual stuff here, but we love the island. We bought this place as a bolthole, although we're here most of the time now. I'll be glad when we…never mind. Tea?' Gemini turned to Mrs Hubbard. 'How are you feeling? Well enough for a cup of tea?'

Mrs Hubbard was almost over the shock of seeing the orange jumpsuit, but she recognised the value of being ill so put a little tremor in her hand as she placed her glass on the coffee table and said, 'A bit better, dearie. Just need to catch my breath. And tea would be lovely, thank you. Penny, there's some shortbread in the car. Why don't you pop out and get it? I think the sugar will do me good.'

Penny caught just the hint of a twinkle in Mrs Hubbard's eye. Ooh, you wicked woman, she thought. Making me pay for it from your shop then snaffling the lot.

'I don't think it will help with your diabetes,' she said matter of factly. 'A nice banana might be better.'

'Not a problem. I'll get you one,' said Gemini, standing up, teapot still in hand.

Mrs Hubbard's twinkle turned to a glare, but Penny took no notice, keeping her eyes on Gemini..

'You've been so kind that I feel embarrassed to ask. Could I use your loo, please?'

For a moment, Gemini looked as though she might refuse. Her body stiffened almost imperceptibly and her grip on the teapot tightened. Then the moment passed and she smiled, gesturing towards the back of the house and saying, 'Down the passage and third door on your right.'

Penny thanked the woman and made her way down the passage. There were four doors on either side, and she immediately began to try the handles. Quietly, she turned the first three, finding them locked. The fourth opened to reveal possibly the poshest utility room she had ever seen. A washing machine stood against oak panelling, the basket next to it overflowing with towels. Who uses that many towels, Penny wondered, peering into the basket. There must be about fifteen in there.

She quietly closed the door and tried the next. This one, too, was unlocked but what lay beyond was entirely unexpected. It was a smaller door, only steel, with a number pad to one side. Jackpot.

If there was one thing Penny had learned about herself over the past year, it was that she was very good at getting into places where she should not be. She had turned this talent into a hobby. Only for fun, mind you. She never had any intention of actually using the skills she picked up from YouTube, wikiHow and some of the lesser known websites. However, surely there was no harm in getting a little real-life practice in from time to time.

She reached into her handbag and pulled out a small makeup pouch. Careful not to spill any on the floor, she loaded a brush with face powder and gently swept it over the pad. The powder adhered to three numbers: 680

Ooh, tricksy ones, thought Penny. At least one of the numbers was used twice, depending on whether this was a four digit or six digit code. Human nature dictated that six digits would often be a memorable date, which narrowed things considerably. In which case, with thirty days in a month, twelve months in a year and a hundred years in a century, the first four digits had to be 0608, 0606, 0808 or 0806 and the last two digits were either 00, 06, 08, 60, 66, 68, 80, 86 or 88. Thirty-six possibilities.

If it was a four digit code, however, this widened the field considerably because people tended to remember a random four digit number far more easily than a random six digit number. Hence there may be no pattern at all. Penny had happily forgotten everything she ever knew about maths, so she had no idea how many permutations were possible. Loads and loads once you started factoring in using the same number twice, she guessed. Yet what she did know was that 8068 was the least used code and if you were trying to hide something behind a steel door, you'd probably pick the least used code.

A total of thirty-seven possibilities, thought Penny. I wonder how many goes I'm allowed. Let's try 8068 first.

She tapped in the numbers and heard a faint click.

Holy guacamole, how cool is that? Got it right first time. The Penny's so bright, you gotta wear shades, she sang in a whisper, then she pushed on the door.

She had been expecting a room but found herself at the top of a set of stairs which led to a brightly lit basement room. As she descended the stairs, Penny realised that this was more basement stadium than room. It was bloomin' enormous. She estimated that it extended at least a hundred metres, well beneath Laird Hamish's estate, but in truth she couldn't see the far end, obscured as it was by a series of obstacles such as crates, crash dummies and even a car.. She was standing in what she thought of as the sciencey bit. Around her were computers and electronic components on desks, glass chambers containing coloured substances and, on a table in the centre, what appeared to be a very strange gun. It was chunky and silver, the sort of thing you saw in movies set in the future, where the hero fires lasers and zaps the baddies.

Penny picked up the large weapon and wrapped a hand around the grip. Instantly, a screen on the side lit up, displaying the instruction, "Insert biometrics". Her heart hammering, Penny gently laid the gun down and made her way back upstairs.

She realised that she had been away for far too long and wondered how she was going to explain this. IBS? Period? There really was no explanation for a long bathroom stay that wasn't embarrassing. She carefully closed the steel door, taking a moment to wipe the powder off the keypad using her cardigan sleeve. Then she wiped the sleeve on her t-shirt.

Then she blew on her t-shirt and wiped it with her other sleeve because how was she going to explain the fact that she had a big, white mark across her boobs.

Eventually, having reduced the white mark to a vaguely lighter patch, Penny tiptoed backwards and began to gently close the other door. So intent was she on hiding the evidence of her snooping, that she didn't sense the person behind her until he cleared his throat.

Penny felt heat stab through her stomach as the adrenaline flood her body, every atom screaming at her to flee. For the tiniest moment, she froze. She didn't turn and she didn't dare run. If she were on her own, fine, but Mrs Hubbard was built for dancing, not running, and she could hardly leave her behind. All these thoughts flitted through her mind in a nanosecond, her brain somehow still multitasking for all it was worth, as the most primal part of it screamed "RUN, RUN, RUN". Penny didn't run. Instead, she clamped her thighs together and jiggled from foot to foot, clawing at the keypad with a trembling hand.

'I don't suppose you have the code for the bathroom, have you?' she asked, forcing as much brightness as possible into her voice. Even to her own ears she sounded a touch maniacal.

'Good try,' said a male voice. 'Didn't work. Now, put the handbag down and turn around with your hands up.'

CHAPTER 12

Sergeant Wilson was alone in the police station. She had sent Easy home a couple of hours ago, urging the lad to "get some sleep and with some luck, you might wake up tomorrow with two fucking brain cells to rub together." She was kind like that. A thoughtful boss who put others' needs before her own. Also, he was doing her napper in with his constant questions.

'Where do you think the laptop is, boss?'

'Are the big boys coming?'

'Are they nearly here yet?'

'What do you think they'll be like?'

'Should I get more biscuits in for them coming?'

'Can we get the IT guys in Aberdeen to look at Henderson's router?'

'Did the Procurator Fiscal speak to Ted Hyatt's solicitor yet?'

'I've never really thought about this before. What's your brain made of?'

It was this last one that had prompted the sending home. She'd always wondered what it would be like to have a child and here she was, spending eight to twelve hours a day with a seven-year-old in a big, hairy body, trying not to let the bugger eat all the chocolate biscuits because he didn't need the sugar high. He was already climbing the walls with excitement about the big boys coming.

The big boys in question were the Major Investigation Team, due to arrive tomorrow afternoon. The caramel wafers were locked in her desk drawer and the ginger snaps were ready and waiting in the biscuit tin.

Sergeant Wilson was starting to doubt that she'd get these murders cleared up before the MIT arrived. She'd started to write a report for them, detailing what she'd done so far. Which wasn't nearly enough.

The problem with being on an island was that everything took for-fucking-ever. Easy's suggestion about the router had actually been quite a good one. If they didn't have the laptop, they could at least see his browsing history. Only they'd need to send the router to Aberdeen or get one of the nerds to the island. Ditto Ian's phone, which they'd found in the Ian and Barley soup at the bottom of the mash tun. God knows how the forsensic wankdoodles had missed that! Technically, she should have put the wet phone straight into an evidence bag, and that would have been absolutely the right thing to do if you could just nip down the road and hand it over to the nerds. However, when these things took several days and a ferry ride to resolve, it was far better to put it into a tub of rice to dry out, put the whole lot into an evidence bag, jab some tiny wee holes in the bag to let the air circulate and prevent the whole thing from turning into mouldy fucking pudding, and hope that nobody questioned the chain of custody.

She looked again at her report on Ian Henderson. She felt like she was missing something obvious. What did she know so far? The man wasn't liked, and his wife wasn't aware of any friends. He was threatening the First Minister because he'd seen her up to no good. Allegedly. She'd interviewed everyone he worked with, and nobody had seen a bloody thing. What else did she have? She had the rota.

Sergeant Wilson brought a copy of the rota up on the

screen. It still said the same thing as last time. New names hadn't magically appeared. She scrolled down, her mind beginning to glaze over as she read the complex pattern of times and duties. Hang on a goddamn minute there. A pattern. Ian wasn't down for lates or night shifts. He was working days. Sergeant Wilson scrolled through the rest of that month's rota. No lates. Just days. In that case, where was Ian going at night? Perhaps he had a girlfriend. That was usually the reason why a man would lie to his wife about not being home at night.

She went back to her notebook and skim read the interviews with people who knew Ian, looking for a mention of a female friend or any reason why he would have been out at night. What was it Anna had said? He was either at work or in the pub. Well, he definitely wasn't at work, so she'd try the village pub. Should she phone Easy and get him to come along? Nah, let the laddie get some rest. He'd only start quoting the rule book at her when she put the blue lights on in case Frankie was out in that bastarding tractor blocking the roads again.

By the time Sergeant Wilson reached the pub, her stomach was sending urgent signals about eating something that wasn't chocolate biscuits. She paused to read the blackboard at the entrance. Food served until 8pm. She checked her watch. 7:55pm.

Elbowing her way to the front of the queue at the bar, Sergeant Wilson roared, 'Bertie! I need a quick word.'

Bertie ignored her and went to take the order of a customer at the far end. At least, that's what she thought he was doing. Right up until the moment he legged it through the back door.

Sergeant Wilson elbowed her way back through the queue and took off after him. For a functioning alcoholic, the man could sprint. In fact, he could probably represent Scotland in the hundred metre hurdles at the next fucking Olympics, she thought, as she watched him clear the cemetery wall.

With a sigh, Sergeant Wilson went back to her police car and drove around to the gate at the other side of the cemetery, just in time to watch a clearly exhausted Bertie come wheezing through the gates. She wound down the window and gave the man a moment to catch his breath.

'That's the problem with a sedentary lifestyle; no fucking stamina. Get in, ye twat.'

Bertie did as he was told and sank, still puffing, into the back seat.

'I wouldn't lie down,' Sergeant Wilson advised him. 'I had Jakey Jackson in the car last weekend and there's still a faint smell of meths and vomit. Why did you run, Bertie?'

'I thought I was in trouble.'

'Why the fuck would you think you were in trouble? I was actually quite polite when I asked for a quick word.'

'That's why I thought I must be in trouble. You didn't call me a moustachioed limpdick and offer to ram a pint glass so far up my arse I'd be picking splinters out of my teeth. Anyway, what did you want a quick word about?'

'I just wanted to put in an order for scampi and chips,' said the Sergeant.

Bertie looked at his watch and sucked at his teeth.

'Sorry. You're too late.'

'Listen here, ya wee unregistered sex offender, the only reason I'm late is because you fucking ran!'

From the back seat, Bertie grinned and gave her a thumbs up.

'There you are. Will the real Sergeant Wilson please stand up, please stand up, please stand up? And you have. Of course you can order your scampi.'

'Right,' said Sergeant Wilson. 'I'll see you back at the pub in a few minutes.'

'What? Are you not giving me a lift?'

'I'm a police officer, not a fucking taxi service.'

Bertie eventually got back to a pub full of people who had

poured their own pints and left the money on the bar. He sent Sergeant Wilson's order through to the kitchen and looked around to see where she was sitting. Good. She was over there by the fire, too far away to see him. He put his foot on the crate of counterfeit vodka and quietly nudged it under the bar, out of sight. He wasn't a bad man; he was a desperate one. The smoking ban, the zero alcohol limit when driving, nearly two years of lockdowns and the rising energy costs had eaten so far into his margins that it was barely worth opening anymore. Hopefully, the Vik Show would give the business the boost it needed to keep going for a few months longer.

Sergeant Wilson glanced over at Bertie and wondered what the shifty bastard was up to. She made a mental note to have a quiet…scratch that…a very fucking noisy word later. For now, though, all her attention was on Stevie Mains, who was sitting across from her trying to figure out what he'd done wrong.

'Was it the time I shoplifted a Mars Bar from Mrs Hubbard's Cupboard? Because I was only twelve, and my mum marched me straight back and made me apologise.'

'Cold.'

'Was it the time I smoked a joint at Scott Mitchell's house and was sick in his dad's shoes?'

'Colder.'

'What about the time I shot Jeff in the arse with an air rifle, and he nearly lost a bum cheek? I know it was really bad, but on the bright side, Karen Green snogged the face off me for being a man of action.'

'Absolutely fucking freezing. Right, I'm not sitting here all day with you asking for your misspent youth to be taken into consideration when you're finally sentenced for being a total bell end. What about the time you were friends with Ian Henderson?'

Stevie let out a sigh of relief and leaned back in his chair.

'Oh, that. Aye, we went…erm,' he paused for a second,

trying to think of a way to avoid incriminating himself. 'We went night rambling together.'

'Night rambling? Is that what they call it these days? Listen, I'm not interested in coming after you for *night rambling*. I'm interested in what Ian Henderson was involved in before he was killed because, between you and me, I have fuck all to go on and if I don't get to arrest someone soon, I might have to speak to your mother about that time you–'

'Okay, okay, you win.'

Surrendering to the inevitable, Stevie Mains recounted his night-time adventures with Ian Henderson.

'I'm getting a bit sick of telling folk about it, to be honest,' he concluded. 'I already told the ginger one over there *and* the reporter.'

Sergeant Wilson followed his gaze and scowled as she recognised the figure in wellies and dungarees chatting with Captain Kev at the end of the bar.

'WEASLEY!'

Half an hour later, Sergeant Wilson finally exhausted her swear word collection.

'I should not be surprised that you…people,' she spat, 'took it upon yourselves to investigate.'

Fiona, who had applied a fair bit of judicious editing to her explanation, was quietly relieved that Sergeant Wilson hadn't enquired too closely about how they'd acquired half the information. She seemed to be content to accept Eileen and Sandra Next Door as some sort of tech geniuses.

'Where's Penny now?' asked Sergeant Wilson.

'I don't know,' said Fiona truthfully. 'I've been trying to get hold of her, but she's not answering her phone.

'Where was she the last time you talked to her?'

This was one of the parts that Fiona had judiciously edited. Sergeant Wilson could just about cope with them taking the grieving Mrs Hubbard back to Elsie's house to get some closure (okay, there may have been some stretching of the truth here too) and she seemed fine with them stumbling across bits of information on Sandra Next Door's computer (just a teensy white lie) but tell her that they were interviewing suspects…well, seismologists would become involved. She wished Penny was here. Penny was a much better lia…editor.

'She was taking Mrs Hubbard to visit someone. Something to do with Elsie,' Fiona said vaguely.

Sergeant Wilson's eyes narrowed with suspicion.

'Something to do with Elsie's murder?'

'No,' said Fiona, recalling the cold water that Mrs Hubbard had poured on their theory of a connection between the Holiday-Homers and Elsie.

When Sergeant Wilson had bellowed her over, Fiona had just taken fresh delivery of the ferry manifest from Captain Kev. She realised that she was still clutching it and that it would make for a nice distraction from difficult questions.

'Here,' she said, handing the manifest to Sergeant Wilson. 'I got it from Captain Kev. If there really was a Russian man on the island, he's probably in here somewhere. Unless he–'

Fiona only just stopped herself from saying, 'took advantage of the helipad at the lodge.'

'Unless he what?' asked Sergeant Wilson.

'I was just thinking that sometimes rich people arrive on private boats or helicopters.'

'Good point,' said the Sergeant. 'That's something I can take care of.'

She plucked her phone from the pocket of her stab vest and dialled a number. Fiona could hear the muffled ring tone at the other end, followed by the voice of a man mumbling, 'Hmmmello?'

'Easy!' barked Sergeant Wilson, 'Playtime's over. Take your pyjamas off and get yourself to the station. Fuck's sake, you tail of a blootered sperm, of course put on your uniform first.'

She hung up, turned to Fiona and said grudgingly, 'I'll take a copy of the manifest and give it back to you later. You lot have actually done a…adequate job for a bunch of fucking amateurs.'

High praise indeed, thought Fiona as she got up to leave. Wait until Gordon hears about this. It'll totally freak him out.

Sergeant Wilson sat alone at the table, the other pub-goers being wise enough to keep their distance. Losers Club had managed to get further in their unofficial investigation than she could in her official one, bound as she was by the rules. Now it was time for the professionals to take over.

She was just about to leave when her phone buzzed. If this is Easy phoning to say he's lost his handcuffs again, she thought, I'll wrap a pair round his scrawny wee neck and chain him to a park bench.

'What?' she roared into the handset. 'Aye, this is she. Eh? You're fucking kidding me? Not again? Right, I'll come now. Where are you?'

CHAPTER 13

Penny and Mrs Hubbard sat on the big sofa, too terrified to move. This was possibly the biggest trouble she'd ever been in, Penny reckoned. The hottest water, the deepest doo-doo, the direst of straits.

She could feel her heart hammering as she listened to the man shouting in the other room. And then there was Gemini, standing guard over them, looking for all the world like an angry tangerine.

'I need a pee,' Mrs Hubbard whispered.

'Can you hold it in for a bit longer?' Penny asked.

'Two cups of tea and a glass of water,' Mrs Hubbard reminded her. 'Ever since Doc Harris gave me these water tablets–'

'Alright. Ask Gemini if you can go.'

'You ask.'

'No, you ask.'

'No, you ask.'

'It's your pee. You ask.'

Mrs Hubbard tentatively put her hand in the air.

'What?' snapped Gemini.

'Please, Miss. Can I go to the toilet?'

'It's Ms. And no, you can't. You'll have to wait until *he* comes back because I'm not leaving *her* alone.'

She pointed accusingly at Penny, who shrank under the woman's angry glare.

They were facing some serious consequences, and not just Mrs Hubbard ruining a good sofa. Penny was about to remonstrate, perhaps even offer to accompany Mrs Hubbard and Gemini to the toilet, when she heard footsteps. The man was coming. She felt Mrs Hubbard's arm slip around hers as the older woman huddled closer, and she sent up a silent prayer. We may never see daylight again and we may spend what little time we have left in captivity but please, God, don't let Mrs H pee the sofa, not when she's this close.

The man towered over them, tall and thin, his shaven head putting Penny in mind of a gangster movie she had recently watched, yet his public school English accent was at odds with his menacing appearance.

'If you're worried now, just wait until you see what I have in store for you,' he told her, flashing her a wolfish grin. 'You'll be leaving us shortly.'

His eyes fell on Mrs Hubbard.

'I don't think we've met,' he said, extending a bony hand. 'Anthony Woodbead.'

'Oh, Mr Woodbead, I'm so sorry,' Mrs Hubbard babbled. 'Here we are making a nuisance of ourselves, and we haven't even offered you a bit of shortbread. Penny, go and get the shortbread from the car.'

'Calm down, Mrs Hubbard,' said Penny. 'Anthony's MI5. Or is it six? He was the one who helped us out when Old Archie was killed, do you remember?'

'No dear. All I remember of that is sitting in cars for hours and needing a pee. Talking of which…' She looked pleadingly at Gemini.

'For goodness' sake,' the woman muttered. 'Come on. I'll take you.'

Once they had gone, Anthony Woodbead asked, 'How on earth did you know about this place?'

'We didn't really know anything,' Penny told him. 'We were looking into the murder of Ian Henderson and found out that he'd seen the First Minister and some Russian gadgie here, the pair of them up to no good. Every lead we had seemed to be pointing us here, so we came to find out whatever we could.'

'And you thought you'd just let yourself into a top secret laboratory on the way to the bathroom?'

'Well, you shouldn't leave top secret laboratories lying around, waiting to be discovered.'

'We don't. We tend to hide them behind steel doors with top secret codes. How did you crack the code?'

'A girl has to have hobbies. Honestly, it was logic and reasoning. You see, if it had been a six digit code…'

Anthony Woodbead listened, fascinated, as Penny explained how she had guessed the numbers.

'…So, if I were you, I'd get one of those biometric systems. Far more secure.'

'If it was up to me, I would have,' said Woodbead. 'Unfortunately, this isn't my facility.'

Their conversation was cut short by the return of a very relieved looking Mrs Hubbard. Gemini still looked like someone had offered her a sweetie and it turned out to be liquorice, but Mrs Hubbard, the island's foremost expert on customer service, was doing her best to elicit a smile from the woman.

'If you get the cheapest toilet roll, dearie, it's not always the best value,' she was saying. 'I stock the good stuff, and if you pop past the shop sometime, I'll give you a roll for free.'

Surprisingly, to Mrs Hubbard's mind, Gemini was unmoved by the offer of free toilet paper. She wasn't sure what else she could say to assuage the woman. Unfortunately, she'd started high, leaving herself nowhere to go in these negotiations. Rookie mistake, she chided herself. Should have opened with a tin of beans.

'Are you going to tell us what's going on here? Are you going to press charges? Are we going to jail?' asked Penny.

'All in good time. I'm waiting for our final guest to arrive,' said Woodbead. There was that wolfish grin again.

While they were waiting for whoever Woodbead had invited, they made awkward conversation. Mrs Hubbard once again tried to interest Gemini in the benefits of triple ply, and Penny delivered a short lecture on how to add zinc to your diet. Woodbead and Gemini didn't say very much at all, not even when Mrs Hubbard suggested shortbread again.

Eventually, there was the sound of footsteps on gravel outside, followed by the cheerful trrrrring of the doorbell, and Woodbead went to answer the door.

Penny's heart sank as she heard a familiar voice. She glanced at Mrs Hubbard and saw that the older woman was almost as pale as she had been during the orange jumpsuit trauma.

Boots tramped across the wooden floor and stopped in front of the two miscreants.

'Was I unclear when I said I'd kick you so far up your arse you'd be shitting kneecaps?' asked Sergeant Wilson. 'Was there some ambiguity? A wee loophole? Yet here you are, breaking into places and interfering with witnesses! What part of mind your own nosy fucking business do you not understand?'

'Martisha Wilson!' exclaimed Mrs Hubbard, standing up and planting herself firmly in front of the police officer, 'If I hear one more vile word out of your mouth, I will be straight round to that care home to see your mother. You should be ashamed of yourself. I'm ashamed of you. We're all ashamed of you. I've lost my best friend of fifty years and I'll be damned if I'm going to sit by and do nothing about it. Now, sit yourself down and shut your trap.'

'There's nothing to even connect Elsie's murder to the

Holiday-Homers,' said Sergeant Wilson sulkily, as she took her place on the sofa.

'There is too,' said Mrs Hubbard. 'The white car.'

'What white car?' asked Sergeant Wilson.

'The one that Jimmy Gupta saw outside her house the day she was killed.'

'That wasn't a car,' sighed Sergeant Wilson. 'It was Nolan Duffy from the dairy out on his milk float. His sister lives across the road from Elsie. Jimmy Gupta really needs to get his eyes tested.'

Penny's heart sank. This meant that they had absolutely no leads in Elsie's murder at all.

'There's still the connection to Ian's murder,' she said.

'Yes, there is,' said Sergeant Wilson, turning to Gemini and Woodbead. 'Which brings us nicely round to what the fuck is going on here?'

'Alright,' said Woodbead, 'I'll explain. The reason I asked you here is because I need you to make sure these two keep their mouths shut. In return, I won't have them arrested and I'll tell you what I can.'

He looked at Penny and Mrs Hubbard, his eyebrows raised as if asking them to agree to keep secret whatever he was about to reveal. They nodded eagerly, relieved that they didn't have a life behind bars to look forward to.

'What I'm about to tell you stays between us. As far as you, Penny and Mrs Hubbard are concerned, I'm only telling you because if you continue meddling, it could be disastrous.

'Remember Mustafa, the man Len hid in his shed? He came to this country to give evidence about a politician who was in the illegal arms trade and people trafficking in Africa. You'll have read in the news about the trial. Well, what you didn't read was that he got a promise of parole in ten years in exchange for passing on valuable intelligence about Andrea Forglen.

'Your First Minister is also involved in arms dealing, except she's on the research and development side. Using a complex web of shell companies and proxies, she set up a company called Dìon.'

'Oh, we know all about them,' said Penny. 'Sorry. Carry on.'

'Dìon has many legitimate contracts, but it's also involved in the shadier side of the arms business. Bribing foreign governments, that sort of thing. They're not fussy about who they do business with. Which brings me to the Wagner Group, a Russian paramilitary organisation or, as some call them, Putin's private army. They're active wherever there's conflict, including Libya where, as you'll no doubt have guessed, our politician friend encountered them during a diplomatic mission.

'Are you with me so far? Good. Dìon has developed something which the Russians have been desperate to get their hands on. It's called a smart bullet; a bullet you can aim at a specific individual, almost like a miniature missile but with the range of an ordinary bullet fired from a high-powered rifle. It will avoid intervening objects and hit only its target. It can change direction or even be given a new target mid-flight, assuming you could enter the command fast enough, and it can work with coordinates or biometrics. Limited uses in battle, though. Shooting round corners, snipers, that sort of thing. However, fantastic for assassinations or taking out those who disagree with you.

'Of course, you can't simply trade arms directly with Russia. Far too many eyes on it. You have to go through a third party, which is where Wagner comes in.

'Andrea Forglen is chasing a multi-million-pound contract to supply the Russians with these bullets and the gun that Dìon developed to fire them. Wagner Group is the middleman. The cushion of plausible deniability, if you will.

'The technology was developed here, far from prying eyes, excepting Penny's of course, by Gemini and her husband, Bentley. They became aware of the deal and, being a tad unhappy with having their creations hawked to the maddest dictator, they blew the whistle.

'We finally had confirmation that the First Minister was feathering her own nest in the most heinous of ways, so we convinced Gemini and Bentley to become Covert Human Intelligence Sources, CHIS to those in the know, and I became their handler. I arranged for hidden cameras to be installed all over the house, which is how I spotted your little foray through the secret door, Penny. The intention was to film Andrea Forglen making her deal, sweep up the middleman then arrest her.

'Obviously, none of this happened because she met the middleman outside to make the deal. We still don't know who he was. However, we were not the only ones watching. Your Ian Henderson overheard her talking one night and, instead of reporting his concerns, he started to send her anonymous threats. Unfortunately for him and fortunately for us, he was quite a stupid man. He carefully cut out letters from the Daily Mail to create his messages. He then posted them to Andrea Forglen, and she contacted us, convinced that some madman was after her. And here comes the stupid. Your chap, Ian, licked the bloody envelopes.'

Woodbead hooted with laughter as the others silently looked on, smiling politely. Once he had calmed down, he continued his tale.

'So, there we have it. One DNA result later and I was sent to knock on his door, warn him off, that sort of thing. He told me to get lost, only a little less politely, and I mentioned the Terrorism Act. That put the wind up the bugger. He denied all knowledge of the middleman, although he did admit to sending the letters, so I seized his laptop. Which reminds me, I still need to get some of our tech guys to take a look, just in case there really is anything on there.'

'You haven't even looked at it!' exclaimed Penny.

'Password protected,' said Woodbead. 'Three strikes and you're out. Just like that keypad. I'll say this, you were bloody lucky there. We'd have been in a right old pickle if you'd locked the thing.'

Mrs Hubbard raised her hand and cleared her throat to attract Woodbead's attention.

'I have a wee question. Did Forglen know about Ian?'

'Good point, Mrs Hubbard, and I think I see where you're going with this. I didn't tell her, but it's entirely conceivable that my superiors might. Only my direct superior knows about this operation, so it's possible that if Forglen asked someone for a favour, they would have given her Ian's name without understanding the wider implications. Once she knew he lived on Vik, well, she would have put two and two together. To answer the question behind the question, yes, the First Minister could have sent someone after Ian.'

'I wasn't being clever,' Mrs Hubbard whispered to Penny. 'I was just being nosy.'

'I think that should be the Losers Club motto,' Penny whispered back.

'What about you, Sergeant Wilson? You've been very quiet. Do you have anything you want to say?' asked Woodbead.

'Just one question,' said Sergeant Wilson. 'Bentley? Who the fuck names their kid Bentley?'

Woodbead's lips twitched, the merest hint of a smile betraying his amusement. Yet his eyes were deadly serious when he reminded his guests, 'This is why you have to stop looking into what's going on here. It puts Gemini and Bentley at risk. We will have other opportunities to catch Forglen, but if she gets even the tiniest hint that we're on to her, she'll shut this place down and move her operation somewhere else. Then we will truly be in the brown stuff.'

A few seconds ago, a thought had occurred to Penny, and she was still mulling over whether she should take the risk. It could land quite a few people in jail, should Sergeant Wilson be so inclined. Yet it could provide everyone with some quick answers.'

'Why haven't you had the laptop examined yet?' she asked.

Woodbead frowned and there was a touch of frustration in his voice when he replied, 'Have you any idea how long it takes to get forensics done on anything from this island? I can't go myself, there are no couriers and Mrs Zheng at the post office told me to come back next Tuesday when she would have a fresh supply of big post bags. "Letters only" she kept shouting at me.'

'I feel your pain,' said Sergeant Wilson. 'Every time a bugger dies under suspicious circumstances here, it takes up to three days to get the fingerprint mannie over.'

Penny took a deep breath. Here goes nothing.

'In which case, how about our tech guys take a look at the laptop? Only you're not going to like it.'

'Why?' asked Woodbead.

'Well, you know the Russian hackers that sent everybody's luggage to Frankfurt? They're at my mum's.'

Penny kept her eyes on Woodbead's, purposely ignoring the low growl emanating from the direction of Sergeant Wilson.

Woodbead held a hand up to forestall the imminent explosion.

'That's not a bad idea,' he said. 'Completely against the rules, of course, but hey ho, any port in a storm. Ha! Funny that half an hour ago I would have sworn you two would be leaving in handcuffs. Just as well I changed my mind.'

'Minds can be changed back again,' snarled Sergeant Wilson.

CHAPTER 14

By the time Penny got home that evening, she was more than ready for bed. Her bones ached for the lovely new mattress. Already, she could imagine snuggling under her duvet and nodding off to a good book. She was currently reading a book called Losers Club by some wag called Yvonne Vincent. It wasn't a patch on her real Losers Club, of course, but it made for an amusing read.

She switched on the living room light and blinked, her eyes slow to adjust to the brightness. Timmy, Hector's border collie, peered forlornly up at her from his basket, reluctant to stir from the stinky warmth of his favourite blanket. It used to be her mother's posh velvet throw but had gone the way of all throws in that it now belonged to Timmy. He did like a good throw.

After some thought, Timmy decided to acknowledge Penny's presence by rolling on his back and showing her his cherries. He was very proud of his cherries and spent an inordinate amount of time grooming and licking them, sometimes even offering other dogs the golden opportunity of a nice long sniff. However, his roll was rudely interrupted by a hand on his collar.

'What have we here, Timmy Wimmy Wooster?' asked Penny, plucking a piece of paper from the dog's collar.

She unfurled the paper and immediately recognised her son's handwriting.

Mother,

Do you still live here? If not, please note that Edith and I will be going to the Show tomorrow and that you no longer have a say in the matter.

However, if you do deign to make a rare appearance, please do not touch the sausage rolls in the fridge. They belong to me and, quite frankly, you have done nothing to deserve them.

I have walked and fed Timmy. Edith is at Jessica's and I shall be taking in the evening air with Danny.

Regards,

Hector
 (your son)

Ooh, sausage rolls, thought Penny. How handy it was to have a son who baked, and surely after all the hard work and lettuce she'd put into shrinking her bottom recently, one…or two…wouldn't do any harm. She briefly considered popping them in the oven, envisioning for a moment the crisp outer shell and soft belly of the delicious pastry. However, she doubted she could stay awake long enough, so made do with the microwave.

A few minutes later, plate in hand, Penny settled into a deck chair and switched on the telly. And that is where Jim and Len found her the next morning, when they called by to find out why she wasn't answering her phone.

'We thought something had happened to you. Fiona said you'd gone to see the Holiday-Homers with Mrs Hubbard and she couldn't get hold of you either. You could at least have called to tell us you were safe,' said Len, his tone almost reproving, as if Penny were still the sixteen-year-old girl who was delivered home in a wheelbarrow by Bertie the barman, having sneaked into the pub and made Kenny Bates' big brother buy her bottles of Hooch all night.

'I didn't know I was *un*safe,' Penny yawned. 'I probably didn't have any reception out at the lodge last night. You know what it's like around here. Did you check with Mrs Hubbard? If she was safe, I was safe.'

'I never thought of that,' said Len.

'Well, you're the grown-up, Dad. You're supposed to figure this stuff out! Anyway, it wasn't very late when we got back, and I have loads to tell you. At least, bits to tell you. I'm not allowed to tell you other bits. Why are you looking at me funny?'

This last was addressed to Jim, who was staring at her like a drunk who'd just discovered the last kebab shop on earth.

'I wasn't looking at you funny,' he protested.

'You were staring at me like this.'

Penny adopted a goofy grin and fluttered her eyelashes.

'I was staring at the sausage roll. Can you hurry up and get dressed? I'm starving and we said we'd meet the others for breakfast.'

Penny looked down at the last night's untouched plate, still balanced precariously on her lap. Sausage roll singular? There should be two.

Timmy watched his human carefully as she checked the plate, then he slowly rolled over. Perhaps she would forget his transgressions if he impressed her with his cherries.

. . .

'You're too much like your mother, that's your trouble' said Sandra Next Door in response to Penny's apology for her lateness.

'I'm not the only one,' said Penny. 'Mrs Hubbard is late too!'

She had sent Jim and Len on ahead to the café, while she detoured to pick up Mrs Hubbard. When she arrived at the house behind the shop, she had found Mrs Hubbard in the midst of a Zoom call with the Hollywood Knitting Club.

'Come and wave hello to Johnny Munroe,' Mrs Hubbard instructed. 'We're making plans for Elsie's funeral.'

She gestured to the tiles on the laptop screen in front of her.

'This is Tom, this is Al and that one there should be Bobby, but he's gone off to get the door. His pal Martin Scor…Scorpion…Scorsomething is coming round with a new pattern for a jumper. Except they call it a sweater. Have you ever heard the like of it? A sweater.'

Mrs Hubbard shook her head in disbelief.

'Anyway, Tom won't be able to make the funeral, but he's going to give a speech at the Oscars, and he said he'd include a wee tribute to Elsie. I told him that would be grand. Elsie would thoroughly disapprove of her name being mentioned on the TV, although secretly she'd be tickled pink.'

Somewhat starstruck, Penny dutifully waved at Johnny, Tom and Al, then told Mrs Hubbard she'd wait for her in the shop. She left Mrs Hubbard offering to book Al in at the B&B in the village, if he could find a wee window in his schedule.

Douglas was in the shop, putting the finishing touches on a giant cake made entirely out of hand soap.

'I've got the bug now,' he told her as he drizzled green washing up liquid "icing" over the top of his creation. 'I think making stuff out of other stuff is going to be my new hobby.'

'Well,' said Penny hesitantly, 'it's certainly different.'

'Aye, it'll make a fine window display provided the sun doesn't come out and melt the lot. Are you waiting for the good Mrs? I'm trying to give her space to process Elsie's passing, but I really need her in the shop this afternoon. It'll be busy ahead of the Show. Do you think you can have her back by lunchtime?'

'Not a problem. I'll drop her home after breakfast,' Penny promised him.

'Thanks. Oh, and the postie's been. Can you let her know there's a parcel for her?'

'Nae bother.'

That settled, Douglas rearranged his face into a scowl and went off to take care of the small queue patiently waiting at the till.

In the end, they were only fifteen minutes late, and not even Sandra Next Door's sniping could burst Mrs Hubbard's bubble.

'So, I says to him, "I know you like a round of golf, dearie, and Vik won't disappoint. There's an excellent course at the park, and it's only a pound for nine holes." I think it was the wee windmill that convinced him. Och, Elsie would be thrilled to bits that Al Cuppachino is coming to her funeral. Well, maybe less thrilled about the funeral part. Oh! Do you think we should take him to Cuppachino? Or would that be tacky?'

Penny couldn't help but smile fondly at Mrs H. She was distracting herself with what Elsie would have called "unnecessary funeral malarkey" yet it was all coming from a place of loyalty and deep affection for her friend. Penny hoped that when she went, she would have someone just as devoted to giving her a good send off. As things stood, Edith and Hector would only notice she'd gone when the fridge was empty.

'Now we're all here, hurry up and get on with the order of business,' said Sergeant Wilson, spearing a piece of Gordon's black pudding with her fork.

'In a minute,' said Penny, who was now busily helping herself to Jim's beans, her dad's fried tomato and Eileen's egg. Waste not, want not, she reckoned. Sadly, negotiations were looking less promising on the sausage and bacon front. Sandra Next Door had already traded her toast for a slice of Fiona's bacon and Gordon was happily tucking into a slice of Sergeant Wilson's square sausage.

'Maybe Len and I should start,' said Jim. 'We've probably got the shortest update. Sod all. The end.'

'Did you speak to Jeanie Campbell, Ernie on the Other Side, Grant Hay and Minky Wallace?' Penny asked.

Jim tried to answer through a mouthful of fried bread, so Len waded in to translate.

'We've cleared Minky, and there's nobody else on the baking competition list who had access to Mrs Hay's kitchen. She pointed out that Grant could have borrowed the recipe if he'd asked, so there's no reason for him to steal it. Ernie on the Other Side survives on Wheels on Meals, so would have no use for the recipe, and Jeanie Campbell spouted a load of nonsense. Sorry, Eileen, I know it's your mum we're talking about.'

'It's okay,' said Eileen. 'She's a handful. Do you want me to have a word with her? My horoscope in the Vik Gazette today said the truth would out.'

'If you think you can get anything out of your mother, be my guest. She told me that people in glass houses shouldn't throw stones then ordered us never to darken her door again.'

'That's weird. She hasn't been nearly as angry since she started having regular sex with your dad, Jim. I think the organisms must be helping.'

Jim, who had just taken a large mouthful of tea to wash down the sausage, suddenly found himself gasping for air, the aforementioned tea streaming from his nose. Fiona and Len rushed to his aid, taking it in turns to vigorously slap his back until the colour of his face receded to what Sandra Next

Door told everyone was "the exact shade of mauve I want for my new bedroom carpet. Stay still for a minute while I take a picture."

'It's alright, folks, panic over,' said Gordon, as Jim sat wheezing next to him. 'My bacon's safe. He only managed to cough on Eileen's fried bread, and nobody wanted it anyway.'

'Orgasms,' said Sandra Next Door, 'not organisms. She's having orgasms with Jim's dad. Oh! Stay where you are Jim. You've gone exactly the right colour for my new curtains.'

Eileen thought for a moment.

'No, I think it's organisms. She got an awful dose of thrush off the gin flavoured condoms and was chucking live yoghurt up there like there was no tomorrow. Oh! Quick, Sandra! Is that the green you wanted for the wallpaper?'

Sergeant Wilson mopped up the last of her egg with a piece of fried bread and decided that if this was what having friends was like, it was just as well she'd scared all the fuckers off over the years. But on the other hand, this bunch of Losers had been quite useful, so perhaps it would be better not to scare them off. It was time to put her diplomatic skills to the test.

'Right, youse lot, are you going to sit here talking about Eileen's mum's fanny all day or…oh for fuck's sake, Jim, get a grip. Penny, bring us all up to speed. And by that, I mean tell me exactly what you twats have been up to.'

Penny looked at the others, her eyebrows raised, silently asking permission to tell Sergeant Wilson exactly how many laws they might have broken. Sandra Next Door, Eileen, Fiona and Mrs Hubbard nodded their understanding, so she took a deep breath and plunged in.

'Full confession. Mrs Hubbard and I pressured a manager at the distillery into giving us the rota and we noticed that Ian hadn't been working late. We made the connection to Stevie Mains. Fiona spoke to Stevie and found out that Ian had overheard the First Minister and some man at the lodge. She also promised a reporter an exclusive, by the way. Jimmy Gupta told us about a white car outside Elsie's, and we got a list of all the white cars on the island. One was registered to the lodge and Jimmy said it was the same as the one he'd seen, even though that turned out to be a milk float. Eileen and Sandra have been getting a group of Russian hackers to research Ian, the distillery and Ian's router. Oh yes, and we had a poke around Elsie's house. We didn't find any leads and before you start shouting at us, we wore…erm…protective clothing. I think that about sums it up.'

All eyes were fixed on Sergeant Wilson, awaiting the inevitable explosion. Correction. All eyes except Gordon's. He had conveniently dropped his fork and was under the table, taking a suspiciously long time to find it. It was, therefore, an enormous surprise when the police officer simply nodded and said, 'I knew the fucking bin bags were something to do with you.'

Everyone stayed silent in case the danger hadn't passed, then a voice came from below the table.

'Is it safe to come out now?'

There followed a yelp as Fiona gave her husband a sharp kick, and Gordon emerged rubbing his thigh.

'Aye, you're safe,' said Sergeant Wilson. 'Truth be told, you got further than me, more quickly than me. Most of it I got in the end anyway, so there's no harm done. Other than the computer stuff, the only thing I could arrest you for is breaking into Elsie's house.'

'No, we didn't break in, dearie,' said Mrs Hubbard. 'She gave me a key years ago so I could feed her budgies. I don't think you can arrest us for that.'

Sergeant Wilson rested an elbow on the table and rubbed her face. She could hardly arrest them for knowingly being interfering bastards in a public place.

With a sigh, she said, 'In which case, let's get to the bit I probably *can* arrest you for. Tell your auntie Sergeant Wilson what the Russian hackers have been up to.'

Sandra Next Door and Eileen exchanged worried glances then began to talk in unison.

'Enough with the stereo,' said Sergeant Wilson.

'You–' She pointed at Eileen. '–fucking Space Cadet over there, start talking.'

Eileen, who under ordinary circumstances would relish her moment in the spotlight, looked like a rabbit caught in the headlights. She sat mute until Sergeant Wilson clicked her fingers and shouted that there were two murders to solve, and she didn't have all fucking day. Gordon eyed Eileen with sympathy as she took a deep breath and, in a trembling voice, started to talk.

'We used a facial recognition thingy on a photo of Ian that Ashov got off his wife. Ian's wife, not Ashov's wife. Because he's not even married. Ashov, I mean.'

Eileen shot a look at Sergeant Wilson, who span a finger in the air in the universally recognised signal of "just fucking get on with it." Eileen got on with it.

'We found a newspaper report from 1969 about a school exchange programme, with a picture of some pupils, and there was Ian in the front row. Except he wasn't Ian. He was Malcolm Johnson.'

Mrs Hubbard, who had been quietly stealing Gordon's toast, spoke up at this point.

'Yes, Len and I know about that. He was at university with us and changed his name afterwards.'

'Why did he change his name,' asked Fiona.

'Never you mind,' Mrs Hubbard told her. 'It has nothing to do with this. Carry on, Eileen.'

'Other than that, there wasn't much on him. Just some stuff in the comments section of the Daily Mail, some of it a bit racist and sexist. He wasn't on the social media, so we couldn't track down any friends. There didn't seem to be any close relatives either. Malcolm Johnson was an only child and his parents died twenty years ago.'

'I spoke to the Chief Warlock of the Freemasons to try and find out more about Ian,' said Fiona. 'Actually, there might be a complaint coming your way, Sergeant Wilson. But in my defence, he was a total wanker.'

'Was it that Alec Carmichael?' asked Sergeant Wilson.

'Yes, him,' said Fiona.

'Aye, you're right enough. Total wanker. Don't you worry your wee ginger head about him, Weasley.'

'Will you stop with the gingerism?' said Fiona, exasperated.

'I will when you stop messing with my investigations. Now, which one are you? Fred or George? I can never tell you apart.'

'Fred!' exclaimed Fiona. 'I mean Fiona!'

'Right, well, tell George over there to stop picking his nose with his fork. He might find a brain cell and shock us all. Keep going, Space Cadet.'

'The next thing we did was look at the distillery. Lots of business things I didn't understand.'

She looked at Sandra Next Door, who took the hint and filled in the blanks.

'It was recently taken over by an American company called Barrois Imperial, and the new owner is Ted Hyatt. There was nothing much on him either. He bought Barrois a few years ago when it was a small cognac producer, before they started branching out into other luxury spirits. There isn't much out there about the company. A few articles in business journals, but they're not one of the major players. Lochlannach Distillery is the company's first distillery and even then, it's quite a small one. The company pays its taxes, makes a decent but not massive profit and supplies to a few exclusive outlets.'

'So far, so boring, Sandra Thatcher' said Sergeant Wilson, faking a yawn. 'Get onto the interesting stuff.'

'Forget it,' said Sandra Next Door. She turned to Penny. 'I won't work with her if she's going to be a cow.'

'I know you are, but what am I?' said Sergeant Wilson sulkily.

'Martisha Wilson! Sandra Next Door! That's quite enough from both of you,' said Len, using his dad voice to absolutely no effect.

Only Penny was scared. Sandra Next Door smirked, and Sergeant Wilson gave Len a pat on the back, as if to say, "good effort."

'I remember you telling us your name was *Polygraph* Wilson,' said Jim out of the blue. 'When did you change it to Martisha?'

'It's always been Martisha. I was being fucking allegorical. Or is it rhetorical? Hyperbolical? Och, something olical.'

'Diabolical?' suggested Sandra Next Door, smiling sweetly in response to the angry glare directed her way.

'Hang on a minute there vet boy. You remembered something!' Penny exclaimed.

'Aye, I'm remembering things now,' said Jim. 'Not much, but I'm getting the odd flash.'

'Do you remember that tenner you owe me?' asked Gordon.

'Nice try,' said Jim.

Sergeant Wilson gave an impatient snort and tapped her fork against her mug of tea.

'Order, order! We are all very happy for you, Jim, now could you please shut the fuck up, thank you very much. Thatch…Sandra Next Door, what else have you and your fellow criminals been up to?'

For a fraction of a second, Sandra Next Door looked as though she might lunge over the table and slap Sergeant Wilson, but she clearly thought better of it because she took a deep, calming breath and resumed her update.

'I'm going to skip Ian's router because the laptop you delivered last night–'

'Stop. Rewind. What laptop?' asked Fiona.

'Goodness, dearie, we forgot to tell you,' said Mrs Hubbard, leaning forward on her elbows as if to settle in for a good old chinwag. 'We were at the lodge last night and Penny broke into–'

'Ahem,' Penny coughed.

'Oh dear, I'm not allowed to tell you that. Anyway, there was this man called–'

'Ahem.'

'Right. Ian saw the First Minister with a Russian. You'll never believe what she was up to–'

'Ahem.'

'Och, how am I supposed to not tell folk? I've never been very good at secrets. To cut a long story short, we found the policeman who took Ian's laptop, and the First Minister really is up to something I can't talk about. Ian was sending her threatening letters because he saw her meeting with a Russian agent and there's every chance she had him taken care of.'

'Well summarised, Mrs H, and top marks for discretion,' said Penny.

'How come you're not allowed to tell us everything?' asked Gordon.

'Oh dearie me, the Secret Service mannie said if Andrea Forglen finds out they're trying to catch her illegally selling weapons to the Russians then the whole operation will be blown'

The words had gushed out of Mrs Hubbard before Penny had the chance to put the cork back in.

'Sorry, dearie,' said Mrs Hubbard. 'They needed to know. And I really don't do well with secrets.'

'That's not true,' said Penny. 'You've managed to keep one.'

A thought occurred to her.

'If Ian was at university with you, that must mean he was in the–'

'Ahem,' said Mrs Hubbard.

'In the what?' asked Sandra Next Door.

'Never you mind,' said Mrs Hubbard firmly.

'Is it some dirty little secret? Were you and Ian an item? Aye, it's fine to talk about other people but when it's about you…'

'That's enough!' said Len sharply. 'What did you find on Ian's laptop?'

Sandra Next Door shot him a mutinous look and would have continued baiting Mrs Hubbard, were it not for Eileen, who exclaimed, 'Porn!'

Everyone stopped what they were doing and stared at her.

'There was an awful lot of porn. I think he liked boobs,' she explained. 'And he was keeping files on people. The Jimmy Gupta file had a spreadsheet tracking the dates that cats disappeared and comparing them with the dates Jimmy ran special offers on sausage rolls. To be fair to the man, it *was* very suspicious. In March, Mr Squeakypaws from 43 Main Street went missing and Jimmy had a special offer on the next day.'

'Jesus Christ,' said Sergeant Wilson, gesturing at Eileen and Sandra Next Door. 'If he liked boobs, then he would have loved you pair of tits. What about any files that might actually be relevant?'

'He had a file on you,' snapped Sandra Next Door. 'You're scared of spiders, sing to your goldfish and sent your sister a Police Scotland baseball cap for her birthday.'

'Aye, well, what's wrong with that? I told her it was only for wearing in the house. Same as the handcuffs I sent her last year.'

'He had files on lots of other people, too,' said Eileen, attempting to distract both women from what was clearly shaping up to be yet another argument. 'Anyone on the island who's not…I don't know how to explain it. If you're not white or you moved to the island within the last fifty years, Ian had a file on you.'

'Stevie Mains said he had a dossier on the Ukrainian cleaner who was murdered a while back,' said Fiona.

Eileen nodded. 'Aleks Antinov. There wasn't much in it. Ian was curious about why a Ukrainian man was here as a refugee on his own. He was suspicious because he couldn't find anything about Aleks' background in Ukraine. Obviously, he was either one of the lizard people or he was the Russian agent that Andrea Forglen met at the lodge. My money's on the first one.'

'What makes you think that?' Penny asked.

'Well, for a start, Aleks was in the Freemasons, and everyone knows that the lizard people run the Freemasons.'

'How do you know he was in the...never mind. I meant why do you think he was the Russian agent?'

'I don't see any other Russiany people running around here, do you?' Eileen said defensively, completely forgetting about the four men who were currently sleeping off the all-nighter they'd pulled to hack Ian's laptop.

'So, your entire evidence is that he was a bit Russiany?'

'Which is why it more likely that he was one of the lizard people. Honestly, Penny, use some common sense.'

Having dropped that little bombshell, Eileen pushed her chair back and wandered off to the counter to order more tea.

By the time she returned, the others had had a chance to ponder the possibilities. Sergeant Wilson said that Easy hadn't found any flights in or out of the island and there were no Russian nationals on the ferry manifest that Fiona had obtained.

'Then he quite possibly was the Russian agent,' said Jim. 'Bugger me with a bar of chocolate, I'd never have guessed that.'

'Ooh, spooky,' said Eileen, settling into her chair, 'I read your horoscope in the Vik Gazette this morning, Jim, and it said there would be a conjunction of Mars and Uranus.'

Jim and Gordon snickered at this, and Eileen looked on, confused.

'It means you'll be confronted by new ideas and will discover fresh ways of thinking,' she clarified.

'Which is what we need now,' Penny declared, giving Jim a sharp kick on the shin. 'Anybody have any?'

Everyone shook their heads.

'That's it then. The end,' declared Sergeant Wilson. 'Leave Andrea Forglen to me and James Bond, okay? Right, off youse all fuck.'

CHAPTER 15

Penny was desperate to get Jim on his own so she could ask him about his memory. Well, ask him about his memory was perhaps stretching things. What she really wanted to know was whether he remembered *her*. Specifically, his feelings about her. A brief flash of panic made her tighten her grip on the edge of the table. What if he remembered everything yet still didn't feel the same way? Could that happen? God, if you have any mercy for a woman who goes to church three times a year and blasphemes fourteen times a day, could you please send it this way because I don't think I can stand this anymore, thank you very much and amen.

In an effort to separate Jim from the herd, she'd offered to give him a lift home. Len began to insist that he would take Jim but Eileen, with the intuition borne of years of shared boyfriend woes, distracted him by saying, 'I heard Mary telling Sandra Next Door that she's going to knock a wall down so you can have a big kitchen-diner. She watched a manly YouTube video on it and the big hammer is arriving in today's post.'

Len gulped nervously and sped off, muttering anxiously about retaining walls.

Sandra Next Door, who had picked up on the subtle undercurrents, said that she would drop Mrs Hubbard at the shop and take Eileen back to Port Vik on her way to the supermarket.

'I'm running out of flour. That Ashov has been gobbling my scones in a way that Geoff never could.'

Jim, ever the fan of a good innuendo, opened his mouth to ask for details but quickly closed it again. Sandra Next Door was not known for her sense of humour and it would be like poking a self-righteous bear with a stick.

'We better go too,' said Fiona. 'Gordon and I have an appointment.'

Gordon went slightly pink, and they exchanged a meaningful glance.

'Men's troubles,' said Jim, giving Gordon a knowing wink.

'Some days I'm never out of trouble,' said Gordon.

'Aye.'

'Aye.'

'So....aye?'

'Aye.'

'Aye, but?'

'No, aye.'

'I'll no…aye?'

'Aye, no.'

'What was that deep and meaningful conversation about?' asked Penny once they'd gone.

'It's obvious,' said Jim with a self-satisfied smile. Sandra-baiting might be off the cards, but he would happily let Penny tie herself in knots.

'How is it obvious? Aye, aye, aye and a couple of nos.'

'Aye, well, if you don't know, I'm not going to tell you.'

'Has anyone ever told you, you're really annoying, Jim Space.'

'Aye.'

'If you two are going to shag, could you not do it here? I'll only have to arrest you and I fucking hate paperwork.'

Sergeant Wilson, to whom undercurrents were what happened when you didn't get your cake mix right and all the fruit sank to the bottom, had not taken the hint and left. In fact, she had just started on her third cup of tea and, Penny wondered, where the hell had she gotten the mug from? Had she taken her own mug?

Sergeant Wilson lifted the "World's Best Sergeant" mug to her lips, took a sip and winked lasciviously.

'She looks at you like somebody stamped on a puppy and you've spent the morning staring at her with your fucking tongue hangin' oot. It doesn't take a detective to see what's going on here.'

'In which case, maybe you could give us some privacy?' Penny suggested, there being no point in denying that she and Jim were long overdue a...frank discussion.

'No can do,' said the Sergeant. 'I need a favour. I need you to find a way to speak to the distillery owner. It's one thing I haven't managed to do, and it will tie off a loose end.'

'Haven't you spoken to him yet?' asked Penny.

'No, the fucker is more tight-lipped than a botched vaginoplasty.'

'Charming,' said Penny. 'What about the reporter that Fiona met? Do you think she could set up an interview with Ted Hyatt and take you along?'

'Much as I'd give my fungal left tit to sneak in there and find out what's going on, it's more than my job's worth. You, on the other hand, are an anonymous intelligence source.'

'I am?'

'You are if I say you are.'

'How do you me want to do this?'

Sergeant Wilson thought for a moment, considering her options, before declaring, 'Aye, that would work. Tell Fred to phone the reporter arsehole. She can say she's sending two reporters who are doing a piece on the distillery for the travel and lifestyle section or some keech. You and Jim can both go.'

'Jim can't go! What if he got another bash on the head?'

'Then it might knock some sense into him. For fuck's sake, I'm not asking you to rugby tackle the cockmonger to the ground and apply the thumbscrews. That's my job. All you need to do is ask a few polite questions. Jim, you can be the photographer. Do you have a camera?'

'I don't know,' said Jim. 'Also, I am here. I can speak for myself about what I will and won't do.'

'Why are we even bothering with this?' asked Penny, ignoring him. 'If Ian was killed by Andrea Forglen, there's no point in looking at the distillery.'

'Oh ye of absolutely fuck all logic,' said Sergeant Wilson. 'Except Space Cadet. That thing about the lizard people was spectacular.

'Right, pin yer lugs back. For a start, the distillery was the scene of the crime and Ian's murder had to have been committed by someone who was able to avoid the security cameras. This is what we in the know call a loose end. He's there at work, playing his wee fiddle, no reason to suspect he's in any danger, everything's as it should be.

'Then there's Elsie's murder. Different method, you might argue, but she's at home, minding her own business, lets someone in, which suggests she doesn't think she's in any danger. Sound familiar?

'We have nothing to link Elsie with Andrea Forglen. Which means that if Andrea Forglen did have Ian murdered but didn't kill Elsie, then there must have been two murderers on one tiny, wee island at the same time. Which is about as likely as me raiding Junkie Neil's flat and finding fucking talcum powder.'

'Then, what you're saying is that the First Minister didn't have Ian Henderson killed?' asked Penny.

'What I'm saying is that this is what we in the know call a shitpuddle. I am left with questions, I have the MIT arriving on the afternoon ferry and I would like some answers before Detective Chief Inspector Fudmuppet pats me on the head and says, 'We'll take it from here.'

'And the new distillery owner told the staff to destroy records. I'd like to know what that's about,' said Penny.

'Aye, that dribbling cat sphincter, Billy Dent, told me.'

'You've been to see Billy?'

'I know far more about what you lot have been up to than you give me credit for, with the added bonus that I can frighten the shit out of a man far better than Mrs Hubbard. The new owner's laying off half the staff and bringing his own people in.'

'That doesn't make sense. Get rid of your experienced people and bring in new ones. Why would he do that?'

'Well now's your chance to find out. Right, off ye fuck, the both of you, and leave me to my tea.'

Penny and Jim drove back to his house in silence. She was wondering how to broach the subject of their relationship. He was wondering what the heck was going on because he had this funny feeling that the First Minister had murdered Ian Henderson. He hadn't been able to keep track of the whole conversation, but that was the long and short of it.

Then there was what Sergeant Wilson said about him and Penny. It couldn't be true, could it? Penny liking him. He was starting to think that before he lost his memory, he'd liked her very much indeed. Warm, funny, caring and sharp as a…a… one of them pointy things you stick in noticeboards – everything about her was amazing. The memory of the ice cream came back to him. He'd been up half the night thinking about it, trying to sort out why he'd had this strong urge to kiss Penny. He looked at her now, confidently steering the car around the bends at Middens Field, little gold earrings glinting in her ears, her hair swept back from her face and her boobs bouncing gently as the car crested the old bridge then bumped back onto the flat at the other side. He shouldn't be noticing her boobs, he thought guiltily, because if she noticed him noticing her boobs, she'd stop the car and make him walk home.

I'm not sure if he's ready yet, thought Penny. If he's starting to remember things, I should probably tell him. But he hasn't actually given any sign that he thinks of me as more than a friend, no matter what Sergeant Wilson said. He's probably already forgotten what Sergeant Wilson said. He used to look at me like he wanted to melt into me. And my boobs. God, he was always looking at my boobs, but it's like he doesn't notice them anymore.

She glanced sideways at Jim, and he quickly looked away.

I wonder what he's thinking, she mused.

Phew, that was a close one, thought Jim.

Eventually, he broke silence, saying, 'Would you like to come in for a coffee when we get to mine?'

'No, but I'll come in and use your loo, if that's okay,' said Penny. 'Too much tea.'

She pulled into Jim's drive and parked behind Phil, the battered Land Rover that had sat unused since Jim had been in hospital. She almost felt sorry for poor Phil, all alone and abandoned. He was such a stoic, reliable beastie, having got them through the torrential storm last year and battled through snow to get Hector and Edith to school over the winter. Penny realised that she would give anything to have things back to normal.

They sat there for a moment, suspended in the silent limbo between arriving somewhere and getting out of the car. That frozen moment before re-entering the hustle and bustle, things to do, busyness and noise of the real world.

Coming to what she hoped was the right decision, Penny took a deep breath and said, 'We need to talk.'

Jim nodded gravely. 'I agree. But can we do it inside because I've just–'

'Oh my word, you can't be serious,' said Penny, leaping out of the car.

She ran to the front door and glanced back to find Jim still sitting in the passenger seat, grinning at her from behind the window. He slowly emerged from the vehicle and sauntered over.

'I had a bet with myself that I could make you reach the front door within five seconds.'

'You're absolutely disgusting. And in my car!'

'Och, no, I didn't really do it, said Jim, unlocking the door. 'Come on inside and I'll make up for it with a chocolate biscuit.'

'You're not supposed to be eating chocolate biscuits, remember? All that weight you put on with the nurses giving you second helpings of ice cream and jelly in the hospital.'

'I have no idea what you're talking about,' said Jim, vainly trying to suppress a smile.

He ushered her into the hall and directed her to the downstairs toilet, forgetting that she'd visited his house roughly a hundred times in the past year. She hadn't been here for about two weeks, though, and was surprised by how quickly he'd redecorated.

'You're well on with the painting. It's all very…green,' she said as she entered the kitchen.

Jim hastily shoved the remainder of a caramel wafer into his mouth and chewed it as quickly as possible, all the time avoiding eye contact with Penny in case he got another telling off.

Eventually, with the aid of a gulp of coffee, he swallowed it down and said, 'Aye, well, I kept forgetting that I'd already ordered the paint, and I ended up with fifteen pots. About thirteen pots more than I needed. I finished the living room then just kept on painting. I'm down to seven pots now, which should be enough to finish the upstairs. Now, what was it you wanted to talk about?'

'Us,' said Penny, sitting down at the table and gesturing to Jim to do the same.

'There's an us?' asked Jim.

'Yes, there's very definitely an us.'

'That's good because I was starting to wonder.'

'What were you wondering?'

'Well, I had a memory yesterday and it made me feel like maybe there was something going on between us.'

'There was. While you were in hospital, we opened up to each other about how we were feeling, and we decided to wait until you came home before we took it any further. You know, what with the hospital not really encouraging snogging and that sort of thing.'

Penny, who had been staring at the table while she talked, glanced up to check whether Jim was on the same page as her or was beset by sheer horror. Jim grinned back. Phew, same page then.

'When you woke up after the brain surgery, I was a stranger to you. I wanted you to love me from the heart, not because I told you and you felt obliged to go along with it.' Penny's voice cracked a little. 'That's why I didn't tell you. Sorry, this is really hard.'

Jim reached out and put his hands on Penny's shoulders, watching as a solitary tear slid into the crease between her cheek and her nostril.

'You did the right thing by waiting,' he assured her. 'It would have freaked me out. To be honest, even though I'm starting to remember, it's still too much. I know it's there, that I loved…love you, but with the memories coming back, my emotions are all over the place.'

'I understand. Shall we leave it as friends for now and if something happens, it happens?'

'I think it's for the best,' said Jim, gently wiping the tear away with his thumb. 'Are you okay with that?'

Every atom in Penny's body screamed "NOOOOOOOO!" but she realised that she would have to be okay with it.

Perhaps so okay with it that someday she would be able to move on and accept that she and Jim could never be more than friends.

Jim looked at the oversized wall clock and smiled.

'We should phone Fiona. I think she might have some news that will cheer you up.'

Fiona sounded out of breath when she answered the phone.

'Hello, Braebank…is that you Penny?'

'Yes. You sound like you've just run the hundred metres. What are you up to?'

'Gordon was waltzing me round the kitchen then fandangoed me out the back door. He dropped me in the cabbages, and now I've got shit stuck to my bum. Quite literally. We fertilised that patch with the contents of the composting toilet yesterday.'

'You sound very happy about it.'

'That's because I have bigger fish to fry. Much bigger. Oh God, I can't keep it to myself any longer. That appointment earlier was for my twelve-week scan. We're pregnant!'

Penny was overjoyed for Fiona and Gordon. She talked babies with Fiona for so long that Jim managed to eat three chocolate biscuits under the radar and was just about to head for the cheese when he heard her say, 'You know that reporter you met? I'm hoping she can do me a favour.'

When she eventually got off the phone, Penny thumped Jim's arm.

'That's for the chocolate biscuits,' she said. 'Don't think I didn't notice. And why do I get the feeling you knew Fiona was pregnant? Was that your vet training kicking in?'

'No,' said Jim, rubbing his arm, 'Gordon told me just before they left the café.'

'The aye no aye conversation? You got all that from aye no aye?'

'Aye.'

Penny gave a little snort and shrugged.

'You amaze me, you really do. Listen, Fiona's going to text me the details, of the interview, not the pregnancy, so you better put the biscuit tin away and start looking for your fancy camera.'

Ten minutes later, Jim sat on his bed, gazing at the tiny screen of the fancy camera as he flicked through the photos. Nearly all of them were of Penny. Days out he didn't remember, parties he'd forgotten and, finally, a close-up of her in her red coat, laughing and eating an ice cream in the snow. A solitary tear slid down his cheek and settled in the crease of his nose.

CHAPTER 16

What would a reporter wear, Penny mused as she flicked through her clothes rail. She noted with some irritation that dust had settled on the shoulders of her clothes and across the tops of the empty hangers. The boxes containing the flat-pack wardrobe were neatly stacked against the wall and she wondered if she should still ask Jim to help her assemble the thing. Since they were to be just friends, it didn't seem right to rely on him all the time. Yet Dad would struggle with something as big as a wardrobe, Hector and Edith would reluctantly help then find some excuse to argue with her and leave halfway through, and her Mum would be…Mum. Perhaps Eileen or Kenny could lend a hand and she could babysit in return.

That settled, Penny picked out a blouse and blazer which she'd wear with her new jeans. Smart casual is the way to go, she thought, brushing the dust off the garments. A reporter has to seem professional, yet friendly and approachable. Now, shoes…

A loud knocking came from downstairs and Timmy gave a single deep woof to warn of impending stranger danger. He didn't actually stir from his bed or take any interest, clearly considering one woof sufficient to warn off any would-be attackers.

'You'd make a useless guard dog,' Penny told him as she made her way to the front door.

Jim was on the step, dressed in his painting jumper and a tatty pair of trousers with so many pockets that he could forge a successful career as a shoplifter. Any security guard who asked him to turn out his pockets would lose interest by number twelve.

'Is that what you're wearing?' asked Penny.

Jim looked down at himself, then back up at her, puzzled.

'Aye. It was this or the gardening jumper. Was I supposed to tart myself up?'

'What about the one I gave you for Christmas? That's quite smart.'

'Was it blue?'

'Yes.'

'I threw out all the blue jumpers. That's why I'm down to the painting jumper and the gardening jumper.'

'For goodness' sake. And the trousers?'

'Not blue.'

'Come in and I'll lend you one of Hector's. Top, not trousers. You're about half a foot taller than him.'

Jim eventually left the house complaining that he felt like "a right eejit" in an Armani sweatshirt that was, admittedly, about twenty-five years too young for him.

'Sorry,' said Penny. 'Since he's been earning his own money, Hector's splashed out on all this designer sportswear.'

'That reminds me,' said Jim. 'Minky's looking for some help in the café. I said I'd let you know for Edith.'

'You remembered that from yesterday?' asked Penny.

'Aye, it sort of stuck. Probably because I had this whoosh of a memory at the same time that knocked me sideways.'

'Oh? What did you remember.'

'It's not important. Keep focussing on taking the Midden

bends at five miles per hour. Have I ever told you that you drive like a granny?'

'About the same number of times that I've told you you're like a boy racer.'

'Aye, well, the car has six gears. We're on the straight now, so you can change up to second.'

They happily bickered their way to the distillery, neither of them noticing that they'd fallen into a comfortable, familiar pattern. It was only when they were leaving the car and Jim said, 'That was a fine argument,' that Penny once more felt the pang of loss.

The woman behind the reception desk seemed to be expecting them because she handed over two lanyards, the words "Visitor – accompanied" emblazoned across the front, then had them sign the visitors book. While she waited for the woman to phone whoever needed to know they'd arrived, Penny flicked through the visitors book, idly scanning the names. She recognised a few locals and there were her mum and dad. Then she flicked further backwards and stopped, gasping as she recognised the name of someone she didn't expect to see.

Before Penny could think on this any further or point it out to Jim, a woman who introduced herself as Lesley arrived and immediately ushered them into an office towards the rear of the building.

'Mr Hyatt will be with you shortly,' she said, with an air of such reverence that Penny would not have been surprised if she'd added, 'His meeting with God is running late.'

They settled themselves into plastic chairs across from a vast, glass desk on which stood only a Mac and keyboard. The room itself was starkly modern, with abstract prints in various shades of grey adorning the white walls. The grey carpet and lack of any personal touches gave the room a cold, impersonal feel. Penny stood up again and wandered to the back of the room where an intricate engraving of the entire distillery site as it was in 1890 hung in an incongruously ornate frame.

'Can you imagine working here all day?' said Jim, joining her. 'It's depressing.'

'It sure is,' said a voice from behind them.

A tall man in a well-tailored grey suit was standing in the doorway, smiling a welcome. He was perhaps in his mid-seventies but with an air of confidence and vigour that made him seem much younger.

'Ted Hyatt,' he said, striding towards them, his hand extended in greeting. 'You must be Penny and Jim. I didn't get your last names.'

Bugger, thought Penny, this is the one thing we haven't prepared for. Her eyes quickly scanned the room before settling on a packet of wipes and some hand gel on a table in the corner.

'Moist and Blobby,' she said, a nanosecond before her brain had the chance to run damage limitation on her mouth.

'Unusual,' Ted commented. 'Penny Blobby and Jim Moist?'

'No, it's Penny Moist and Jim Blobby,' Penny corrected him, ignoring her brain which was now urgently signalling that she might very well be a twat. Jim was signalling the same thing, if the twitch of his lips and discreet nudge in the ribs were anything to go by.

'Please, please, sit down,' Ted said, gesturing towards the plastic chairs. 'Has anyone offered you a beverage? No? Lesley! Lesley! Bring a pot of coffee! Or would you prefer tea? Lesley!'

'Coffee's fine,' said Penny, interrupting before poor Lesley found herself juggling pots and cups.

'Coffee's fine!' shouted Ted.

Penny had expected him to sit behind the desk, but instead he pulled up a third plastic chair and sat beside herself and Jim.

'We haven't had time for a makeover yet, so things are still pretty basic,' he explained. 'Alrighty, I guess you have some questions for me. First, can I ask when this piece is likely to be published?'

'Not until next month at the earliest,' Penny lied smoothly. 'We're running a feature on dolphin watching spots on the Northeast coast first.'

'That's good. I'll be done by then,' the man muttered to himself.

'Done?' asked Penny.

'I mean we'll be more organised. Have the capacity for more visitors. Now, these questions of yours, Miss Moist? Sorry, is it Miss or Mrs Moist?'

'Mrs,' said Penny, hiding her growing mortification behind a lengthy search of her handbag for the list of questions that Sergeant Wilson had emailed to her earlier.

She had made some amendments to the questions, feeling that "are you a murdering fudgebucket?" might not set the right tone. Sergeant Wilson had managed to replace all her swears with non-sweary words that sounded exactly like swears and clearly considered this sufficiently diplomatic.

'Before I begin,' said Penny, regaining her composure, 'can I ask about your accent? I noticed a Scottish twang in there.'

Ted Hyatt's eyes twinkled with delight as he smiled broadly and said, 'Well observed, young lady. I was born in Glasgow and moved to the States when I was quite young. You can take the man out of Scotland, but you can never take Scotland out of the man.'

He gestured around him, as if to encompass the whole building.

'That's why I bought this place. I'm getting old and I missed my roots, so when it came up for sale it seemed like the gods were trying to tell me something.'

'Do you still have family in Scotland?' asked Penny, aware that she was straying somewhat from the murdering fudgebucket questions.

'Some distant relations. We don't keep in touch. But I

brought my boys over so they could see where their old Pops comes from.'

'Are they here now? It would be great if we could get a photograph of you together. The two generations set to take the whisky industry by storm.'

Penny nudged Jim, who looked like he had fallen into a trance.

'Oh, aye,' he said. 'Hang on, I'll get the fancy camera out.'

'Unfortunately, the boys aren't here,' said Ted. 'You'll have to make do with a picture of me.'

He stood up and went to the door, coming back a few seconds later wearing a Stetson. Sitting at his desk, he moved the computer and keyboard aside, put his feet on the glass surface and crossed his legs. As he leaned back, the cuffs of his trousers rose to reveal a pair of tartan cowboy boots.

'Here we are, Mr Blobby. An American businessman in Scotland.'

As Jim made his way around the desk, taking photographs from different angles, Penny consulted her script and continued to ask questions. Towards the end, the beleaguered Lesley appeared with a large pot of fresh coffee and a plate of shortbread. Penny noted that it was the same brand she had taken to the lodge, and she wondered how Mrs Hubbard was holding up on what was likely to be a very busy afternoon in the shop.

Eventually, the questions having petered out, Ted offered them a free tour of the distillery and summoned a minion to assist. The minion in question was a young American woman who seemed quite nervous and far less well-informed than Penny would have expected of a guide.

'It's my first week,' she confided. 'My first job, in fact.'

'Yes, I heard that Mr Hyatt is replacing some of the staff with his own. He didn't seem concerned when I asked him about it,' said Penny. 'Any idea why he's laying experienced people off?'

'I don't ask questions,' said the woman. 'I get my instructions and do my job. I'm sorry, Mr Blobby, you can't take pictures in here, but I can send you some stock pictures later.'

She stuck to the script for the rest of their visit, never leaving their side until she waved them off at the main entrance.

Once in the car park, Jim turned to Penny and said, 'Mrs Moist and Mr Blobby?'

Penny finally let out the bubble of laughter she'd been holding in every time someone had addressed Jim.

'Sorry. I went blank and they just fell out of my mouth.'

'In a world of Smiths and Joneses, you go for Moist and Blobby. I suppose we should go and see Sergeant Wilson. Let her know what we found out.'

'Yes, but don't mention Moist and Blobby. She'll never let us live it down.'

'Oh look, Easy, it's our intrepid reporters, Lois Moist and Clark Blobby,' said Sergeant Wilson, locking a packet of KitKats in her desk drawer with a key she kept on a long chain around her neck.

'Oh lordy, how did you find out?' asked Penny.

'Because I am the all-seeing, all-knowing Sergeant Wilson. Plus, Robbie Bates saw you and he told Kenny, who told Eileen, who told Sandra Next Door, who told Mrs Hubbard, who told me when I went into the shop to get KitKats. Don't worry, your secret's safe with…everybody.'

'I thought the MIT were arriving today,' said Penny in an attempt to change the subject.

'Don't try to change the fucking subject,' said Sergeant Wilson. 'And yes, they're here. Detective Chief Inspector Fudmuppet has sent them up to the distillery while the man himself has gone into town to look at Elsie's house. It has been made very clear to me that I should carry on helping old ladies across the road or whatever else passes for policing out here in the sticks. They weren't even interested in a briefing.

Swept in, ate a whole packet of Ginger Snaps then fucked off again.'

'Didn't you tell them about the First Minister?' asked Jim.

Sergeant Wilson spoke slowly, as if addressing the village idiot. 'No, we were sworn to secrecy, remember?'

She shook her head in disgust and resumed her normal bark. 'Anyway, Woodbead made the mistake of telling Mrs Hubbard, so they can probably hear it off half the village by now.'

'Well, we've spoken to Ted Hyatt,' said Penny. 'Did you know he's Scottish by birth? Most of it was quite boring, though. He's over here with his sons, setting things up. What you heard about him replacing the staff with his own is true. We spoke to one of them, but she wasn't too keen on giving us information. She seemed quite nervous and gave the impression that she wasn't doing the job by choice. The only other thing that might be weird is that Ted Hyatt said something about being done in a month. He claimed that he meant getting the distillery ready for more visitors, but I don't know, it sounded like he was planning something.'

'Did you get any photos? Sandra Next Door says they haven't been able to track down any online.'

'I emailed them to you on the way here. Turns out I've got a *very* fancy camera,' said Jim.

Sergeant Wilson turned to her computer and checked her emails.

'Have you looked through these?' she snapped. 'What sort of camera do you have? One of them plastic ones for four-year-olds that plays a tune when you press the buttons?'

'I don't know anything about photography,' Jim protested. 'Penny says I took it up last year when I bought the fancy camera, but I had to read the manual in the car on the way there so I'd remember how to turn the thing on.'

Sergeant Wilson spun the monitor around and scrolled through the photos. Ted Hyatt's face was shaded by the

Stetson and the focus was off, rendering him almost unrecognisable in most of the photographs.

'If you screw your eyes up and stand back, you can see Scooby Doo,' Jim commented.

'If I wanted a fu–'

Sergeant Wilson's rant was cut short by Penny, who said, 'Never mind that. Do you want to hear the really interesting thing we found out?'

'It had better be the name of the murderer in two-foot-high letters above the police station or you pair of donkey fannies will be spending the night in my cells.'

'For what?' asked Jim

'For wasting police time.'

'If you'd stop shouting and just listen for a minute,' Penny suggested, holding up a hand to prevent a further outburst. 'When we signed in at the distillery, I flicked through the visitors book and guess whose name was there the day before Ian's murder.'

'If I wanted to play guessing games, I'd help Easy revise for the Sergeant's exam. Spit it out.'

'It was Elsie.'

CHAPTER 17

'Ooh, that was lovely,' said Penny. 'I always feel so relaxed afterwards.'

'Me too,' said Jim. 'It's a pity we don't smoke. I could almost go for a cigarette right now.'

'I know what you mean. That last bit, though.'

'Aye. I think I might have pulled out too quickly.'

'It was worth it. The end part always takes you into another world.'

'Finishes you off nicely.'

'Are you two for real?' asked Edith, peering down at the supine figures on the living room rug.

Penny scootched onto her elbows and smiled up at her daughter.

'Jim's doctor said yoga would be good for him.'

'Honestly, it's like living with Fifty Shades of Grey.'

'Are we talking old people sex?' asked Jim, 'Because I'll have you know that I've retained full colour where it matters.'

'Oh my God, you two are disgusting,' said Edith, grabbing Timmy's lead and pushing his bottom out of his basket. 'Come on, you hairy lump. Walkies.'

Timmy wasn't too keen on moving. In his view, he'd been doing an excellent downward dog and, anyway, outside was full of the wet stuff that made his bum cold. Reluctantly he put a paw out of the basket. Then put it back in again. At least he'd made the effort. Although not enough for the human, he realised, as he felt himself lifted bodily from the basket and deposited on the floor. With a doggy sigh, Timmy allowed himself to be dragged across the floorboards to the front door.

'Come on, other hairy lump,' said Penny. 'We better get to the Show. They'll have judged the cakes by now and Mum will be dying to talk about it. I hope she doesn't win. She'll be unbearable.'

By the time they reached the Show, the light rain of the morning had been replaced by the warmth of the afternoon sun. Deep grooves had been carved into the grass by the vans and lorries delivering their loads to the stalls and fairground rides, and the muddy ruts made for slippery going. A veteran of many past Shows, Penny wore shorts and wellington boots. A combination that does nothing for the knees and thighs, she thought to herself, stepping over a plastic bag which had become caught in the glutinous trail of a prize-winning tractor.

The Show was in full swing, with dogs leaping through hoops in the event area and three small girls bobbing and whirling, their kilts flying as they competed to win the Highland dance trophy. The crowd moved towards the road in response to the distant thrum of drums and bagpipes, and Penny moved with them, dragging Jim behind her.

He hadn't been quite as prepared for the boggy conditions and found himself the Torvill to Penny's Dean, sliding behind her, gripping her arm tightly in an effort to stay upright.

The sound of the pipe band grew closer, the excitement mounting, until the Pipe Major rounded the corner and the thrum of the pipes and drums vibrated through Penny to her very core.

Exhilarated, she shouted, 'I love this. I can feel it in my heart and in my tummy.'

Jim, who was clinging onto the fence for dear life lest he spend the rest of the afternoon picking mud off his jeans, laughed with the sheer joy of her. Swept away by the music and the moment, he let go of the fence and pulled Penny towards him, his face descending towards hers and his eyes closing.

For a moment, he thought he must have slipped. He suddenly found himself sitting in the mud, wincing as cold liquid seeped through his jeans. The pipe band were in full flow now, the drums beating out the rhythm and the bagpipes skirling Scotland the Brave. Jim looked up at the crowd of legs in front of him, expecting to see Penny there, her hand outstretched to pull him up.

Except Penny wasn't there. Jim looked behind him to see her stalking towards the prizes tent and quickly scrabbled to his feet to go after her, cursing the mud that now covered his hands and knees.

He caught up with her at the entrance to the tent, grabbing her arm and spinning her towards him. The flush of excitement that had warmed her face when the pipe band arrived had now become a flush of anger.

'You have no right,' she shouted at him. 'You don't get to lead me on like that. I said we'd be friends to give you space.'

'I'm sorry. I got carried away. Please, Penny.'

'I've been breaking my heart over you for months now and it took every ounce of self-control to step back. If you don't want me, that's fine, but don't toy with me. It's not right and it's not fair.'

'I'm sorry,' Jim pleaded again. 'I didn't mean to.'

But it was too late. Penny had wrenched her arm away and was running towards the cake tables and her mother. Having heard the altercation, Mary glared at Jim and put a comforting arm around her daughter.

Realising that there was nothing he could do except let

Penny simmer down and hope that she would eventually forgive him, Jim sighed and turned back towards the pipe band, only to be blocked by a clipboard being thrust into his chest.

'You're late,' said Len.

Seeing Jim's look of bewilderment, he clarified, 'The big vegetables. We better get a move on. Things are getting quite heated in there.'

'But Penny–'

'Yes, yes,' said Len. 'I saw what happened. She has her mother's temper, but she'll calm down once you've apologised a gazillion times. I'm even allowed to use Mary's body wash again, provided I ask permission. So, that's two life lessons for you today; never lead a girl on and never use Chanel No. 5 on your bits and blame the rash on the new washing powder. Now, hurry up because I think Geordie Barnes might be about to punch Robbie Bates over a giant marrow.'

Jim took the clipboard and followed Len into the tent, studiously avoiding eye contact with Penny and Mary. His mind was mostly elsewhere, yet he gamely assigned points for size, firmness and quality. He resolved marrow-gate by awarding a joint first prize and gave Fiona and Gordon a complicit wink as he pinned a winning rosette to Fiona's statue of Madonna made entirely from carrots.

After an hour of making polite conversation on such riveting subjects as cabbage speckle and whether Mr King's cucumber clown was acceptable because the nose was a tomato and everyone knows that a tomato is a fruit, Jim glanced, for what must have been the hundredth time, towards the cake tables. Penny was still there, consoling Mary for being runner up in what he suspected must be the "inventive but inedible" category. Not once had she caught his eye, so taking this as a sign that she was unlikely to calm down today, he handed his clipboard to Len and began the long walk home, only stopping at the entrance to greet a harassed-looking Mrs Hubbard, resplendent in a sequinned pink dress and wellington boots, who had lost her Douglas somewhere between Hook the Duck and Guess the Weight of Stevie Mains.

'You look tired dearie,' she said, patting him on the cheek. 'Get yourself off for a rest. By the way, we came second in the ballroom dancing. My Douglas stood on the hem of my dress and there was nearly an incident. Nearly, not actually, which is just as well because my good knickers are in the wash.'

She toddled off, carefully holding the hem of her dress up as she picked her way through the mud and completely failing to spot her Douglas, who was staggering away from the Hoopla stall, almost completely hidden behind the giant pink teddy bear that he was struggling to carry.

Penny stayed at the Show, but her heart was no longer in it. The twins appeared, demanding money for the waltzers, and she dutifully lost the argument about why Hector should not have to pay for himself if Penny was subsidising Edith. She made a note to self to march Edith into Cuppachino tomorrow and insist that Minky hire the lazy minx.

Eventually the crowds and the noise became too much. Penny bought four large candy flosses and handed one to each of her precious people, saying, 'Have a lovely afternoon, you gorgeous lot. I have a headache coming on, so I'm going home for a lie down.'

Despite their protests that she should stay to watch Timmy compete in the laziest dog competition, she made her way to her little cottage by the harbour, switched her phone to silent and lay on the bed.

'The bed that Jim made,' she whispered into the silence of the empty house. 'What a damn pickle this is.'

Penny awoke with a start, her heart thumping wildly as she felt the breath on her cheek. The rancid smell hit her next, coming in short, panting waves.

'Timmy,' she groaned. 'You nearly frightened the life out of me. What time is it?'

She pushed the dog off her chest and switched on the bedside lamp. Good Lord! Nine o'clock.

Timmy gave a small whine and looked at her pleadingly.

'Alright, hairy lump. I get the message.'

She padded downstairs and let Timmy out into the small back garden. The twins must have dropped him off and gone out again, she reasoned. They better not have gone to the marquee dance or there would be hell to pay. Nevertheless, she nipped back upstairs where a quick check of Edith's bedroom revealed a suspicious absence of glittery shoes.

'Little buggers,' she said, retrieving her phone from the bedside cabinet. 'I bet Mum gave them money for it, too, the traitor. She'd never have let me go at seventeen.'

She called Edith and listened to the chirpy voicemail message telling her, "If this is a party invite, keep trying. If not, leave a message. Luvs ya!"

She fared no better in her attempts to call Hector. "One is dreadfully busy and important. Please don't clutter up my life with your trivial concerns." She loved him very much, but sometimes it was like living with a hormonal Jacob Rees-Mogg.

Penny dialled her mother's mobile, letting it ring and ring. No reply. She dialled her father's mobile with the same result, so she tried the house phone. Again, no reply. Weirder and weirder. Was this some sort of horror movie where she went to sleep, woke up and her whole family had disappeared? Penny laughed at the ridiculousness of it.

'There's only one way to find out,' she told Timmy as she let him in the back door. 'Go and look for them all. Sorry, boy, you're going to be stuck in on your own for a while. Shall I leave the telly on for you? There's a very good thriller on BBC1.'

Before jumping into her car and speeding off to the marquee dance in the hope of locating her disobedient offspring, Penny walked a few doors down to Eileen's cottage. It was almost identical to hers, except that Eileen and Kenny had added a porch by the back door to accommodate the mountain of coats and trainers which could have kitted out a small country.

Penny let herself into the porch and knocked on the back door. It was with some relief that she found her friend home and in the middle of a raucous game of Charades with Ricky and Gervais, the four hackers and Anna Henderson.

'In you come,' said Eileen. 'Kenny went to the pub for some peace and quiet. The boys and I are thick as mince and the others only know about Russian stuff, so I think we were doing his head in. He gave up halfway through Pictionary and said even the pub on Show night would be less stressful.'

'I won't stay,' said Penny. 'I'm trying to track down Mum, Dad and the kids. Have you seen them?'

'Not since the Show this afternoon. Your mum told me what happened with you and Jim. Are you okay?'

'Not really. I'll live, I suppose. If you hear from any of them, can you ask them to call me?'

'Will do, Rubber Duck,' said Eileen, giving Penny a quick hug. 'Let me know when you find them.'

Some enterprising soul had laid boards across the mud leading towards the marquee. Girls hyped up on pre-drinks shivered in tiny dresses as they teetered over the uneven path, trying not to catch an unwary heel which would bring their night to a premature and very mucky end.

The end will probably be mucky one way or another, thought Penny, as she eyed the teenage boys who were showing off like Lynx-ridden peacocks, their legs ridiculous in impossibly skinny jeans. Oh, to be young and horny.

Feeling distinctly old and very out of place in her shorts and wellies, Penny approached the guardian of the marquee;

the man in the neon yellow jacket who was keeper of the tent and god of the little blue hand stamp.

'I don't have any money,' she shouted above the persistent thump, thump, thump of the music inside. 'I only want to see if my kids are here.'

'What?' shouted the man.

'My kids are missing!'

'Five pounds!'

'No, I just want to see if my kids are inside!'

'I don't have any change!'

This was clearly getting her nowhere. Desperately, Penny looked around for someone she knew. Perhaps they could lend her the entrance fee. Everyone she could see was under twenty-five and she didn't recognise any of them.

The man at the entrance was becoming somewhat agitated now and signalling to her to move along. Realising that she was blocking the entrance, she smiled apologetically at the queue behind her and stepped away. There was nothing for it, she decided, she'd have to do the traditional thing and sneak in under the ropes.

Away from the main area, it was dark and even the deep treads in her wellies couldn't prevent a few precarious wobbles during the short walk to the rear of the marquee. This was not going to be pretty, she mused, lowering her bare knees to the grassy swamp. Mud squelched into the tops of her wellies as she scrabbled around the bottom of the tent, searching for a gap in the pegs which firmly anchored it to the ground. Eventually, she felt some give in the fabric and bent down, trying to lever it up far enough so that she could squeeze through. Unfortunately, the crew who had erected the thing had been very thorough, and there was barely enough room to squeeze her head through. Thus, a few seconds later, Penny found herself staring at a sea of legs, her head inside the marquee and her mud-stained body outside.

Anxiously, she cast around for a familiar pair of legs in the jiggling morass. The flashing lights and the constantly shifting sea of limbs made her task almost impossible. This was pointless, she decided. How on earth did she think she could recognise someone by their–

'Mrs Hubbard!' she yelled, spotting a familiar pair of support stockings, an incongruously sequinned pink hem swirling around them.

'Mrs Hubbard!'

Penny looked around for something she could throw to get the woman's attention, before remembering that her arms were firmly pinned outside the tent.

'Mrs Hubbard!'

She turned her head and discovered a conveniently discarded plastic pint glass. If she could juuuuust grasp the rim with her teeth, ugh, disgusting, okay, one, two, three, twist aaaaand flick.

The glass quickly ascended then just as quickly descended, landing a few centimetres from her nose and splattering her with stale beer dregs in the process.

Penny strained her neck, trying to reach the glass for another go, but it was useless. Yet all was not lost. She was just about to give up when she heard a voice above her.

'Is that you, Hector's mum's head?'

'Oh, hi Danny,' she shouted, trying to sound as nonchalant as a beer-covered disembodied head could.

'Are you trying to sneak in without paying, Hector's mum's head?' yelled Danny, his eyes twinkling with mischief.

'I'm looking for Hector and Edith,' Penny bellowed back. 'Have you seen them?'

'Yeah, I think they've gone outside. They're with a couple of older guys.'

'What?'

'I said they've just gone–'

'No. The older guys. Who are they?'

'Dunno,' Danny shrugged, seemingly unconcerned that the most precious beings on earth, fruit of her lady parts, most cherished cherubs and disobedient wee twerps, might be outside right now being taken advantage of by older guys.

Penny tried to withdraw her head from the gap in the tent so that she could rush to the aid of her little darlings but found that a vacuum had formed between her knees and the swamp below.

'Can you push?' she shouted.

'What?'

'My head. I'm stuck. Can you push me backwards.'

Danny squatted down and, putting his hands on her face, gave her a hard shove. It did the trick, and Penny felt herself slide backwards in the mud until, with some difficulty, she was able to stand up.

'There's no point in trying to sneak in. They have it battened down tight this year,' said a voice beside her.

'I got that, thanks,' she told the pimply youth who had emerged for air long enough to deliver the warning.

She left him trying to swallow his girlfriend's face and skidded her way back towards the front of the tent, just in time to see a pair of glittery shoes that she was convinced must be Edith's disappear into the dimly lit street beyond the entrance to the park.

Penny raced after what she hoped was her daughter, performing a neat pirouette as she slid off the mud onto the dry land of the street. Where had Edith gone? She looked left, right, left again. Why didn't the council put proper lighting in this street? Curses on the penny-pinching jobsworths.

Further down the road, two pinpricks of red light punctured the gloom and Penny saw headlights illuminate the road. Someone had started a vehicle. She raced towards what she could now make out to be a large, dark-coloured van.

'Edith,' she screamed.

The van roared off before she could reach it, leaving only a trail of exhaust fumes in its wake. Penny followed, cursing the wellies that had been such a help in the muddy park but were now a hindrance.

'Edith!'

But it was no use. The van sped around the end of the road, and she heard the distant roar as it gathered speed along North Street.

Panting and clutching the stitch in her side, Penny made her way back towards the park. She had to make sure it was Edith. She had to find Hector. Jeeze, she had to find out just what the heck was going on.

Drawing level with the spot where the van had been parked, she saw something glinting in the glass verge and her heart lurched. She bent down to take a closer look and, with mounting horror, picked the object up. In the dim light of a distant streetlamp, the object sparkled in her hand. A solitary glittery shoe.

CHAPTER 18

'Have you seen Hector and Edith?' Penny yelled at anyone who would listen, perfectly aware that she looked like a lunatic with her beer-sodden hair and muddy legs.

The crowd queueing outside the marquee paid her no heed, intent as they were on jostling their way through the entrance to the alcoholic delights awaiting them inside.

'Please.' Penny screamed in desperation. 'Hector and Edith Moon. Has anyone seen them?'

'They went off with a couple of big lads,' said a skinny girl who was smoking what Penny's nose told her was most surely a joint.

'Jessica,' said Penny, her relief at recognising Edith's best friend outweighing her instinct to threaten to tell the girl's mother about the joint. 'Do you know where they went?'

Jessica airily waved an arm in the direction of where the van had been moments earlier.

'Somewhere down there. Mind you, Edith had a face like a slapped arse. I don't think she was too happy about being hauled out for being underage.'

'Underage?' asked Penny, confused. 'Were they bouncers?'

Jessica shrugged her emaciated shoulders and scratched what Penny suspected was an infected tattoo on her thigh.

'Dunno.'

'Was Hector with her?'

Jessica nodded then glanced at her phone, which had pinged to let her know that a notification had arrived. She swiped the screen and snickered at whatever teenage shenanigans were happening on Snapchat stories. Conversation over. Jessica had more important things to do.

Penny left her and went back to the park entrance, away from the crowds and the music. Her heart in her throat, she phoned the twins again. Once more, the calls went to voicemail. She didn't normally swear, not even in her own head, but quite a few eff words were racing through her mind right now as she tried to push down the rising panic in her gut. Someone had taken her babies.

With trembling hands, she called the one person who could help. The brrr brrr at the other end seemed to go on for minutes, although in all likelihood it was only a few seconds.

'Hello, Police Scotland.'

'Easy? Is Sergeant Wilson there?'

'Sergeant Wilson is very busy right now,' said Easy, licking the remains of a chocolate hobnob off his fingers.

Sergeant Wilson was, in fact, currently receiving the dressing down of her life for failing to pass on the information about the lodge. He could hear her shouting, 'I am very fucking sorry that you marched in here and didn't so much as consult me for a briefing…Sir.'

'Can you get her for me? It's urgent,' Penny pleaded.

Easy, who was enjoying the show far too much to let it be interrupted, said, 'I'm sorry, she said she didn't want to be disturbed.'

'It's Hector and Edith. I think they've been taken–'

But it was too late. PC Easy Piecey had hung up.

Penny scrolled through her recent calls and dialled her parents' numbers again, a tiny irrational spark of hope convincing her that Mary and Len must have picked up the twins. The people in the van were visiting one of the houses nearby. It was all a big coincidence, and the shoe didn't even belong to Edith. Damn. Still no reply. Where were they? There was no way that she was going out to Valhalla in the midst of a crisis, only to find them tucked up in bed.

She called Sandra Next Door, hoping the woman would relent in her war of attrition against Mojo, the begonia shitting cat, and find it in her heart to check up on the cat's owners. Again, no reply. Sandra and Geoff were probably out with the Show committee, celebrating another successful year.

Eileen, thought Penny. Maybe she can…do what? Penny didn't know what her best pal could do, but she had to reach out to someone for help. She was losing any semblance of composure, standing there covered in mud, her face awash with snot, tears and stale beer.

She was almost babbling when Eileen answered the phone and at first her friend couldn't understand her.

'Rubber Duck? Slow down. What's the matter.'

'Two men have taken Hector and Edith.'

Penny's voice was a high-pitched squeak as she tried to control the hiccoughing sobs that threatened to break through the thin veneer of self-control. Her back ached with the strain of it, and she slid down to sit against the fence, any thoughts of dog poo danger in the grass verge suppressed by the urge to do something, anything, to protect her children.

Eileen had been here before. She shuddered as she recalled the primal horror of discovering that her own children had been taken. The rush of adrenaline she felt upon hearing the agony in Penny's voice made her face prickle, as if something had cut the circulation to her cheeks and chin.

'Where are you?' she asked.

'The park. They went to the marquee dance, and someone took them away in a van,' Penny squeaked. 'I found Edith's little shoe. She loves those little shoes.'

'Oh God,' Eileen breathed, deciding that now was not the time to remind Penny that Edith's feet were a size eight. 'Stay there. I'll phone Kenny to drive you back here.'

After she'd relayed strict instructions to Kenny that she didn't care if he got arrested for drink driving, he was to get Penny and drive her car home right now, Eileen called Sergeant Wilson.

'Hello, Police Scotland.'

'Easy, it's Eileen Bates. Is Sergeant Wilson there?'

'She's not available right now,' said Easy, one ear on the phone and the other straining to hear how DCI Fudmuppet responded to being called a pudden-headed monkey stain.

'It's urgent. Penny's kids have been '

But it was too late. Easy had hung up and gone back to the Saturday night entertainment.

Eileen switched the kettle on and briefed Anna and the hackers on what little she knew. Reaching into the depths of the dresser, she found the packet of posh shortbread that Mrs Hubbard had given her for Christmas and checked the use-by date. Och, only a couple of months. It would still do. She tipped the entire packet onto a plate and warned the others that they were not to touch even so much as a crumb. These were for her Rubber Duck.

Penny stumbled through the back door, ignoring the usual protocol of "muddy wellies live in the porch," and collapsed into a kitchen chair.

'I couldn't find anyone to help me,' she wailed between sobs. 'Easy hung up on me.'

'Easy is a pillock,' said Eileen, passing Penny a mug of sweet tea. 'Tell us what happened.'

Penny recounted how she'd seen what she thought was Edith leaving the park and had followed.

'And they must have put them in the van. Why would anyone take Hector and Edith? It's an island, for God's sake. How far do they think they can run with two teenagers in tow?'

Penny had calmed down a little now and was starting to think more rationally.

'Did you get the number of the van?' asked Eileen.

'Of course I did. I'm not a complete idiot. But what use is the registration number to us if we can't even get hold of Sergeant Wilson to trace it?'

'There are four people here who can,' said Eileen, gesturing at the hackers.

'Why didn't I think of that?' howled Penny, overcome by a fresh wave of tears. 'How come you're the sensible one? I'm supposed to be the sensible one.'

'What's the number?' Eileen asked gently.

'ZA17CKW'

Eileen nodded at the hackers. 'Leave it with us. We'll find out who owns the van. Have you called Jim?'

'I'm not speaking to him right now,' said Penny sulkily.

'Because he tried to kiss you? I think you've got bigger things to worry about. Here,' Eileen handed Penny a towel from the top of the washing basket she'd been intending to lug upstairs for the past three days. 'Shower that mud off you and I'll ring Jim.'

By the time Penny came back downstairs, clean and wearing a pair of Eileen's yoga pants, Jim was sitting at the kitchen table, tucking into the plate of shortbread. Eileen felt so sorry for him after his head injury that she could deny him nothing.

'Shall we get in the car and drive around looking for the van?' he asked, hoping Penny wouldn't screech that she was never getting in a car with him again.

There was no screeching. Penny simply nodded miserably and helped herself to a coat from the pile in the porch. It was only as she was steering the car up the lane towards Port Vik High Street and felt the sleeves creep up that she realised she was wearing Ricky's school anorak. Not even this could raise a smile.

'At least driving around feels like I'm doing something,' she told Jim. 'Did Eileen tell you about Easy?'

'Aye. She's going to try the station again and if Easy's still being a pillock, she's going to get Sandra Next Door to drive round there and put his balls through a mincer.'

'We should try my mum and dad's place before we start randomly driving around. I couldn't get them on the phone. They're probably in bed, but I'm not worried about wakening them up. They need to know what's happened.'

'Fine. Have you got a key in case they don't answer the door?'

Penny pointed to the big handbag on the floor by his feet.

'Ha! I haven't seen the Bag of All Things for a while. I once asked you if you had any chopsticks and, lo and behold, a pair appears out of the bag.'

'Another memory?' asked Penny, trying to keep her tone even.

'Aye,' said Jim awkwardly. 'I did a lot of thinking today and a few things came back.'

They lapsed into an uncomfortable silence for the next couple of miles, only talking again when Penny pulled onto the gravel drive in front of her parents' bungalow.

The house was in darkness and Penny had a sudden sense of foreboding as she turned her key in the lock. The front door swung open with an ominous creak and Jim felt for the hall light switch. Penny could hear the click as he flicked it, but nothing happened.

'Oh God,' she whispered.

'Do you have a torch?' Jim asked, thinking that he wouldn't be surprised if she pulled a standard lamp from that bag.

Penny nodded and ran back to the car to find the torch she had stashed away for emergencies. Vik winters were long and harsh, and no islander would venture out without a snow shovel and a torch. She had decanted the snow shovel from the boot when she'd taken her mother shopping back in May, but there was the torch, stuffed into a corner next to the emergency chocolate.

Jim took the torch from her trembling fingers and shone it into the hall. They crept forward, the eerie stillness of the house unsettling them both. A quick sweep of each room revealed no trace of Mary and Len.

'Where could they be at this time of night?' said Penny.

'Aye, it's not like them,' said Jim. 'Where's the fusebox?'

Penny pointed to the hall cupboard.

'In there. It was in the loft, but they had it moved when they rewired last year.'

Jim nodded and opened the cupboard door. A moment later, light flooded the house, causing Penny to screw her eyes against the sudden brightness. She heard Jim gasp and almost fell as he stumbled backwards into her.

'It's only a bit bright. It'll pass in a minute,' she assured him.

'No,' he said, his voice unusually strained. 'Look!'

Penny slowly opened her eyes, giving them a few seconds to adjust, then screamed as the body in the cupboard toppled towards her.

'Dad!'

CHAPTER 19

'Call Doc Harris,' shouted Jim. 'He'll be down at the Show on standby with the paramedics.'

Penny could barely hold her phone steady enough to scroll to Doc Harris in her contacts list. She tucked her elbows in and gripped the device, trying to bring the trembling under control.

Fortunately, Doc Harris picked up almost immediately.

'Have you checked for a pulse?' he barked.

'It's there, but it's weak. He's breathing. There are no obvious injuries.'

'Put him in the recovery position and keep him warm. The paramedics are on their way to you now.'

'I don't even know the recovery position,' said Penny, starting to panic that she might make things worse.

'Put him on his side and tilt his head back to keep his airway clear,' said Doc Harris, less terse now that he knew Len was still alive. 'If he stops breathing, administer CPR. Do you know how to do CPR?'

'I do,' said Jim.

Penny looked at him quizzically. Last year, when Captain Rab had almost died, Jim had been fairly clueless.

'Gordon taught me after that thing with Captain Rab,' he clarified.

'The memories are positively flooding back,' said Penny, unable to hide the slightly bitter edge to her words.

'Aye, as I said, I did some thinking today. Never mind that. Help me roll him over.'

They sat with Len until the paramedics arrived and it was only once he'd gone that Penny's shocked brain realised that something was missing.

'Mum!' she exclaimed.

'Definitely not in any cupboards,' said Jim. 'I checked them all while you were seeing your dad off. Fucking hell, Penny. This is…fucking hell.'

Penny's phone rang and she snatched it off the floor where it had fallen when she was helping Jim to roll her father onto his side.

'What?' she shouted, taking no time to check the name of the caller.

'It's only me,' said Eileen timidly.

'Sorry, Eileen. We got to mum and dad's to find dad half dead in a cupboard. They've just taken him to the hospital now. No, I don't know what's happened. Mum's missing too, and I'm worried sick. Any word at your end from Hector and Edith? I left them both a message to call you if they couldn't get hold of me.'

There it was again. That absurd sliver of hope that the twins had merely gone astray.

'No, nothing,' said Eileen. 'Kenny nipped past your cottage and there's nobody there. He's taken Timmy back to ours. The reason I'm phoning is that the hackers have traced that registration number. It belongs to Minky's son, Zack.'

'Zack Wallace? Why would he be taking Edith and Hector? He's only a few years older than them. And where could he have taken them?'

'I don't know. You'll have to ask Minky. Do you have her number?'

Penny turned to Jim.

'Minky was one of your suspects from the Peppermint Slice investigation. Do you have her number?'

Jim looked blank.

'No, I don't have her number,' Penny told Eileen. 'Do you know anyone who'll have it?'

'Hold up there, Sherlock,' said Jim. 'I don't have it, but your dad has been keeping all his notes and evidence in a little blue book. It'll be in there.'

'We're fine, Eileen. The number's probably around here somewhere,' said Penny. 'I think it's time Sandra Next Door went round to the police station, though. If you take care of that, Jim and I will contact Minky.'

By the time Penny came off the phone, Jim was already in the living room hunting through drawers.

'It won't be here,' said Penny. 'It'll either be in the kitchen Drawer of Doom or, if he didn't want mum interfering, it'll be in his shed.'

She sent Jim to the shed while she searched the Drawer of Doom. She didn't bother sorting through the jumbled mass of takeaway leaflets, radiator keys and chargers. She simply removed the drawer and tipped the whole lot onto the kitchen table. The blue book was there, sure enough, tangled up in the lead of some long-forgotten appliance. However, this was not what caught Penny's eye. It was the folded sheet of notepaper which interested her. Why would her parents tape a note to the bottom of the Drawer of Doom?

Now was not the time to be worrying about such things, not with Zack Wallace inexplicably making off with the twins. Part of her was relieved that it was a local kidnapper and not some sex trafficking gang from…from…Auchnagatt. Jesus, what was she thinking? Auchnagatt was a lovely little village, far too good for the likes of sex traffickers. Stop rambling to yourself, Penny, and get on with the job of finding them then ripping the heart out of whoever hurt Dad. She pulled the piece of paper from the underside of the drawer and rammed it in Ricky's school coat pocket.

Leafing through her father's notebook, even in her frantic state she couldn't help but be impressed by how thorough he'd been in his investigation, if a little over-enthusiastic in his suspicions of the bakers. She quickly came to the Minky section and found what she'd been looking for; Minky's telephone number neatly inscribed in her father's precise handwriting. You couldn't be a former bank manager without getting very good at writing numbers clearly.

Jim returned from his search of the shed just as she was about to dial.

'Do you want me to talk to her? I met her the other day and it might help if she's speaking to someone she knows.'

Penny nodded and handed him her phone. A few seconds later, she felt a tiny sense of triumph bleed through the fear that kept an unrelenting grip on her heart. Minky had answered on the fourth ring.

'Minky? It's Jim Space. We met the other day at your café. Aye, aye, aye. We're looking for…aye, aye, no. ZA17CKW. Aye. Have you any idea where…aye, no, no, aye aye. Aye, thanks.'

Penny could happily have taken every one of those ayes and shoved them down Jim's throat. Why did he have to be so annoying? Why couldn't he have a conversation like a normal person?

Jim hung up, his expression grim.

'She confirmed the van is his. She gave it to him for his seventeenth a few years ago.'

'I thought she gave him a car,' said Penny. 'It was all over the island about him getting a car despite crashing Randy's tractor into the shoe shop window.'

'Aye, no, she bought him a van because…never mind, it doesn't matter now. I think I know where Zack's gone. Minky gave me a list of his usual places, but only one of them makes sense. Sort of.'

. . .

Mrs Hubbard was a teensy-weensy bit tiddly. She and Douglas had gone to every marquee dance since they were in their twenties, fifty years ago. The Show was the highlight of their year, not just because it brought in additional trade to the shop, but because they both loved dancing. It made little difference to them whether it was Mozart or Drake, they had dancing and they had each other. It was all they needed.

That afternoon they'd left the Saturday girl in charge, donned their glad rags and almost skipped out the door. Nevertheless, it was now getting late, and the marquee was filling up with the post-pub crowd. If previous Shows were anything to go by, trouble would soon follow, and the police drafted in from Aberdeen would have no hesitation in sweeping up any offenders. Neither Mrs Hubbard nor her Douglas felt like being accidentally swept up alongside them, so they called a Vikster to take them home.

The house was in complete darkness when they arrived, and as she stumbled against the hall table, Mrs Hubbard was cursing herself for forgetting to leave a light on.

'It's fine. I've got it,' said Douglas, flicking the switch.

Mrs Hubbard surveyed the damage. The house phone lay on its side on the floor, along with three bills they had both been ignoring for days and a parcel.

She slowly bent to pick up the items, letting loose a very long burp on the way down. Giggling, she scrabbled around the floor, her coordination less precise than she'd expected. She managed to grab the phone and parcel before straightening up and judiciously kicking the bills under the table.

'Even if we can't see them,' muttered Douglas, 'we still have to pay the buggers.'

Mrs Hubbard ignored him. She was peering blearily at the writing on the front of the package.

'S'addressed to me,' she declared, slurring her words. 'Have you been buying presents?'

'Why would I buy you a present and post it to you?' demanded Douglas. 'Why would I buy you a present when we have a shop full of boxes of chocolates? Why would I buy you a present full stop? It's not your birthday and it's not Christmas.'

'Lurgic and reasnin. What about romances and s'prises?'

'I told Penny to let you know there was a parcel for you.'

'She didn't say nuffin.'

Mrs Hubbard made to sit on the stairs but missed her intended target and landed with a bump on the bottom step, still clutching the parcel.

'Well, f'you didn't send it, who did?'

'Open the thing and find out,' said Douglas, wearying of being the sober one.

Mrs Hubbard picked half-heartedly at the string, knowing that if she took long enough with the knot, Douglas would give in and get some scissors. Her legs were in no mood for walking right now. They were like someone else's legs. Alien legs, their lumps and bumps forming tiny hills and valleys beneath the wrinkled support stockings, their feet encased in shiny, red dancing shoes. They put her in mind of the witch in the Wizard of Oz. The one who got splatted under the house. T'was a lovely film, Wizud Oz. Used to watch every Christmas but not on telly now.

Douglas woke her up a minute later by waving a pair of sewing shears under her nose and grumbling, 'Here, Sleeping Beauty. Do you want me to open it for you?'

Mrs Hubbard scratched her nose and looked up at him through half closed eyes.

'Maybe leave it til mornin . Too tired,' she yawned.

'Och, I've gone and got the scissors now. Hand it over.'

Douglas deftly snipped the string and the tape securing the parcel. Turning it over, he carefully removed the brown paper and laid the contents on the stairs next to the good Mrs.

A childhood of wearing hand-me-downs and waking up to ice on the inside of the bedroom window had taught

Douglas the value of things. A good piece of wrapping paper should never be wasted. He carefully smoothed out the creases, intending to keep it to use another time. So intent was he on returning the paper to its original state that he paid scant attention to his wife's muffled, 'Oh!'

Eventually, the wrapping paper smoothed and neatly folded, Douglas looked up to find Mrs Hubbard clutching a letter, tears streaming down her cheeks.

Now entirely sober, she gazed back at him and, a sob catching in her throat, said, 'It's from Elsie. It's her diary.'

Sandra Next Door was in no mood to be trifled with. She lifted her knuckles to the glass panel in the police station reception and set it rattling in its frame.

Several loud raps later, the panel suddenly slid back and Easy's startled face appeared in the gap, his eyes widening at the sight of the angry woman who, caught mid-knock, had narrowly missed punching his nose.

Sergeant Wilson's comparison of Sandra Next Door with Margaret Thatcher wasn't too far from the truth. Her stiff, blonde bob and the steely determination in her eyes made her an imposing figure, someone with whom Easy was ill-equipped to deal.

He rapidly shut the hatch, leaving Sandra Next Door standing mouth agape, her carefully planned tirade replaced with an anti-climactic, 'Eh?'

A moment later, the hatch opened again, and Sergeant Wilson's face appeared, far less startled and far more scowly than Easy's.

'This better be good,' she snapped. 'Fudmuppet in there has been kicking my arse all night and he's an inch away from suspending me.'

'Easy?' asked Sandra Next Door, momentarily diverted from her mission by the thought of Constable Piecey kicking anyone's backside, let alone Sergeant Wilson's.

'No! DCI Fred Moffat from the Major Investigation Team. Fud Muppet.' Sergeant Wilson spread her arms and shrugged, as if it were obvious. 'Anyway, make it quick. I'm in the middle of a creative writing session on what you lot have been up to, and I have to hand the report into Fudmuppet by midnight.'

'I can't believe you're sitting here writing a report. Why haven't you called Penny or Eileen?'

Sergeant Wilson's expression changed from one of disgruntlement to one of baffled innocence.

'Why would I need to call them?'

'Because they've been calling you. Repeatedly. Hector and Edith have been kidnapped by Zack Wallace, Penny found Len half dead and stuffed into a cupboard at home and Mary's missing.'

'For fuck's sake. Why am I only hearing about this now?'

'Because according to Easy, you were not to be disturbed. Well, I'm disturbing you. Phone Penny!'

Sergeant Wilson tapped into some hitherto undiscovered well of self-restraint and shot a look of pure malice towards Easy, who was currently sitting at his desk taking an intense interest in his computer monitor.

'I'll deal with you later,' she told him, the quiet tone and absence of swearing far more menacing than the bawling out he was expecting. 'Get your kit on. I'm phoning Penny, then we're going out to find her mum and the twins.'

She was about to head for her locker when a commotion behind her made her turn. Mrs Hubbard's flushed face had appeared at the hatch. She was looking rather the worse for wear, Sergeant Wilson noted. Her smooth, grey curls had puffed out into a demented frizz and black trails of mascara ran down her cheeks. Douglas stood behind her, his sullen, calm stoicism a stark contrast to Mrs Hubbard's agitated bobbing and throat clearing.

'Sergeant Wilson!' she shrieked.

'Does it never fucking end with you people?' Sergeant

Wilson asked. 'Can it wait? There's full on hell here and I don't have time to stop.'

'You have to stop. Stop now!' Mrs Hubbard demanded. 'You'll want to see this.'

She thrust a loosely wrapped package through the hatch and Sergeant Wilson took it, eyeing Mrs Hubbard suspiciously.

'Have you been on the sweetie juice again?'

'Open it! Just open it! It's evidence!' shouted Mrs Hubbard, her tone shrill.

'For God's sake woman, bloody open it,' said Douglas, then turning to his wife, he added, 'Calm down, Minty. You getting yourself worked up isn't helping.'

Sergeant Wilson reached into a drawer and pulled two rubber gloves from the box inside. Having slid them on, she spread that day's Vik Gazette over the counter and laid the package on it. Carefully, she removed the paper and set it aside before examining the contents. She was holding a diary and a letter. The letter was slightly crumpled and smudged, Mrs Hubbard's mascara-tinged tearstains distorting the ink. The message within was a short, hurried scrawl, yet Sergeant Wilson could almost smell the fear coming off the page.

Dear Minty,

This is my insurance policy in case something happens to me. I thought it would be fine, but someone came looking for me today. We are not safe. None of us are safe. Read my diary. Everything you need to know is in there. As soon as you have read this, run. Warn the others and get off the island. Tell Sergeant Wilson. She has to know what's going on so that she can protect anyone left behind. He might come after their families, you see. He's that evil.

. . .

Elsie

'Read the diary,' urged Mrs Hubbard. 'Start at the day Ian Henderson was killed.'

Only a few pages had been completed before the entries stopped on the day of Elsie's death, yet this was enough to convince Sergeant Wilson that Hector, Edith and Mary were in grave danger. And if Penny had somehow figured it out and gone after them, then Len might be the only survivor of this clusterfuck.

CHAPTER 20

Penny felt the tyres slip on the damp surface of the road as she rounded the corner into the distillery car park. Jim clutched his seatbelt, trying to keep from lurching into the window.

'Have I ever told you that you drive like Mario on his man-period?'

'No, you usually get annoyed with me for going too slow.'

'I can't remember that, but I take it all back, whatever I said.'

'It's quite nice being compared to Mario for a change.'

'Aye, well, you've got the moustache for it.'

He clung on through a stomach-churning swing around the car park then jolted forward, the seatbelt cutting into his shoulder as she slammed on the brakes and performed an emergency stop directly outside the tall, wood and glass front door.

Penny didn't hesitate. She sprang from the vehicle, ran to the door and began tugging on the handle. It was locked fast. She pressed her face against the glass panel, her eyes raking the interior of the building for any sign of light.

'It's completely dark,' she told Jim, who arrived a few seconds behind her.

Looking up, she spotted the security camera high above them.

'Do you think they're inside watching us?'

'God knows,' said Jim. 'You'd think they'd have set the security guards on us by now.'

'Not if they're up to no good. Hyatt has probably fired them and replaced them with his own people. There must be another entrance. You go round that side, and I'll go round this one. Phone me if you find a way in.'

Penny glanced at her phone. The screen was black. She swiped it, but there was no response.

'Damn. All those calls earlier must have drained the battery. Just go round then meet me at the back.'

'I'm not leaving you on your own,' said Jim.

'And I'm not arguing about it,' she hissed.

Penny moved away, gesturing to Jim to go in the direction she had indicated. She made a quick pitstop to grab the Bag of All Things from the car then headed off around the perimeter of the building.

She hadn't gone far when she came to a set of low, rough stone buildings. She pulled the torch from her bag and shone it on the one closest to her. Set deeply into the stone was a large door with the words "No.1 Duty Free Warehouse" painted neatly upon it, the letters stark white against the wood. She tried the handle. Locked, darnit. She pressed an ear against the door, listening intently for any sound of movement, but there was nothing.

Making her way along the row of buildings, she repeated the process and found each one locked and silent. Jeeze, if you were going to kidnap people and take them somewhere in the middle of the night, you'd surely pick a creepy old building full of barrels and spiders.

When she reached the back of the building, she found Jim already there.

'Tell me you have a way in,' she said, her clipped tone turning the plea into an instruction.

'I found a way in, but you won't like it,' said Jim. 'There's a big air vent back there. There's an emergency exit below it, although I doubt we can get through that. They're usually made of toughened glass to stop ejjits like us breaking in. The vent above it doesn't seem as secure. I don't know where it leads, Penny, so don't blame me if we end up getting smothered to death in a ton of barley.'

'I don't care if we get smothered to death. At least I'll have tried to do something,' she told him.

'What about me?' asked Jim, a little offended that he didn't count.

Penny gave this question about half a second's due consideration.

'Are you ever going to be a twat again?'

'Probably,' said Jim, suspecting that honesty might be the best policy here.

'You're right. You probably will. Never mind, I'll do my best to save you from the man-eating barley anyway.'

The banter had distracted her from the panic while they'd walked around the side of the building to the spot where Jim had seen the vent.

Penny dug into the Bag of All Things, feeling for the familiar object she had been carrying ever since the night she was attacked at Hélène's. She carried it partly for safety and partly because it was very handy should she ever have to break into places again. Which, given her history of being a crime busting nosy beggar, was entirely possible.

She put the Swiss Army knife between her teeth, turned to grip the wall and said, 'Gig uch a leg uck.'

'Eh?' came Jim's bewildered voice behind her.

Penny removed the knife and repeated, 'Give us a leg up.'

'Ah, right,' said Jim, cupping his hands to boost her towards the vent. 'I always hoped that the first time I'd hear you talk with your mouth full would be because my–'

'Finish that sentence and I'll kick you in the head,' said

Penny, wobbling precariously as she tried to find the correct tool to unscrew the vent.

'I was going to say, "because my wallet was empty from buying you ice creams," but you had to go and spoil it with your filthy mind.'

Penny was standing on Jim's shoulders now, deftly loosening the screws which attached the vent cover to the wall. She knew that Jim was trying in his own unique way to keep her calm, and to some extent it was working, yet she was so close to getting inside this damn fortress that her entire world had narrowed to these screws and what lay on the other side of them.

Finally, the last screw came free, and Penny wrenched the vent cover away from the wall, tossing it aside and ignoring the surprised yelp from Jim, whose head it narrowly missed. It was just as well the cover did miss, because Penny used his head to give her the extra few centimetres she needed to pull herself up and into the gap.

Bugger, she thought, there's another cover on the inside. Obviously. Well, this one would have to be removed with brute force. Thank goodness they built these walls thick. She wedged herself in tightly then stuck a leg out, pulling her foot back to deliver as hard a blow as she dared without sending herself flying backwards onto the ground, or Jim, below.

Three solid kicks were all it took to send the cover spinning into the darkness inside the building. She reached backwards, whispering to Jim to pass her the bag and torch. She had no idea why she was whispering. If there was anyone in the building, all the banging and clattering would have long since alerted them to her presence. Yet the eerie stillness of whatever lay beyond seemed to demand whispering.

A thought struck Penny. Why was it so quiet? She knew from her recent tour as Mrs Moist that the machines worked through the night, grinding and stirring and pumping to turn the barley into the amber liquid that would eventually find its way to all corners of the world. Yet she could hear nothing.

She shone the torch into the room and discovered to her relief that it was the small exhibition area. Scrambling down from her hole in the wall, she ran to the emergency exit and opened it to admit Jim.

'It's okay,' she assured him. 'Nothing more dangerous in here than an interactive history of the distillery.'

They made their way out of the exhibition area towards the inner workings of the building, with Jim moaning, 'Bugger me. I remember thinking the place was a maze when we did the tour, and that was going forwards. But doing it backwards...I'm not sure I can cope.'

'Shut up and follow me,' hissed Penny, still keeping her voice low.

Together they explored the distillery as quickly as two people with a proper torch and a phone torch could. They opened doors, lifted bags and checked inside cupboards, but found no sign of Mary or the twins.

'Fuck,' said Jim. 'If they're not here, then they must be in one of the other places Minky suggested. I really thought this would be it.'

They were in Ted Hyatt's office where, having established that the distillery was devoid of people, they'd thrown caution to the wind and switched the light on.

Penny looked around in the desperate hope that they'd missed something...missed what? Her mother's lifeless body in a corner? Don't think like that, she chided herself. The room was as sparsely decorated as it had been on their last visit. Even more so, because the monitor which had loomed large on the glass expanse where Ted had rested his tartan cowboy boots, was now missing.

'Why would his computer be gone?' she asked, not expecting an answer.

She was not disappointed. Jim merely grunted a quick "dunno" and unlocked his phone. He sat down on one of the plastic chairs, staring at the screen, seemingly oblivious to Penny, who was agitatedly prowling the room while she racked her brains for inspiration as to the whereabouts of her family.

'I mean, we don't even know that it was Zack who took Mum. There might be a simple explanation for her disappearance. Although she'd hardly stuff Dad in a cupboard. Not unless he'd done something really, really wrong like use her cashmere scarf to clean up cat sick, and even then, she only stopped talking to him for three days. What do you reckon the chances are of there being two kidnappers on the loose? There were two murderers. Or so we thought. But it has to be one murderer now, doesn't it? Because Elsie had been on the distillery tour just before she and Ian were killed. And Zack works at the distillery. And Zack definitely took Hector and Edith. Do you think Zack's the murderer?'

'Are you actually breathing between sentences?' asked Jim. 'Stop talking for a minute and look at this.'

He held up his phone and Penny gasped as she saw the image on the screen. Jim had opened one of the photographs he'd taken of Ted Hyatt and zoomed in not on the man himself, but on the computer monitor beside him, where a picture of a woman lying on a tiled floor was displayed. Even if the skin on her neck had not been red and mottled, her blank, lifeless eyes would have told the viewer everything they needed to know.

'Elsie,' gasped Penny. 'But…but why?'

'Why would Ted Hyatt have a photograph of Elsie's corpse on his computer?' said Jim, finishing the question for her. 'I don't know. At least it answers your question about why his computer is gone. He must have nudged his mouse or something to wake it up while I was taking the photos then realised after we were gone that Elsie's picture was on there. I was too busy trying to work the fancy camera to notice at the time and didn't even look at the photos properly afterwards, just emailed copies to myself and Sergeant Wilson. I expect he got rid of his computer once he knew he'd slipped up.'

'If Ted killed Elsie and was worried about us finding out…

sorry, I can't see the connection. Okay, he must have something to do with both murders. I just can't understand what that has to do with Mum and the twins.'

'Me neither. I suppose he could have figured out who we are and come after your family to stop you telling anyone. Although, if he was willing to murder Elsie and Ian, you'd think he would have bumped us off too. Plus, why come after your family and not my dad? I know my dad's fine because I was with him when Eileen rang to tell me about the twins. We could go round in circles all night with this, and we don't have time for it. I was going to call Minky again to ask if she had any other information about Zack, but there's no phone reception here. We should look around outside for a landline.'

'I don't think we need one,' said Penny.

She was standing at the back of the room, gazing at the engraving of the distillery which had so fascinated her on their first visit.

'Look,' she said, pointing to an area set back from the main building. 'The old distillery workers' houses. They've been empty for years, but Mrs Hubbard told me the other day that she'd heard it from Paula McAndrew, who heard it from Mrs Gunn, who heard it from Billy Dent that the houses are being renovated to be sold as holiday homes.'

'Oh, that won't go down well with the islanders,' said Jim. 'Mind you, it joins a few dots. Minky didn't say Zack worked *for* the distillery, just that he was working *at* the distillery. You asked earlier about her buying him a van instead of a car. She told me it was because him and his friend, Jordan, got jobs on a building site.'

He stopped talking. Penny had already sprinted out of the room, and he could hear her feet clattering towards the main entrance. He hesitated for a moment then ran to the entrance to help her break out of the building.

Neither Jim nor Penny noticed the security camera turn to follow their movements as they once again ran around the side of the distillery, this time heading for the path which would take them to the row of houses that stood beyond a line of trees at the back.

Their progress was impeded by a high chain-link fence, its expanse broken only by a wrought iron gate. Jim threw himself at the gate and scrambled over, ripping a hole in his fleece when the pocket caught on the top of a bar. Cursing, he landed heavily on the other side and stood for a moment, getting his breath back before turning to check that Penny had made it over. She hadn't. She was calmly closing the gate behind her and, even though he couldn't make out her face in the dark, he could feel the waves of smugness coming off her. For such a little person, she could be hugely irritating.

Together, they set off through the trees and along the rough track towards the houses. They were only a few metres from the first house when Jim held a hand out to stop Penny.

'Get behind me. I'm bigger than you, so if somebody attacks us, I have a better chance of fighting them off.'

Remarkably, given the trials and tribulations of the past half hour, Penny still had her Bag of All Things. From it, she extracted a personal alarm and a bottle of spray.

Jim's eyes widened in surprise.

'Is that pepper spray? Aren't they illegal?'

'You've just helped me break into the distillery and cause quite a lot of criminal damage, and you're worried about pepper spray? Anyway, it's not pepper spray. It's the chilli oil I bought at the loch café the other day.'

'For cooking,' she added.

'You're a scary woman. Way worse than Sergeant Wilson.'

They hurried along the row of dark houses, Jim shining the torch on the ground to pick out the jumble of builder's debris in their path. Suddenly, he came to a halt, and Penny grunted softly as she almost collided with his back.

'Here,' he whispered. 'They wouldn't have been working on Show weekend and there hasn't been much rain until today.'

The ground outside the middle house had been churned

into a muddy sludge and, judging by the number of footprints, at least four people had traversed it quite recently.

Penny looked up and shone her torch on the front of the building.

'I think the bars on all the windows might be a giveaway as well.'

She took her Swiss Army knife out, fully expecting to have to break in. However, as they got closer, they saw that the door was ajar. Rather than have to root through the bag to find it again and not trusting the shallow pockets of Ricky's school coat, Penny slipped the knife beneath the tight sleeve elastic that was doing its utmost to cut off the circulation to her forearms.

Jim gently pushed the door, wincing as the hinges creaked a warning of their arrival. His heart racing and his fists tightening in anticipation of attack, he stepped into the hall. If whoever was here hadn't known they were coming before, they certainly knew now. Despite this, nothing happened, and he cautiously let out the breath he'd been holding in since that first creak. Beside him, Penny was tense, holding her alarm and bottle of chilli oil in front of her. He could hear her breathing rapidly through her nose.

Stairs loomed before them, and Jim could dimly see the hall disappearing towards other doors. There was little choice left. They had probably lost the element of surprise, so their only advantage now was speed. They needed to cover as much ground as they could, as quickly as possible.

He pointed towards the stairs and whispered, 'You take the upstairs and I'll take the down. Move fast but stay quiet. If anything happens, pull your alarm and I'll come straight away.'

Penny nodded and took the torch from him before putting a tentative foot on the bottom step. She could feel some give in the boards beneath her and wondered how many steps she could take before her foot went through the wood. Sticking to the side of the staircase, she began to ascend.

When she had been in the hallway with Jim, she had put the faint odour down to the rot that the house must surely contain after standing empty for so many years. However, as she got closer to the top of the stairs, the smell of putrid meat became stronger, making her gag into her sleeve. She flicked on the torch and saw three doors, one to her right and two ahead. A bathroom and two bedrooms, she thought. A fourth, narrower door, was clearly a cupboard, and her nose told her that the source of the stench was behind this door. What was it with these people and stuffing folk in cupboards?

No way am I opening that, thought Penny. I don't care if Mum's in there large as life, I am not opening door number four. Mrs Hubbard has watched all the crime documentaries, and she would agree.

She tried door number one. At first, she thought it was locked, but a hard shove told her that it had merely been stuck, years of damp and neglect leaving it swollen in its frame. Her efforts, however, were for nought. A quick once over with the torch revealed a bathroom containing nothing but cracked porcelain, cobwebs and dead woodlice.

'Door number two,' she whispered to herself. This wasn't a movie. Her family couldn't be behind the last door. It had to be this one. Her muscles throbbed, both from tension and the struggle with door number one, yet the adrenaline pumping through her system mercifully dulled the pain to a low-level ache. Trying to heed Jim's advice to move quickly, she pushed the handle and stepped back, her senses hyper-alert to the threat from inside.

The door clattered back, its hinges screeching their complaint, and Penny raised her torch, expecting at any moment for Zack Wallace to come rushing at her. All her focus was forward. There was nothing but that door and whatever lay in the darkness. Her torch beam flickered and a tiny part of her brain, the bundle of neurons that had somehow remained in control despite every insanity that this night had thrown in her path, that spark of common sense asked when she had last changed the batteries.

Fuck. Her eyes strained to see the room as the torchlight grew dimmer. She stepped forward, frantically sweeping the room for a sign, anything please God, that her precious people were still here, still breathing, still alive. There it was again, the needle of hope pricking her subconscious.

She stepped towards a bundle of…something…in the corner and reached her hand out to touch the corner of the object. It was a blanket, thrown over something soft.

The fear at what she would find underneath made her feel physically sick, yet she yanked the edge of the blanket and aimed the dying torch at the object. A large teddy bear sat propped against the wall, its eyes glittering in the torchlight, a thick layer of dust covering what would once have been pink fur.

Fuck, thought Penny for the second time. Her breathing was coming in fast gasps, and she could feel pains in her arms. The tight sleeves? A heart attack? More likely a panic attack, she decided, recognising the signs from when she'd left her cheating wankpuffin of a husband.

The adrenaline wasn't helping with the panic attack. Her limbs were trembling uncontrollably and the darkness at the edge of her vision was closing in. Hang on. No, that was just the failing torch. She was definitely still conscious because she could hear Jim banging about like a big clumsy lummox downstairs.

Keeping her eyes fixed on the creepy teddy, she slowed her breathing. In through the nose, out through the mouth. One, two, three, four, five.

Okay, that would have to do. She was on the move again, heading towards door number three, hoping against hope that the twins were in there. Her hand reached for the door handle and her brain did a small double take as her fingers met air. She directed the torch beam at where there should have been a handle but where there was only a hole.

Penny groaned. Jim's warning to be fast and quiet was rendered pointless, not least by the racket he himself was making. Well, if there was no door handle, then there was only one way to do this; batter it down. She didn't plan. She didn't pause. She charged as hard as she could at the door, feeling a spike of pain in her shoulder as it loudly protested that barging open door number one had been quite enough, thank you very much.

The door didn't burst open, but she felt the wood give. It was probably soft from damp, like the stairs. She kicked the lower panel, and it gave way. A few more kicks and she had made a hole large enough for her to crawl through. Why she had continued to cling onto the Bag of All Things, she didn't know, but she dumped it now, the hole being too small for both her and the bag. Still clutching chilli oil, alarm and torch, she clumsily scrambled through the gap and waved the beam of light around the room.

There! Oh, thank God and all the very saints and angels, they were there. Her mum and her two precious, precious cherubs, whom she would never let out of her sight again, were in the middle of the floor, hogtied and gagged, but wriggling and alive.

Unfortunately, adrenaline which had powered her on so far, now failed her. So focused was she on what was ahead, that her senses had forgotten that there was a behind. She didn't sense the figure looming out of the darkness until pain exploded in the back of her head and she lurched forward onto the filthy carpet. This time, the blackness at the edge of her vision was real, and it was closing in. Just as the blackness became complete, Penny's finger twitched on the object in her hand and the alarm began to shriek.

CHAPTER 21

Jim was faced with three doors and the cupboard under the stairs. He decided to check the cupboard first as it was least likely to contain anything scary. Unless they'd stashed a dead body in there, of course. Which, he reflected, was entirely possible given what the bastards had done to Len. Plus, the smell. It was only after Penny had gone upstairs that he realised what was bothering him about the smell. Given the number of dead animals he had handled over the years, he should have recognised it straight away. He hoped he was wrong, but if he was right, he hoped the source of the stench was down here so that Penny didn't have to deal with the trauma of it.

He steeled himself for what he might be about to see and opened the cupboard door. If he hesitated even for a second, he knew he would simply shut the door again, so he shoved his phone torch through the opening and looked. His breath left him in a laboured hiss. The worst thing in here was the spiders. Big buggers with fat bodies and thick legs that scurried away from the light at an almost impossible speed. Jim shuddered and closed the door before any of the wee monsters could escape. A little part of him wondered whether he would rather have found the corpse.

On he crept to the first door, the bare floorboards beneath his feet creaking in protest. He readied his phone torch, determined to search the room as quickly as possible and move onto the next. If he was honest, it wasn't only that he wanted to find Mary and the twins. This place, the darkness, the smell, they were creeping him out. His brain was sending urgent fight or flight signals to his body and judging by the urgent hammering in his chest, most of them involved flight.

His grasp on the handle was firm as he turned it and shifted his weight forwards to push on the door, however his own forward momentum was to be his undoing. The door was suddenly pulled open from the other side, sending Jim stumbling into the room beyond. It took his mind a moment to catch up with his body and he found himself tripping over his own feet, his spatial awareness in disarray. Somehow, he managed to stay upright, careering instead into the wall beyond. Damp plaster crumbled and his shoulder was driven into the brick beneath, the impact sending pain shooting down his arm to his fingers, which reflexively opened and dropped the phone.

Jim rolled against the wall, instinctively moving away from his opponent's line of fire and he felt the thud of something hitting the space where his head had been a moment before. He barely had a split second to glance at the dark figure, silhouetted as it was by the light from the phone, before the attacker raised his arm and struck again. Jim ducked beneath the blow then charged forwards, but not quickly enough. The man grunted and dodged Jim's flailing fist, rocking back on his heels before raising his arm once more and viciously lashing out with what Jim could now see was a baseball bat. It missed Jim's ear by millimetres, sending him scurrying backwards, towards the centre of the room.

There was no time for his assailant to regroup as Jim immediately sprang forward, his left hand grappling at the arm holding the bat while his right hand landed a hard punch in the man's stomach. The bat hit the floor as the attacker doubled over, gagging and wheezing, but Jim didn't stop. That flight response was now all fight, and he jerked his knee upwards to deliver a blow to his opponent's jaw. The spray of blood hung suspended in the beam of light from the phone and the man slowly collapsed to the ground.

Throughout the fight, not a word had been spoken, the blows punctuated only by a series of grunts and the heavy breathing of two men entirely focused on beating the living daylights out of each other. Jim decided it was time to remedy this. He retrieved his phone and directed the light at the man's face.

He was just a kid. Tall, skinny, early twenties, his face pock-marked by the scars of teenage acne. His mouth was twisted into a bloody grin, a gaping hole where, until a minute ago, there had been two front teeth, and his eyes glittered with malice

'What the fuck have you done with them?' Jim snarled. 'You better not have hurt them you wee bastard, or I'll–'

'You'll what?' said a voice behind him.

Jim was about to spin round to face this new threat but felt his arms grabbed by strong hands and twisted behind his back. A sharp jerk upwards caused his fingers to once again release their grip on the phone, and he had no choice but to bend over to relieve the pressure in his shoulders. He could see the legs of two men and considered kicking backwards, but they were wise to this ploy and kept their legs out of reach, using the armlock to turn his body towards the voice.

The men released the pressure just enough to let Jim straighten up a little and he heard a click. Instantly, he was almost blinded by the powerful beam of a lamp. His pupils, used to the dark, immediately constricted and despite the danger, Jim found himself screwing his eyes tightly shut against the sudden glare.

'I thought Zack had you there,' said the voice, a note of amusement in the transatlantic drawl.

'Hyatt!' spat Jim, struggling to open his eyes so that he could properly face the bastard.

'Indeed,' said Ted Hyatt, seemingly unconcerned. 'Pleased to meet you again, Mr Blobby.'

Jim's eyes were slits, but at least he could now see the fucker. He struggled forward, intent on violence, only to feel the pressure on his shoulders increase as the men either side of him raised his arms a little.

'There's no point in trying anything,' said Hyatt. 'Elvis and Brayden are trained in physical combat. Unfortunately, Zack here is not.' He eyed Zack with disgust then continued, 'Let's hope that Jordan fared better with your friend upstairs.'

Panic swept through Jim. Shit, Penny! He struggled harder, but the agonising burn in his shoulders only caused him to bow lower.

'Penny! Penny! Run!'

The men pushed his arms a little higher. Christ, at this rate his arms were going to pop out of their sockets. He didn't care. He writhed in their grip, frantically lashing out with a foot and managing to connect with the side of a knee. He felt the hand on his right arm loosen as the man's leg buckled and he took the opportunity to drop to the floor, dragging the other man with him.

'Never find yourself on the floor in a fight,' his father had told him, 'and if you do, remember that first one up is the winner.'

He tried to stand but left arm man was still clinging on, tucking himself tight into Jim's back and pushing harder and harder, setting the nerve endings in Jim's shoulder screaming for relief.

'Have you never heard of personal space?' Jim roared, rolling over and trapping the man beneath him.

He tried bouncing up and down, anything to shake the bugger off, yet still he was trapped in that iron grip. The delay had allowed time for the first man to get up, and Jim suddenly froze at a sharp prick in his neck. He risked looking down and saw the evil blade of a zombie knife, its lethal tip disappearing beneath his chin.

'Let go, Elvis,' said Brayden. 'I got him.'

Jim lay still as Elvis slid from beneath him. He could feel the tip of the knife pressing hard on his skin and knew that one wrong move would result in an early demise. He realised that even if he had wanted to, he was no longer capable of pushing himself up. The pain in his shoulders was almost unbearable, any movement of his arms nigh on impossible. He sighed and sagged back, resting his head on the floor.

'That's my boys,' said Hyatt. 'They make their old dad proud every day.'

'What do you want with us?' gasped Jim.

'In a word, revenge. You see, fifty years ago, some of your little island friends were my friends. My followers, you could say. In those days, we were like one big, happy family, praying and living together. We were on a mission to change the world. Only, they stopped believing and became corrupted–'

'You mean the Red Path cult?' asked Jim. 'Aye, I know all about that. They told the police about the inner circle planning to hijack a plane or something, then everyone got arrested and they got put into witness protection on the island, while the leader fucked off to carry on the cult in America and Canada. Old news, pal. Hang on, though. If they were your followers, that must mean you're…'

'Not Ted Hyatt. Well done! I expect your dad will have mentioned me. I'm Thaddeus Height, Leader of the Red Path, although I prefer to be known as The Bridge. And of course, you're Jim Space and she's Penny Moon. Ridiculous names.'

The transatlantic drawl was gone, to be replaced by a menacing Glaswegian growl.

Jim snorted. 'Aye, well, you call yourself The Bridge, so I think you're ahead on that score. Anyway, you fell for Blobby and Moist, and they're even worse.'

'Don't be an imbecile. I knew exactly who you were, you meddling pair of shites. I came to this island with the intention of slowly removing my enemies and every trace of their bloodline, one by one. It took years to hunt them and now I'd get the pleasure of the kill. However, best laid plans and all that jazz, things have had to be…accelerated. Now, what is taking Jordan so long?'

No sooner were the words out of Hyatt's mouth than an ear-splitting shriek rent the air. Penny's alarm. Jim started to get up but a sharp pain in his neck and the fact that his arms no longer seemed to obey the commands of his burning shoulders made him reconsider. He glanced at Brayden, squatting above him, and the man bared his teeth, returning Jim's look with a glare of pure malevolence.

They waited and waited. The siren continued and continued until eventually, it abruptly stopped. There followed a long, drawn-out silence. Jim strained his ears, listening for any sound of Penny upstairs. All he could hear were some muffled thumps, then a man's voice shouted, 'It's okay. I've got her.'

Heavy footsteps sounded on the stairs, and the man that Jim assumed was Jordan came into the room. He was a heavy-set lump of adolescence, perhaps a couple of years younger than Zack, and he too was armed with a baseball bat. He glanced at his friend then shifted his gaze to the bat on the floor and, finally, to Jim.

'Looks like I missed a good fight there,' he commented, before turning to Height and saying, 'I've tied her up with the others Mr The Bridge. She's out for the count, so she'll be nae bother.'

'Excellent,' said Height. 'You and Zack can go now. We'll take it from here.'

'Alright, Mr The Bridge. And about our money?'

'I'll be leaving tonight. It will be sent on, have no doubt of that.'

Once Zack and Jordan had gone, Height turned to his

captive and, as if they were a couple of old friends sharing a fireside gossip, said, 'Now, where were we? Oh yes, things moving faster than intended. I'd planned to, let's say, *disappear* people, slowly but surely. A couple of fishing boat accidents here, a car crash there, but then Elvis got a little ahead of himself, didn't you son? Recognised Ian Henderson and thought he was doing me a favour by giving him what, even by my standards, was quite a gruesome death.

'We had a long chat about that, didn't we Elvis? Thou shalt not kill unless daddy tells you to. That's the trouble with kids these days. No patience.'

Height spread his arms and shrugged, like a fellow parent asking if he was being unreasonable. Jim didn't respond, so Height continued.

'Thanks to Elvis, the spotlight was on the distillery. I'd walked past Elsie while she was taking the tour and wondered if she recognised me. I recognised her, of course, the sour faced bitch. After Ian's death, I knew it wouldn't be long before she put two and two together, so we took a family trip to Elsie's house.

'Then you two came sniffing around. Billy Dent told me who you were. It's a bloody waste. Not killing you and Penny's family. I mean, I spent millions buying this place, thinking I could finally settle down, bring all my followers over, quietly murder a few people in my dotage, then you bastards have to spoil it. Why couldn't you have minded your own business?'

Jim didn't answer. He knew that he was mere seconds away from death. The pieces had slotted into place, and he wouldn't be around to tell anyone. God, it was so annoying when villains told you everything then killed you.

Height nodded at Brayden, giving him daddy's permission to kill, and Jim felt the knife bite down on his neck.

'No!' he shouted, his mind frantically scrambling for a way to play for more time.

More time for what? They were out here in the middle of

nowhere and not a soul knew where they were. The fear swooped in, and he could feel his bowels begin to loosen. Death was quite literally frightening the shit out of him.

Braydon paused and looked at his father, who nodded once again. Jim wanted to scream, he wanted to roll over and somehow get to his feet, but he was frozen, his arms no longer having the strength to push him, his voice trapped in a constricting throat, his breath coming in shorter and shorter gasps. Jesus, if the guy didn't kill him, he'd probably die of positional asphyxiation.

Then there was a voice at the door.

'Did one of youse leave the distillery door open because that's a fucking waste of electricity? Your heating bill must be enormous.'

In a flash, Braydon leapt to his feet and ran at Sergeant Wilson, Elvis hard at his heels.

'I don't think so, twatmonkey,' she said, casually pulling the trigger of her taser.

Behind her, Easy did the same and in the blink of an eye, both brothers were on the ground, twitching to the beat of the volts.

Six police officers squeezed past Sergeant Wilson and Easy, heading straight for Height. He ran to the window and swept aside the curtains, only to come up against the very bars he had installed to keep his prisoners in.

'Take him away!' shouted Sergeant Wilson, gleefully giving the trigger another wee squeeze, just for the hell of it. 'Do you like dancing lads? Craig Revel Horwood would give you a ten for those moves.'

She was suddenly barged out of the way by a frantic woman in a purple school coat. Penny collapsed to her knees beside Jim and threw herself onto his chest.

'I thought I'd lost you,' she sobbed. 'I could hear him running his mouth off, and I knew he was getting ready to kill you, but there was nothing I could do.'

She hugged him tightly and Jim yelped as pain shot through his shoulders.

'Sorry, sorry,' sniffed Penny, sitting up to examine his wounds. 'Oh God, there's blood all over your neck. Did he get you? Talk to me, Jim.'

Again, she pushed her head into his chest, this time listening for a heartbeat.

'I'm okay,' Jim croaked. 'I'd hug you back, but my arms aren't working. Actually, could you get off? You're making it worse.'

Penny sat up again and gave him a weak smile.

'Doc Harris and the paramedics will be here in a second. They're seeing to Mum and the twins. Mum's in a state. They beat her really badly. Hector and Edith are okay, though. It looks like they were drugged…roofied or something. They're still a bit out of it.'

'How…you're all…did the police let you out?'

Despite the exhaustion that was now creeping over him, Jim's mind was feverishly trying to sort out the timeline. Penny could almost see the cogs turning, followed by a flicker of self-doubt.

'It's okay. Your poor brain hasn't jumbled things up again. I'd tucked the Swiss Army knife into the sleeve of Ricky's coat and as soon as Jordan left, I managed to wriggle it out and cut us all loose.'

'Let me guess,' said Jim. 'You saved the day.'

'Not really. Height was so busy talking that I was able to get everyone downstairs and out of the house. Thanks for keeping him distracted, by the way.'

'It wasn't on purpose, you know. Once he'd started, the bugger wouldn't shut up.'

'You're still a hero in my eyes. I can't ever remember being as scared as I was when we were sneaking down those stairs. Lord knows how Sergeant Wilson knew we were here, but I've never been so glad to see her in my life. She'd rounded up the cavalry that were policing the Show, and here we all are.'

'I've never been so glad to see *you* in my life,' said Jim. 'Listen, I need to tell you something…'

But his words were lost as two paramedics gently nudged Penny aside and began tending to his wounds.

CHAPTER 22

'You were fucking lucky that Penny's alarm went off when it did,' said Sergeant Wilson, helping herself to a handful of chocolate mice. 'We knew you'd gone to the distillery, but Fudmuppet was ready to call it a day when we couldn't find you. "Get the dogs in from Aberdeen in the morning," he said. "Over my hairy arse," I told him. Not that my arse is hairy, mind. No, it's all peachy smooth down there, even my–'

'I don't think we need that level of detail,' snapped Sandra Next Door.

'Oh, I don't know,' said Gordon. 'Carry on, Sergeant Wilson. Peachy smooth, you were saying.'

Fiona elbowed him in the ribs and deftly snatched the bag of chocolates from Sergeant Wilson's hand. There were worse cravings, she supposed.

'Bugger me with a swollen tonsil, there'll be no chocolates left at this rate!' Jim exclaimed.

'You don't want swollen tonsils, dearie,' said Mrs Hubbard. 'You've enough on your plate with a couple of dislocated arms. How about a nice, healthy strawberry instead of chocolate? You've been looking a bit…beefy lately.'

Jim sat in the hospital bed and smiled. Other than sore shoulders and a few stitches on his neck, he was fine. Doc Harris had only kept him in overnight as a precaution, but this hadn't prevented his friends turning up en masse, armed with enough snacks to keep the thieving seagulls on the ferry occupied for a week.

'Tell me about the diary,' he said, hoping to distract Mrs Hubbard from the topic of fruit long enough for Fiona to slip him a chocolate mouse.

'Not much to tell, dearie. She wrote that she'd recognised Hyatt as Thaddeus Height. Not at first. She thought he looked familiar, and it was only when Ian Henderson was killed that she realised who he was. It's been half a century and we've all changed in that time, I suppose. But you don't spend a couple of years in the Highlands hot housing with a maniac then forget about it.

'Ian was with us in the Red Path, although I think he was more interested in saving his own skin than bringing some of the more radical members to justice.

'It was Elsie's diary that led us to the distillery. I took it straight to Sergeant Wilson, yet I'm still kicking myself. If I'd opened the parcel when it came, none of this would ever have happened.'

'You can't blame yourself, Mrs Hubbard,' Fiona soothed her. 'It was a set of unfortunate circumstances.'

'Aye, she can,' said Sergeant Wilson.

Sandra Next Door looked like she was about to intervene, and the Sergeant held up a warning finger.

'She can blame herself if she likes. She can tear herself apart, gnashing her teeth and moaning about what could have been. It'll change nothing, and we'll still lo…lo…what's the word that means a bit more than like?'

'Love?' suggested Fiona.

'Aye. That one. We'll still that one her. You're a good woman, Mrs H, or at least you're not an arsewazzock.'

'That's the nicest thing you've ever said to me,' said Mrs Hubbard, giving the Sergeant a fond smile.

'It's the nicest thing I've ever said full stop. Just don't tell anyone or they'll think I'm going soft. Anyway, Losers, the good news is that we picked up Zack Wallace and Jordan Jamieson this morning, trying to board the ferry with a van load of cannabis plants. The bad news is that we've still to identify the body in the cupboard.'

'Poor Minky,' said Jim. 'She's the best of that family. Talking of which, my dad and Jeanie are coming in later to visit myself, Mary and Len.'

'Has Penny visited you yet?' Gordon asked Jim.

'She and Eileen are down the hall with her mum and dad.'

'Is she coming later?'

'Aye.'

'And you're no…?'

'No.'

But you'll…'

'Aye.'

'Aye?'

'Aye.'

'And she'll say?'

'No.'

'Aye?'

'Maybe, aye.'

But maybe aye?'

'Aye.'

'Glad we got that cleared up.'

'Aye.'

Penny sat between the two hospital beds, her head turning back and forth like she was at the centre court in Wimbledon.

'That was a dreadful thing to do,' said Len. 'Low, even by your standards.'

'What do you mean, by my standards?' shouted Mary. 'I'm not the one growing cannabis in the garden shed.'

'That reminds me. Penny, will you water my plants while I'm in here?'

Len had had a mild heart attack after answering the door to Zack and Jordan. They had burst into the house and attacked both him and Mary, using the opportunity to beat Mary until she gave them the combination to the safe under the bed. Unfortunately, or fortunately (Penny wasn't sure which) Mary had also told them about the cannabis plants in the shed. They had stuffed Len in the cupboard, then bundled Mary, her valuables and the contents of the shed into Zack's van.

Jim had forgotten about Len and Elsie's little side-hustle, which is why he hadn't noticed anything amiss when he'd searched the shed for Len's book. Penny had only discovered the missing plants that morning and didn't have the heart to tell her father that his drug-dealing days were over. If Len hadn't woken up when she was berating her mother for stealing Mrs Hay's recipe, she wouldn't have told him about that either.

Mary opened her mouth to say something and Penny shot her a warning look.

'The doctor says he has to have peace and quiet, Mum. You're only allowed to share a room on condition that you both behave yourselves.'

'I was just going to say that technically it was Jeanie Campbell who stole the recipe,' said Mary indignantly.

'Because you asked her to,' said Len.

'I was *borrowing* it. How else was I going to win with my apple and bechamel slice? The base had to be just right. I don't know what you were thinking of, Penny, snooping around the bottom of my kitchen drawer like that. Your father is angry with me when he's supposed to be resting and it's all your fault.'

'I was looking for Dad's notebook so I could come and save your life! Which I did.'

'I'm glad you found it,' said Len. 'Ashamed of your mother and proud of you. You saved us all.'

'Jim saved you as well,' Penny reminded him.

'And another thing,' Mary declared. 'What are you going to do about Jim? He can't just go around kissing people and saving people willy-nilly. Before you know it, you'll both be seventy-eight and a couple of old maids.'

Penny smiled at the thought of Jim being an old maid. People might have called Elsie an old maid, but it wasn't true. She'd happily rubbed along with Old Archie for decades, neither of them ever living together. She'd had good friends and the respect of everyone who knew her. Penny would happily settle for that.

'I'm not doing anything about Jim,' she said. 'We'll be friends, that's all.'

'I always thought you'd be great friends,' said Eileen from the doorway, 'Only with more shagging.'

'Exactly!' exclaimed Mary. 'A shag would do you the world of good, wouldn't it Len. Len? I said, a shag would do her–'

'I heard you, dear. The whole hospital probably heard you. Leave them alone to sort it out between themselves. Is that my newspaper, Eileen?'

Penny left her father doing the crossword and her mother chatting to Eileen. Mary's face was covered in bandages, and Penny could have sworn that as the door closed behind her, she heard her father mutter, 'It's a pity they don't do bandages for the mouth.'

She felt the back of her head, where a nurse had gently snipped away the hair and applied stitches to the wound. She hadn't realised that she'd bled so much until she'd removed her clothes and saw the ruined mess that was once Ricky's school coat. Doc Harris had wanted to keep her in overnight but agreed to let her go home with the twins as long as she didn't drive and called him immediately if she noticed any signs of concussion. She couldn't drive anyway. Her car was back at the distillery, behind a barrage of police tape. The Bag of All Things, however, had made it through and, with the help of a borrowed charger, she was able to call a Vikster to carry her, Hector and Edith safely home.

There would be a big talk with the twins later, but first she had to visit Jim. If last night had taught her anything, it was that life was too short to fanny around. She needed to tell Jim that she was fine with being friends. She'd accept friendship and he need never worry or feel awkward around her. She would move on, and her heart would surely follow. Someday.

He was sitting up in bed when she arrived, surrounded by his adoring fan club and Sergeant Wilson. There seemed to have been some sort of picnic going on, judging by the number of sweet wrappers that littered the bed covers.

Gordon grabbed an extra chair from the adjoining room and Mrs Hubbard insisted on swapping places so that "the man and woman of the hour can sit together."

Her friends bombarded Penny with questions, curious to find out exactly what had happened and anxious for news of Len, Mary and the twins. She recounted the story, giving a distilled version of the witness statement she'd narrated to Easy that morning. The lad was surprisingly good at taking witness statements, or perhaps he was being extra careful because he was in Sergeant Wilson's bad books.

The easy chatter and gentle teasing between friends cheered her up immensely.

'Your baldy patch is nearly as good as mine,' Jim joked when she showed him her stitches.

'At least my hair covers it. When are you going to get your hair cut? It's starting to look ridiculous.'

And so it went, the happy back and forth, the banter, the gossip. Penny knew that she was blessed to have these people in her life and that it was selfish to want more from Jim. The love and the dreams had to be packed away in a box and pushed to the back of her heart, where they would mellow until the day she could unpack them, and all that would be left was friendship.

Her thoughts were interrupted by Gordon, who cleared his throat and said, 'We have to be going now. We'll see you all at the church hall on Wednesday.'

Fiona looked at him curiously, surprised by his sudden desire to leave.

'We can stay a while longer,' she said.

'No. We need to be on our way. Can we give anyone a lift? Sandra Next Door? Mrs Hubbard? Sergeant Wilson..no, you'll have the police car.'

Penny noticed that he didn't offer her a lift. Perhaps he was unaware that she was currently without a vehicle. However, Sandra Next Door and Mrs Hubbard eagerly accepted his offer, so there was no room for her even if she'd wanted to go.

There was a general clearing out and Penny realised why Gordon had wanted to leave so abruptly when she overheard Fiona saying, 'Why are you so desperate to go all of a sudden?'

'Because Jim wants to talk to Penny alone.'

'How do you know that?'

'Because he told me.'

'When did he tell you?'

'Well, you were there!'

'You only had one conversation with him.'

'Aye.'

'And it consisted mainly of aye, no and maybe.'

'Aye.'

'And you got all of that from aye, no, maybe?'

'Aye.'

They wandered off, following Sandra Next Door, Mrs Hubbard and Sergeant Wilson down the corridor, and suddenly it was just Penny and Jim.

'You wanted to talk to me, then?' she asked him.

'Aye,' said Jim.

She only just stopped herself from punching his shoulder.

'I'm not Gordon. You're going to have to do better than "aye" if you want to talk to me.'

Jim took a deep breath and looked down at the bed cover, surprised to see his fingers picking nervously at the edge of the sheet. He'd given a lot of thought to this conversation, although admittedly some of the thoughts were a bit hazy because they were thunk yesterday.

'When we talked the other day and you said we could be friends, I agreed because I thought it was the right thing to do, not because I didn't want to be more than friends. God, if you only knew how much I wanted to disagree with you! The first memory I got back was of you, Penny, and it took my breath away. Ask your dad. I was a mess.

'Even before that, the feelings were there. I forgot everything, and it was very confusing at first, but the more I saw you…like, it was coming from a place deep, deep inside that never really forgot. I thought that maybe it was me who liked you more than you liked me. Or maybe it wasn't real, and I was imagining things. All this stuff going on that I couldn't fathom and that I couldn't tell the one person I wanted to tell. But when I remembered, and you told me that you felt the same way…fuck. I couldn't saddle you with me. Who knows if my brain will ever fix itself.'

'It's not your decision to make,' Penny told him, her eyes brimming with tears. 'The decision to accept a saddling is *mine* to make. Stop smirking. I know that sounded rude.'

'Oh Christ, darlin', I've made a right mess of things.'

'We both have. Is there a way back, do you think?'

'A way back, no. A way forward, yes, I hope so. If you'll have me.'

'I'd go forward into anything with you by my side, in case you hadn't noticed.'

'Then we go together.'

'Together.'

'You're going to have to do the kissy bit. My arms…'

Penny laughed and wiped away her tears then finally, finally, she leaned forward and put her lips to his.

A voice at the doorway whispered, 'I knew it. Great friends. With shagging.'

EPILOGUE

Half a century ago, I sat next to this shy, wee, skinny lassie on our first day at university. We got talking, then we went for lunch and before long, we became the best of friends. She may have seemed timid to others, but on the inside there was steel. If you were in trouble, you'd want Elsie by your side. If you were in a muddle, Elsie would sort you out. She didn't panic, she didn't judge… okay, she judged. She'd purse her lips and give you that look; the one that said she knew that you knew better than to do whatever it was you weren't supposed to be doing. And if you crossed her, she was the quiet master of revenge. Nothing terrible, mind, but I think her false teeth had more adventures than she ever did. Few of us escaped finding Elsie's false teeth somewhere unexpected.

'And on the subject of adventures, of those she had many. By now, you all know about the cult we joined at university. It's not a secret anymore since we caught that man. I won't sully Elsie's sacrifice by saying his name. Believe it or not, we were happy on the cult farm for a long time until things went…wrong. Jeanie Campbell was the one who spotted the money being syphoned off, but we all played our parts in gathering the evidence and, without Elsie, I'd never have had the courage to walk ten miles to the village to tell the police. She kept me going every step of the way and has ever since.

'She was fiercely brave and loyal. When they put us into witness protection on the island, she organised us and helped us get started in our new lives. In those first days, the library was the place to be. Of course, there was no internet, so Elsie had us all learning the skills we'd need from books. The houses that Len, Mary, Sandra Next Door and Geoff live in – we built those, and many others around the island.

'Elsie may have been the quiet one and, let's be honest, a little stern, but her heart was full of love. The man she met at university, Archie, was the only one for her. It was an unusual relationship by today's standards. They never married and they never lived together, yet I dread to think what went on in that library van.

'Later in life, Elsie made a new set of friends when we all signed up to Losers Club. She'd settled into a quiet routine of selling "special medicine" to the old folks from the back of her library van and thought that her adventures were far behind her. She could not have been more wrong. I doubt that she ever imagined herself doing surveillance, hunting lost treasure and solving crimes. To her, it was the stuff of her beloved novels.

'Through her adventures with Losers Club, she met Johnny Monroe and together they founded the Hollywood Knitting Club. It's a measure of the woman she was, that Johnny and his friend, Al Cuppachino, have come all the way from America to be with us today. Like many waifs and strays over the years, she took Johnny under her wing and was so proud of him when he mastered jumpers.

'Even in death, Elsie took care of us all. The day she died, she sent me her diary and warned us to leave the island. She pointed us to the distillery and the man who was plotting to send us all to our graves. She helped save lives.

'She was my friend and told me she was grateful for that. Well, I am profoundly grateful for her friendship and everything she brought into my life. She asked that I remember the best of times with her because those are the ones that really count. I've talked about some of those today, but they are only the big things. The small things, like sneaking into the park and having a go on the swings aged sixty-three, could fill a book.

'There's a phrase they use at the distillery for the whisky that evaporates while it's maturing. By that I mean the good stuff that goes to the heavens. They call it the angels' share. In Elsie, we have lost someone truly good. In Elsie, the angels have their share.'

Mrs Hubbard looked around her at the crowd gathered in the pub to celebrate Elsie's life and smiled through her tears. Then she raised her cocktail glass.

'To Elsie.'

MRS HAY'S PEPPERMINT SLICE RECIPE

Base

- 225 g crushed Digestive Biscuits
- 1 tbsp caster sugar
- 115 g butter
- 3 tbsp cocoa powder
- 50 g dark chocolate
- A puckle o' secret ingredient fae Len's shed (optional & only if legal)

Peppermint Filling

- 375g icing sugar
- 2 tbsp butter
- 2 tbsp milk
- 2 tsp peppermint extract
- A wee drappie o' green food colouring

Chocolate Topping

- A fair thochtie (at least 200g) o' dark chocolate
- 1 tsp cooking oil

- Grease and line a medium sized baking tray with greaseproof paper.

- In a pan, melt the butter, sugar, cocoa and chocolate. Add the crushed digestives to the melted mixture and stir until combined.

- Using a wooden spoon, press the mixture into the tray until you have an even finish. Chill for at least 1 hour.

- Sift icing sugar and add rest of peppermint filling ingredients then spread over the base. If it's too thick to spread, add a wee skite o' boiling water. Chill for half an hour.

- Melt chocolate and oil together. Spread evenly over the peppermint filling and leave to set. Cut into squares.

For those not familiar with Scottish imperial measurements, a drappie is a drop, a skite is a very small amount (in this case a teaspoon), a puckle is a lot, a thochtie is some and a fair thochtie is quite a lot. My mum's recipe book is full of such precise instructions.

And once you're done making your peppermint slice, you'll want a great muckle dod for your fly cup (och, just Google it).

AFTERWORD

I hope you enjoyed this book. If so, I would be grateful if you could take a moment to pop a review or a few stars on Amazon.

You can hear more about my books and get access to exclusive material by subscribing to my newsletter via my website, https://theweehairyboys.co.uk . You also can drop me a line using the contact information on the website or treat yourself to a signed copy of one of my books.

Did you know that there's a Losers Club on Facebook for fans of the Losers Club series? Yes, you really can join Losers Club, although our fellow Losers are far more interested in cake and chocolate biscuits than diet sheets. I think it is best described as a warm, friendly and creatively bonkers place. Please do join us.

Other than this you can find me at:

Facebook Growing Old Disgracefully (blog)

Yvonne Vincent - Author

Instagram @yvonnevincentauthor

Threads @yvonnevincentauthor

X (Twitter) @yvonnevauthor

Tik Tok @yvonnevincentauthor

Amazon Yvonne Vincent Author Page

Until the next adventure.

Yvonne

ALSO BY YVONNE VINCENT

Losers Club

The Laird's Ladle

The Angels' Share

Sleighed

The Juniper Key

Beacon Brodie

The Losers Club Collection: Books 1 - 3

The Losers Club Collection: Books 4 - 6

The Big Blue Jobbie

The Big Blue Jobbie #2

Frock In Hell

You can find all of these via my website at https://theweehairyboys.co.uk or on Amazon.

Printed in Great Britain
by Amazon